S0-AIA-851

"I think we should have coffee and our conversation somewhere else, Mrs. Cosgrave."

Bristling with irritation, the prime minister's wife gestured toward a door beside a corner fireplace.

Samantha turned on the bathroom taps and the shower, settled a radio on the WC cistern and switched it on. She patted the rim of the bath. "Sit here with me, Mrs. Cosgrave. We need to be close to one another."

When Mrs. Cosgrave had done as she'd asked, Samantha put her mouth close to her ear and murmured, "If you want to keep secrets, don't talk about them in this house. Take a walk outside, or bury your whispers beneath background noise."

Mrs. Cosgrave gave her a wide-eyed stare. "I'm the wife of the prime minister. What you're suggesting is unthinkable. I—"

"You're the prime minister's widow. Your husband's been murdered. They'll want to hear everything that's said by the people who visit. I'm going to disclose things you'll probably wish to keep secret. I'm going to reveal my own involvement in it all. If that were widely known, I'd be in danger...."

RAYMOND HAIGH

is the author of the Samantha Quest series, which includes the books *Gigolo, Dark Angel, The Doll Doctor, The Spider* and *Resurrection*.

RAYMOND HAIGH

RESURRECTION

W✪RLDWIDE®

TORONTO • NEW YORK • LONDON
AMSTERDAM • PARIS • SYDNEY • HAMBURG
STOCKHOLM • ATHENS • TOKYO • MILAN
MADRID • WARSAW • BUDAPEST • AUCKLAND

If you purchased this book without a cover you should be aware that this book is stolen property. It was reported as "unsold and destroyed" to the publisher, and neither the author nor the publisher has received any payment for this "stripped book."

Recycling programs
for this product may
not exist in your area.

ISBN-13: 978-0-373-06288-1

RESURRECTION

Copyright © 2012 by Raymond Haigh

A Worldwide Library Suspense/October 2013

First published by Robert Hale Ltd.

All rights reserved. Except for use in any review, the reproduction or utilization of this work in whole or in part in any form by any electronic, mechanical or other means, now known or hereafter invented, including xerography, photocopying and recording, or in any information storage or retrieval system, is forbidden without the written permission of the publisher. For information, contact: Five Star Publishing, 10 Water Street, Suite 310, Waterville, Maine 04901 U.S.A.

This is a work of fiction. Names, characters, places and incidents are either the product of the author's imagination or are used fictitiously, and any resemblance to actual persons, living or dead, business establishments, events or locales is entirely coincidental.

This edition published by arrangement with Harlequin Books S.A.

® and TM are trademarks of the publisher. Trademarks indicated with ® are registered in the United States Patent and Trademark Office, the Canadian Trade Marks Office and in other countries.

www.Harlequin.com

Printed in U.S.A.

RESURRECTION

ONE

THE SKY WAS vast, the air cold and clear, the image of distant grass and tarmac sharp in the telescopic sight. Clovis swept the gun along the elevated stretch of road, moving it towards the hairpin bends that would slow the car. He steadied it on a fence post, located where the nearest bend turned into the straight, and checked the range-finder: a little more than six-hundred yards, close enough for accuracy, close enough for the rounds to retain some energy, but far enough away for him to escape before the escort could respond.

He'd been lying in frost-whitened undergrowth for almost an hour. The many layers of clothing beneath his overalls, his heavy boots, his balaclava and gloves, were no longer keeping out the cold and he was aching with it. Behind him, hawthorn bushes screened the rising ground. After fifty yards they gave way to birches, then came the mature forest trees that covered the crown of the hill. Before him, the distant road curved over meadows on a low flood embankment. Beyond the road, a conifer plantation, dark and brooding in the pale winter sunlight, swept up the far slope of the valley.

This was for Carl, the cousin who'd been as close to him as a brother. Carl, who'd been loyal and generous, who'd begged him to join the family business yet held no grudge when he'd refused. Carl, who'd welcomed him like a hero when he came home on leave, who'd taken him to his clubs, introduced him to the girls who

worked there, all pretty, some beautiful; warm affectionate girls, girls who'd been generous with their favours
to a battle-hardened squaddie. And there'd been good
food and plenty of drink and a car: always something
decent, something top-of-the-range.

He could never forget the others, the cousins and
uncles who'd died and the widows, mothers and sisters
who—like him—still grieved. But Carl was uppermost
in his mind. This was pay-back time for the heartless
bastard who'd sanctioned the plunder and killing that
had stripped the family of its wealth and left Carl dead
in a cellar full of starving....

A black Jaguar XJ and a dark-green four-by-four had
appeared around the first hairpin bend. It was him. No
mistake. The dark bands around the armoured windows
were the give-away. They made the sidelights seem like
panda's eyes and spoilt the look of a beautiful car. He
held the Jaguar in the telescopic sight, tracking it as it
navigated the second bend. Through the windscreen he
could see the driver and a security man sitting beside
him, then the limousine turned into the straight and
presented its side. The passenger in the back was visible now, less distinct but displaying his famous profile.

The car was six-hundred yards away and accelerating.
He had to allow for bullet travelling-time and the movement of the target. He aimed the weapon, squeezed the
trigger, felt the recoil against his shoulder and winced at
the deafening roar of the exploding cartridge. As he let
out his breath he saw the rear side-light shatter and the
shadowy figure jerk as if tugged by a rope. He'd been
lucky; with a moving target, you had to be lucky. The
car suddenly picked up speed, lurching away from danger. He squeezed the trigger again and again, emptied
the magazine as he tried to put all five rounds through

the shattered window. At least one should have killed the arrogant bastard.

The green four-by-four slowed to a walking pace—two men tumbled out and scurried into the long grass beside the road—then it sped on to rejoin the Jaguar. The men would have heard the shots echoing across the valley, seen glass fly from the near-side window. They'd have realized he was up here, on the hillside. He wanted that. He wanted to lure them in this direction.

Leaving the heavy rifle on its tripod, he crawled through the bushes, then rose to his feet and ran on between the birches, circling the edge of the forest until he came to a stream that rippled down the hillside beneath a film of ice. He splashed along its stony bed, heading with the flow, the shallow water hardly covering the soles of his boots. He'd practised this a dozen times, familiarized himself with the terrain, prepared himself. Lower down the hill, below the birch trees and hawthorns, the banks of the stream rose higher: high enough to hide him as he doubled back towards the elevated road. The men who'd leapt from the four-by-four would be advancing up the hill now. It wouldn't take them long to find the gun, then they'd probably climb up to the woods that swept over the hill and rolled on to the village of Enderley.

Down in the valley the stream meandered across flat meadow-land, and the trees and bushes lining its banks formed a tunnel that screened him from view. He ran on, boots crunching through the thin ice, splashing in the shallow water. The exertion had warmed him, driven the chill from his body, it made his heart pound and his breathing painful. When he could make out the embankment through the tracery of twigs and branches he slowed, began to move stealthily, so as not to alert anyone who might be watching and waiting by the roadside above. Another hundred yards and he was moving between concrete walls that funnelled into a culvert conveying the stream beneath the road. Crouching down, he entered the tunnel and crept towards the circle of light that marked the far side.

High banks and overhanging branches still concealed him when he emerged. He continued along the bed of the stream, moving around the conifer-covered hill, until the bushes thinned and the banks lowered, then disappeared, leaving the water to flow on into a wilderness of shallow ponds and marshy grassland.

Bracing himself, he climbed the steep hill and plunged into the gloomy plantation of pines. Hidden now, he paused and looked back. He could just make out a solitary figure striding along the distant road. The security men would have found the gun. They'd probably alerted superiors, called for assistance and for aerial surveillance.

He turned and ran on. Here, pine needles carpeted the ground beneath the evenly spaced trees and the going was easier. His ruse to double back towards the road, to head in the direction they'd least expect, had worked. He'd not been discovered and he'd made good progress, better than on his practice runs. He began to feel calmer. His breathing became easier.

Fifteen minutes later, he emerged from the plantation and skirted the isolated farmhouse his grandparents had tenanted. A place of happy childhood memories, it was abandoned and disused now. Every time he'd passed it on his practice runs, the decay and dereliction had saddened him.

Soon he began to hear the first faint sounds of cars and lorries. Keeping close to boundary hedges, he crossed two fields. The rumble and roar of traffic was loud now. He tugged off his balaclava, crawled through a gap in some bushes and looked down into a maintenance compound that huddled against the face of a rocky cutting. His prostrate body was level with the roof of a latrine block. Beyond the latrines, closer to the mesh fence that separated the compound from the motorway, stood the site manager's office, a canteen and a row of metal storage sheds. He glanced around. The office and canteen seemed empty, the yard deserted. The men would be out at this time, working along the coned-off section of highway, widening it, laying channels and drains, erecting barriers and fences. He swung his legs over the edge of the rock face and clutched at the grass while he lowered himself, found a foothold, then dropped down on to the concrete.

His van was in the plant enclosure, parked beside one of the excavators. He walked over to it, unlocked the side door, slid it open, took a spanner and a wad of cotton waste from a tool box, then climbed on to the tracks of the huge yellow machine. He wiped the glands on the shovel cylinders then glanced at the wad. It was dry. The new seals were holding. He applied the spanner to nuts, gave them a final tightening, then wiped his hands and stepped into the cab. He started the engine, revved it and operated levers. The huge steel shovel glided out and swung down until it was poised above the concrete. He glanced at a gauge. The hydraulic pressure was steady and within limits. Everything was normal. He drew the shovel back, killed the motor and stepped out on to the steel tracks.

'How's it going, Barry?'

He glanced up. The site manager was standing on the steps of the latrine block, fastening his visibility jacket.

'It's all fixed. Good as new.'

The manager strolled over. 'Have you taken a look at the tarmac spreader? The cylinders on the drag bars are—'

'Repaired it. I stayed on last night. The electricians rigged up a light for me.' Barry Clovis jumped down from the tracks and crossed over to his van.

'Thanks Barry, I'm grateful. We're falling behind and I can't afford any down-time on the plant.' The manager gave the stocky sandy-haired mechanic an appreciative smile. Barry was a real diamond. You couldn't do better than hire an ex-army man. Brisk, business-like, efficient; they knew their trade, they understood hydraulics, they were used to big machines. 'Where are you heading now?'

'Home, meal, warm bed.' Barry gave his hands a final wipe on the cotton waste then tossed it into the van and slid the side door shut. When he'd climbed up behind the wheel, he looked back at the manager. 'Pump on the small digger's a bit tired. Another month or two and you ought to be thinking about a replacement.'

'Order one and fix it,' the manager urged. 'Warn me when you're coming and I'll tell them to leave the digger in the compound.'

Barry slammed the cab door, started the engine, then reversed down the side of the latrines. The manager waved. Barry Clovis pulled away, drove past the canteen, the office and the metal sheds, then headed along the coned-off hard shoulder. He accelerated, matched his speed to the motorway traffic, then drifted out on to the main carriageway, behind a Polish lorry. He'd done it. He'd done it for Carl. What was left of the family had begun to avenge the dead. He'd fired the first shots. His involvement had ended. Others would take over now.

Tears pricked behind his eyes. His memories of that awful night were still vivid. The women had been told to stay at home. He'd gone with the men to the funeral parlour; gone to pay his last respects to Carl. They'd gathered around the open coffin. The undertakers had been discreet, placed Carl's hands beneath the shroud and covered his face with a square of white brocade. Carl's father was numbered amongst the dead, so his Uncle Henry had done the honours and lifted the cloth. He remembered the shocked intake of breath as if it were yesterday; he remembered the anguished groans that had sounded in every throat, the muttered curses and the calls for vengeance. He'd fought for his country in Iraq and Afghanistan. He'd seen his share of maimed and mangled bodies, but nothing had prepared him for the sight of the face that stared up at them from the coffin. Rats had gnawed away the lips, exposing teeth and gums; they'd fed on a cheek and the nose, devoured an eye and taken the forehead down to bullet-shattered bone. Carl, more than a cousin, more a beloved brother, his one true and faithful friend, had been horribly disfigured in death.

Barry wiped his eyes with the back of his hand and prayed to God that the man who'd ordered the sequestration and authorized the killings was lying dead in his car.

TWO

THE WOMEN IN the outer office glanced up from their keyboards, an expectant smile on every face. Marcus invariably passed the time of day, exchanged pleasantries, paid them charming and outrageously flattering compliments. And his attentions were all the more welcome because his manner was so gentlemanly; welcome because, despite his advancing years, he was still an impressively handsome man. His dark curly hair was hardly touched by grey, his blue eyes were wickedly bright, his posture erect, his smile engaging. He had no smile for them this morning—no pleasantries. His gaze was distracted and remote, his expression grave. Without sparing them a glance, he strode past the half-dozen desks and stepped into the PA's office. They heard Miss Purbright exclaim, 'Major Soames! Please go through. Miss Fallon's expecting you.'

Footsteps muffled by thick carpet, Marcus approached the heavy walnut door, gave a warning knock, then entered.

Loretta Fallon was standing by the window, arms folded beneath her breasts, gazing out over the cold darkness of the Thames towards the sunlit London boroughs beyond. When she turned her tired grey eyes registered pleasure. 'Come on in, Marcus. Any developments?'

'Nothing significant, ma'am. The Met have lifted the roadblocks around Enderley village, but they're still searching barns and outhouses, and they've got four teams combing Howden Woods. They've got the gun; killer left it at the scene. Probably too big and heavy to run through dense forest with. Sniper rifle, powerful weapon, half-inch bore; been wiped with formaldehyde to obliterate DNA traces. Gunsmiths are dismantling it so the lab technicians can swab the hidden parts, but they're not expecting to find anything.'

'What kind of sniper rifle?'

'British: Accuracy International AS50 loaded with armour-piercing rounds and fitted with a laser range-finder. Serial number's been checked. It's army issue. Went missing after an ambush in Afghanistan, two years ago.' He frowned in a concerned way at the tall slender woman with the tied-back iron-grey hair. Lack of sleep had given her face a waxy pallor and the flesh around her eyes was puffy and dark. The past twenty-four hours had aged her.

Loretta stifled a yawn. 'Anything else?'

'Security people at the scene are convinced the killer escaped through Howden Woods; probably had transport waiting in Enderley, the large village a couple of miles away. It all seems to have been carefully planned. The car and the escort were taking a detour around motorway maintenance works between junctions twenty-one and twenty-three. They'd been doing that for the past six weeks, every time they made the run.'

'Cardinal rule: keep changing the route. They'd got complacent, they were ignoring procedures,' Loretta observed scathingly.

'It gets worse,' Marcus went on. 'Took them nearly an hour to get road-blocks up and a chopper in the air. The killer would have been well away by then.' He watched Loretta move from the window and perch on the edge of her desk. Her jacket had been tossed over the arm of a chair, her navy-blue skirt was creased, her usually pristine white blouse crumpled. 'How did the meeting with the Emergency Committee go, ma'am?'

'Better than I expected. No recriminations: no talk of apportioning blame. The politicians were too shocked for that. Cosgrave's widow's been driven to Chequers and put under protection. Deputy Prime Minister's taken over; she chaired the meeting.'

'How did she cope?'

'Seemed a little unsure of herself; understandable really. Home Secretary was very supportive.' Irritation suddenly overrode the tiredness in Loretta's voice. 'Didn't we have *any* intelligence about this, Marcus?'

He lowered himself into a chair beside a conference table. 'It would seem not, ma'am. Mycroft's team are trawling the database, running key-word searches on all the recent intercepts, but they've not come up with anything so far.'

'Emergency Committee seem to think it's a response to Cosgrave's tough line on Iran; the blockade, increasing sanctions, all that talk about using military force.'

'They'd harass us with suicide bombers, ma'am. Assassination isn't their style.'

'Are there any would-be bombers at liberty after that last wave of arrests?' Loretta rounded the desk, sank into her chair and allowed her head to fall back against the leather. She closed her eyes. 'Home Office is insisting on a very muted response; there's to be no suggestion that this might be Islamic militants. On top of so many arrests, the house searches, detentions without trial, they're afraid unproven accusations could lead to rioting.'

'Rioting?' Marcus raised an eyebrow.

'"A serious breakdown in community relations" is what the Home Secretary actually said, but he meant rioting.'

'Did they say when they were going to release the news? It's been twenty-four hours. Surely they can't—'

'Noon, today. Deputy Prime Minister's making a statement on television, then the Metropolitan Police Commissioner's going to brief the media.'

'That should help to distance us from it, ma'am. Where's the body being kept?'

'Makeshift morgue on an airbase about twenty miles south of Stockport. Bullets tore through the head and chest, caused a lot of damage. Commissioner said the back of the car looked like an explosion in an abattoir. They've decided the car's going to be crushed and incinerated when the investigation's over: not fitting to have something a British Prime Minister died in put on public display. It's under guard in a hangar for the time being.'

Loretta and Marcus gazed at each other without speaking. Appalled by the enormity of the event, they were wondering what it might mean for the Department, what it might mean for them.

Stifling a yawn, Loretta said, 'Edward Ashton buttonholed me after the meeting. Mrs Cosgrave's been going through her husband's private papers. She's discovered he'd made regular payments into a bank account she didn't recognize: fifteen-hundred a month. She phoned the bank, but they were evasive, so she talked to Ashton: Ashton and her husband were lifelong friends, they confided in one another. Ashton knew quite a bit about it, knew Cosgrave had called us in a while ago, but he didn't have the stomach to tell the widow who the payments were being made to. He just told her it was something to do with a security problem we'd been involved in; said he'd ask me to give her the information.'

Marcus stiffened his shoulders. 'That business with the missing child. What was he called? Benjamin: Benjamin Hamilton. Quest won't want that can of worms opening again.'

'She dealt with it. She knows all the sordid little details, and it would be woman to woman. Contact her, Marcus; fix up a meeting between her and Cosgrave's widow at Chequers.'

'Quest might not be co-operative, ma'am. God knows how many Bassingers died when she was searching for the boy. She won't want that made known.'

'This is the Prime Minister's widow we're talking about; surely she'll realize the information's confidential. After all, it's not something she'd want her husband to be remembered for. Is Quest still in our employ?'

'About a month of that short-term contract left to run.'

'Persuade her, Marcus. There's going to be a detailed enquiry when the panic's over. We've got to appear helpful. The last person we want to offend is the Prime Minister's widow.'

There was a knock on the door and a white-haired woman in a green woollen dress stepped into the room. 'Your car's waiting, Miss Fallon.'

'Thanks, Gemma. Tell the driver I'm coming down.' Loretta rose and reached for her jacket. 'I need sleep, Marcus. I'm heading home. Hold the fort. Call me if things develop.'

VELMA LOATHED THESE men, hated it when they came to the house dressed in their dark double-breasted suits and expensive ties, fragrant with deodorant. Clothes and perfume couldn't hide the fact that they were no more than a couple of hired thugs; Henry's minders and enforcers. It wasn't so much their brutish arrogance—they were always deferential and respectful to her—it was the bold way they looked at her: lingering lustful looks that embarrassed her and left her feeling soiled. Henry didn't mind. He laughed when she complained about it. It gave him pleasure when other men coveted the things he owned: this big detached house, his Bentley, his Rolex watches, his diamond rings. Her.

And a growing awareness that she was no more than a possession to him was making her feel afraid. Drifting into her forties now, she knew she wouldn't go on looking like this much longer. With every day that passed, the grooming took a little longer, demanded a little more care. She was a depreciating asset. When she'd lost her shine, she'd be disposed of, replaced by a newer model. And the way Henry kept going on and on about finding a woman for this entrapment scheme, a woman who was attractive and refined, who could seduce an educated and cultivated man, worried her. So far he'd had no success and his impatience was growing. Every day that passed she became more afraid he might ask her to do the job. That would confirm her fears. She would know that she no longer meant anything to him.

Velma led the men across a blue-carpeted hall, past an impressive flight of stairs, down a passageway and into a breakfast room. The house was still very much as Henry's wife had left it: gleaming white paint, expensive wallpapers, carpets, curtains, the carefully chosen furniture, everything coordinated and stylish. Mona had had good taste and the money to indulge it. No point changing things for the sake of it; no point unsettling Henry. But she'd insisted on buying a new bed, and she'd had the master bedroom redecorated. It would have been tasteless to lie with him in the bed he'd shared with his wife.

Henry Bassinger was sitting at a table cluttered with the remains of a meal. A tall broad man, his eyes, nose, mouth and jaw were big and intensely masculine; his greying hair thick and wavy, his eyebrows dark and bushy. Dressed in a black silk dressing gown and crimson Paisley cravat, he was eyeing them over a newspaper.

'You wanted to see us, Mr Bassinger?' James Cleaver's cockney voice was nervously respectful.

Henry nodded. 'Park yourselves.' He glanced at Velma. 'Could you fix some more coffee, love?'

She returned his smile, gathered the breakfast things on to a tray and trotted into an adjoining kitchen. Moving as quietly as she could, she placed the tray on a worktop and began to prepare the coffee, all the time straining to catch what the men were saying.

She heard a rustling as Henry tossed his newspaper aside, then a voice so deep it made the air tremble demanded, 'Have you found me someone? It's been weeks. The flat's almost finished. I want a woman in there and ready for business before the end of the month.'

'We've checked the two houses in Birmingham, the clubs in Leeds and Manchester,' Cleaver said, 'but there's no one suitable, Mr Bassinger.' The second minder, the one called Conrad, added, 'Half of them can't speak English. We have to teach them the basics so they can understand what the punters are asking for.' His whining voice was cringingly apologetic. 'And you said you wanted a woman with a bit of class, someone who could be taken anywhere, but classy tarts register with escort agencies, they advertise on the internet, they're independent.'

'Bollocks, Conrad. You've got forty or fifty women to pick from. There's got to be one that's half-decent, someone we can smarten up.'

'You said not too young, Mr Bassinger,' it was James Cleaver talking again, 'not too old, attractive, refined. The one or two that came close were East Europeans. They can't speak a word of English. They couldn't hold a simple conversation. You wouldn't be able to explain what you wanted them to do.'

The kettle began to rumble to the boil. Velma found clean cups, and while she was spooning coffee into the pot heard James Cleaver say, 'Terry Gurdin's got a woman who might be OK. Latvian. He fancied her himself, so he kept her in his flat. He's getting tired. Tried to introduce her to a few select punters, but she started kicking and screaming. Now she's got difficult, the way they do. She'll cook and clean a bit, but that's about all. He's been thinking about having her sorted: inviting a few blokes round to show her what it's all about. If she was willing, she could be what you want.'

'You've seen her?'

'Once or twice, just after Terry brought her over. She looked good, very smart, handled herself well. Been to university in Latvia. Sort of girl you could take home to mother, if you know what I mean.'

Henry growled, 'She speak English OK?'

'Perfect; educated voice, just a trace of an accent. She wasn't what you'd call a bundle-of-laughs. Fact is, she was hard going, not really interested in anything you had to say. Found her a bit—what's the word?—disdainful: yeah, snooty and disdainful. Terry was really taken with her, but you could tell she wasn't bothered about him. I knew he'd have trouble.'

'Would he let her go?'

'Probably be glad to, for a consideration.'

Velma bustled back into the breakfast room, slid the tray on to the table and began to rattle cups into saucers. Conrad Hartman stared brazenly at her hips and thighs sheathed in a black skirt. James Cleaver gazed at her breasts, impressive beneath a scarlet satin blouse. There were women of every size shape and colour in the houses they managed, in every state of undress; why on earth did they have to stare at her like this?

'Want you to do something for me, Velma,' Henry growled huskily. It was as if his throat were lined with rusty nails; his huge chest a rumbling drum. She flashed him an apprehensive smile and her hands shook a little as she poured the coffee. 'Want you to go with James and Conrad to Manchester, take a look at a girl, talk to her, see if she's suitable, find out if she'd be willing.'

'You want me to go today?'

'This afternoon if James can set it up; if not, tomorrow. If you think she's OK, James and Conrad will do the deal with Gurdin.'

'You want me to bring her back?'

Henry nodded.

'But where would we put her; the flat in London's not ready yet? We—'

'Bring her here,' he said.

'Here, to this house!' An outraged look had settled on Velma's face.

Henry began to smile. 'Give you a chance to find out what she's like, get her sorted, make sure she knows what she's got to do.' Velma was looking at him with shocked eyes. Her chin was trembling. He laughed. It was a gentle laugh, a laugh that told her he understood her displeasure. His voice softened, rustled like dry leaves. 'I won't be here, love,' he explained. 'I'm going to Dublin with the boys for a few days. Flat's going to be finished on Friday; Stanley promised me. You can get her settled in before I get back.'

'Dublin? With Mark and Lewis? Are their wives going?'

'Just me and the boys. Conference on asset management.' He smiled. 'We need to get away for a few days.'

Her body relaxed. They were going to put themselves where they could be seen by law-abiding, respectable men. They needed an alibi. And two days ago, Henry and his sons had flown to Amsterdam for a pointless meeting with diamond merchants. Something was happening.

'I want you to take care of this for me, Velma. I want you to deal with the girl, set her up in the flat, make sure she's got some decent clothes, keep an eye on her.'

'What if it doesn't work out? What if she turns out to be useless?'

'She'll get her papers and her air-fare home. But do your best with the girl. I've waited long enough. I want this sorting.'

Velma nodded, returned his smile, then finished arranging cups in saucers. James Cleaver was rocking back on an expensive ebony and gilt dining chair, his ankle hooked over his knee. She watched his gaze slide from her breasts to her hips.

The girl had to be suitable. Henry wouldn't wait much longer. He was obsessed with this scheme and he'd run out of patience. She was sure that if the girl couldn't or wouldn't do the job, he'd tell her to do it. She'd overcome her scruples and done some dodgy things for Henry, but she wouldn't act the tart. She couldn't bear the humiliation.

THREE

HELEN COSGRAVE GAZED down into the courtyard. Frost sparkled on Hygeia's head and shoulders; it whitened the four-leafed-clover-shaped island of grass that surrounded her pedestal. The rather demure-looking goddess was facing the gates where guards, bulky in body armour, were cradling guns and looking out across the park. Helen had always thought the statue should face the house, as if offering the occupants a benediction. Did the gods of ancient Greece offer benedictions, or did they just demand sacrifice? During her first stay here, one of the staff had told her Hygeia was the goddess of health—or was it wealth? Thinking and remembering were so difficult now; her mind was like a dark pool, frozen on the surface, chaotically turbulent in the deeps. The staff had taken endless pleasure in acquainting her with the secrets of the house, and she'd had to appear delighted to receive each and every little tit-bit of information, but remembering it all....

Chequers: she'd never liked the place. Right now her heart was crying out to be in her own home, surrounded by her own things, where she could grieve and weep in private. They'd insisted on bringing her here; rushed her here with indecent haste. They'd said it was to ensure her safety, reminded her she was the Prime Minister's wife. Wrong. She was the Prime Minister's widow now. What a sad and chilling little word widow was: widow's weeds, widow's mite, widow's stoop. There was nothing uplifting about the word widow.

She'd discovered things about her husband, things she'd had no knowledge of. A woman was coming here to talk to her, a woman who knew her husband's secrets. It had been arranged. The man who'd telephoned had been so charming, so understanding, his gentleness had reduced her to tears. He was called Major Marcus Soames. He'd told her there were no records; no documents in files. Her privacy was assured. This woman he was sending was the only living person who knew why and to whom her husband had been making those payments for more than seven years.

Helen reached for her bag, took out her powder compact and studied her reflection in the tiny mirror. God, she'd aged. And her hair needed styling and tinting. Perhaps they'd bring a hairdresser to her now Lawrence's death had been announced. She clicked the compact shut and dropped it in her bag. She must try to stay calm and composed and look her best, for Lawrence's sake. She smoothed the skirt of her grey woollen dress, then checked the clasp of the diamond brooch she'd pinned just below her left shoulder. Lawrence had given her the brooch when they'd won the last…

Something caught her eye. There it was again, a distant flash of brilliant red between the beeches, way across the frost-whitened parkland. It was one of those low-slung sports cars, moving excessively fast. This must be her. The charming major had kept his promise. The woman who was privy to her husband's secrets had arrived.

SAMANTHA QUEST RISKED a glance at the house: Elizabethan, the real thing, not some stockbroker's pastiche.

Bigger than she'd expected, it was built from russet bricks with stone-mullioned windows and high gables. Ornate chimneys rose out of roofs of small red tiles. She smiled. So, this was the historic pile where Prime Ministers were supposed to relax and entertain the great and the good.

She shifted down the gears, braked hard, swung the Ferrari around a bend and allowed it to rumble to a stop in front of tall gates. A blue-uniformed guard approached, peaked cap tugged down over his eyes. She lowered the window. *Police* was stencilled across his bullet-proof vest; pouches bristled and handcuffs dangled from his belt. He was clutching a Heckler and Koch sub-machine gun. The lever on its stock had been set for a three-round burst. Formidable.

'May I see your pass please, miss, and your ID.'

'I've just shown them to the men who searched the car at the road block.'

'I'd like to see them again, if you don't mind, miss.'

Samantha dipped into the bag on the passenger seat, plucked out a leather wallet and passed it through the window.

'Would you mind removing your sun-glasses, miss.'

'Must I?'

'I have to check your identity, miss.'

This was the thing that concerned her, why she'd tried to refuse when Marcus had asked her to visit Helen Cosgrave. She hadn't wanted to be seen and remembered by every Tom, Dick and Harry. The name on her documents was false, but that hardly diminished the risk, especially if they discovered why she was here.

His eyes widened when she tugged off the glasses. After a quick glance at the photograph in the wallet, he handed it back and gestured towards the house. 'Enter the courtyard, drive up to the door, then climb out of your car and leave it unlocked. Someone will come and take you in.' He stepped back, unclipped a two-way radio and began to mutter into it.

The gates were set between brick pillars capped by pinnacles of white stone. Guards, sub-machine guns slung from their shoulders, heaved them open. Samantha let out the clutch and snarled into the high-walled courtyard. After circling a statue on a quatrefoil lawn, she parked beside the entrance door, snatched up her bag and climbed out. Guards were standing in narrow pedestrian openings in the courtyard walls. They had their backs to her. The one on her right was gazing out over rising ground towards Beacon Hill; the one on her left had a view across rose gardens that had been reduced to a wintry tangle of prickly black stems behind low box hedges. Samantha studied the statue on the pedestal. The young woman seemed to be shivering in her flimsy robes, clenching her pert little buttocks against the cold. The low winter sun offered no warmth, but its brightness made the statue cast a long shadow across the frosty grass. Samantha gathered her furs about her throat, and her breath made misty clouds in the cold clear air.

The door opened and a grey-haired man, portly in a black pinstriped suit, smiled out at her. 'I understand you have an appointment with Mrs Cosgrave?'

She nodded.

'Please come inside. Mrs Cosgrave's waiting for you in the Hawtrey Room. May I have your name so I can announce you?'

Samantha gave the name on her ID cards, 'Grey: Georgina Grey.' Then, heels tapping on flagstones, followed him across the entrance hall. Portraits, mostly ghostly faces peering out of a varnished brown gloom, decorated panelling that had been scraped and cleaned until it had taken on the colour of bleached bones. The man tapped gently on a door set deep in masonry architraves, then led her into a large comfortable-looking room where a fire was blazing in a stone fireplace.

Helen Cosgrave rose from her armchair beside the fire, a surprised expression on her face. What a coat the woman was wearing! So much silver fur, massed around the shoulders, spilling down to a hem just above her ankles. And the purple stockings and purple suede and snakeskin shoes! Johnson wouldn't like those heels stabbing into his floors.

'Miss Georgina Grey, Mrs Cosgrave.'

Helen Cosgrave extended a hand and continued to stare, fascinated, as the woman swept around a sofa and came towards her. Black hair, abundant and straight, was trimmed just above her shoulders; a deep fringe almost covered her brow. Large sun glasses, like iridescent mirrors, concealed her eyes, and her mouth glistened, vividly red. What she could see of the woman's skin was pale. She watched her unbutton a purple glove and tug it off and felt warm, soft fingers take her hand.

'I've asked for coffee to be brought through. Would you care for coffee?'

Samantha glanced around the room. More panelled walls, an expanse of oatmeal-coloured carpet, overstuffed sofas, half-a-dozen armchairs with red-tasselled valances, all covered in a beige fabric that had a bold red pattern. 'I think we should have coffee and our conversation somewhere else, Mrs Cosgrave.'

'You don't like the Hawtrey Room?' Surprise tinged with indignation registered in Mrs Cosgrave's rather brittle voice. 'Edward Heath refurbished it when he was prime minister. He chose the fabrics and all the furnishings.'

'Politician, pianist, yachtsman, conductor of orchestras, *and interior decorator.*' The crimson lips parted in a smile. 'Edward was a man of many parts, Mrs Cosgrave. It's not the room. It's quite charming. I'll explain later. Your bedroom, perhaps: could we go there?'

'I really can't imagine why.' Mrs Cosgrave didn't bother to hide her irritation. How dare this person tell her where they should talk?

Samantha continued to smile at the slender woman with dark brown hair and frightened eyes. In the flesh she seemed smaller than she did in her rare appearances on television. Right now she was looking vulnerable and ill at ease. 'Let's go up there, and I'll explain,' Samantha said, then stepped aside.

Helen Cosgrave glanced at the attendant as she strode towards the door. 'Tell Jennifer not to bother with the coffee, Angus,' she snapped, then swept out of the room, turned through an opening and began to climb an ancient flight of stairs. Unable to help herself, she turned and took another curious look at the black-haired woman who was following her. The dark glasses made her inscrutable; her husky voice was soft and low and strangely compelling. 'That's a rather overwhelming coat,' she said. 'Is it real?'

'It's not an illusion, Mrs Cosgrave. It's real.'

'I mean,' Mrs Cosgrave insisted tetchily, 'is it real animal fur? I can't bear the thought of God's defenceless little creatures being killed and made into coats.'

'The winter pelts of Siberian wolves. And if you'd seen a pack attack and devour men and horses, I think you'd want them all killed, skinned and sewn into coats.'

As they rounded the top of the stairs Samantha added, 'It was presented to me by the Russian Minister of the Interior: a gift from a grateful Russian people.'

'Really! And why were they so grateful?'

'Just politician's rhetoric. They probably weren't grateful at all. I resolved a terrorist problem.'

They were walking down a long book-lined gallery where oatmeal coloured carpet and dark Persian rugs covered creaking boards, where ornate brass reading lamps gleamed on tables set between blue and gold arm-chairs and sofas. Perhaps the multi-talented Edward had given the long gallery a make over, too.

Mrs Cosgrave led them into a high-ceilinged room dominated by a four-poster bed. A dressing table arranged in front of a tall window was strewn with letters and documents and a few cosmetics. Face powder had been spilled beneath its small oval mirror.

'Is there a bathroom?' Samantha tugged off her gloves, pulled at silk tapes, allowed her coat to slide from her shoulders and tossed it on the bed.

Bristling with irritation, Mrs Cosgrave gestured towards a door beside a corner fireplace. Her gaze was suddenly drawn towards Samantha's long-sleeved purple dress. The bodice and waist were close fitting, the skirt full with a hem just above the knee. It had an expensive look, a look of utter perfection. It made her feel dowdy.

'Does this work?' Samantha reached for a portable radio on the bedside table.

'Of course it works. I listen to the news when I'm dressing; come up and listen to the play in the afternoons.'

Samantha picked it up. 'Let's take it through with us.'

The en-suite bathroom was small, white-tiled and windowless, probably formed in what had once been a linen store. Samantha turned on the taps and the shower, settled the radio on the WC cistern and switched it on. She patted the rim of the bath. 'Sit here with me, Mrs Cosgrave. We need to be close to one another.' When Mrs Cosgrave had done as she'd asked, Samantha put her mouth close to her ear and murmured, 'If you want to keep secrets, don't talk about them in this house. Take a walk outside, or bury your whispers beneath background noise.'

Mrs Cosgrave gave her a wide-eyed stare. 'I'm the wife of the Prime Minister. What you're suggesting is unthinkable. I—'

'You're the Prime Minister's widow. Your husband's been murdered. They'll want to hear everything that's said by the people who visit. I'm going to disclose things you'll probably wish to keep secret. I'm going to reveal my own involvement in it all. If that were widely known, I'd be in danger.'

Helen Cosgrave could see the distorted reflection of her face in the woman's dark glasses, feel the warmth of her shapely young body in the perfect dress and catch its fragrance. She knew the perfume, but couldn't remember the name. Lawrence had bought her some, years ago. It was unbelievably expensive. He'd never repeated the gesture.

Samantha reached up and slid the glasses off.

Mrs Cosgrave flinched. Dear God, those eyes! So large, so luminous, such a vivid green; they seemed to sear into one's soul. Glancing away, she said, 'I suppose they've told you I've been going through my husband's papers, that I've discovered regular payments were being made into a bank account I don't recognize. When I questioned the manager at the bank, he was very evasive; said he couldn't reveal the name of the account holder. I understand you know about these payments. Were they being made to you?'

'Not to me, Mrs Cosgrave.' Samantha gazed at her for a moment, then asked, 'How much do you want to know?'

'Everything.'

Samantha leaned closer. 'Parliamentary election time, eight years ago, you told a priest, a Father Ryan, that your husband needed some help in his constituency office.'

'Did I? It's so long ago, I really can't remember.'

'Father Ryan mentioned it to a parishioner, a young woman. She was eighteen, waiting to take up a university place in the autumn. She contacted your husband, or your husband's election agent, and she was given the job. She was called Rachel Hamilton.'

Mrs Cosgrave tried to meet Samantha's gaze, found it too disturbing and looked down at her hands again. She began to twist her wedding ring on her finger.

'Your husband had an affair with her. She became pregnant. He persuaded her to have an abortion, but the priest and her parents talked her out of it. Eventually she went with her mother to a private maternity home somewhere on the south coast. When they came back with a baby boy, the mother said the child was hers; an unexpected late pregnancy. Your husband paid for the nursing home, paid for a doctor to attend Rachel at the birth, then made monthly payments to Paula, the girl's mother; she'd agreed to care for the child. He arranged with the doctor who attended the birth for Paula's details to be entered on all the documents, and she and Rachel's father were named as the parents on the birth certificate. I was told the payments were a thousand pounds a month when the child was born. Your husband increased them over the years. When I was involved, they were about fifteen-hundred.'

Mrs Cosgrave studied the young woman's face. The green eyes were calm, the expression relaxed. She certainly wasn't in awe of her or the house and, judging by her remarks, seemed contemptuous of politicians. Collecting her thoughts, she asked, 'And why did you become involved, Miss Grey?'

'The little boy went missing; it was thought he'd been abducted. Paula Hamilton made appeals on television. She also approached your husband and begged him to do something. I think he feared someone suspected he was the father, that they'd have tests done and when they had proof use the knowledge to bring pressure on him.'

'Pressure? Why would anyone want to—'

'A year earlier there'd been a big trial involving most of the male members of a criminal family called the Bassingers. The Crown Prosecution Service botched it. Only one Bassinger was jailed. The government, your husband's government, ordered a very aggressive sequestration of the man's assets: property, works of art, cash, an ocean-going yacht. It was a face-saving thing for the Home Office, and the Bassingers were desperate to have it stopped. Your husband feared they might blackmail him, and asked the security services for help. I was assigned to recover the child.'

'And did you?'

'Yes. Alive and unharmed.'

Mrs Cosgrave closed her eyes. The hissing of the shower, the gurgle of water in the outlet, the voices on the radio, were making concentration difficult. How could the man she'd lived with, slept with, loved and supported, have kept a secret like this? She suddenly felt incredibly tired and confused. 'Where is the child now?'

'I returned him to his grandmother, Paula, the woman he thinks is his mother. They live in Stockport.' Samantha gazed at Helen Cosgrave. The revelation had clearly dismayed and distressed her. Beneath the grey dress, her slender body was visibly shaking. Samantha made her voice gentle. 'Do you want to know any more, Mrs Cosgrave?'

'The child's real mother, the little slut who seduced my husband after she'd been given a job, where is she?'

'Dead, murdered by the Bassingers during the search for the boy.' After a silence, Samantha added, 'She was barely eighteen, Mrs Cosgrave. She was young enough to be your husband's daughter.'

'I'm not sure what you're implying, Miss Grey. She was old enough to know right from wrong. She could only have been in the constituency office for a few weeks. She was a slut.' Mrs Cosgrave fixed Samantha in a haughty stare. 'Was she attractive?'

'Yes.'

'In what way was she attractive?'

'She was young, fair-haired and blue-eyed. When I met her she was about twenty-three. She'd had a child, put on a little weight, but she was still very attractive.'

'You're saying she had a good figure?'

'Yes.'

Mrs Cosgrave looked down at her hands again. She'd long realized that Lawrence had begun to find her slenderness unappealing. But clothes looked their best on slender women, and she'd always been a well-groomed, elegant companion. And she'd supported and encouraged him, devoted her life to him, this man who'd had secrets, who'd been unfaithful to her. The sound of running water invaded her thoughts. *Woman's Hour* was murmuring out of the radio. The presenter and her guests were giggling about some special tights that were supposed to reduce cellulite on thighs. She glanced at Samantha. 'You said you were concerned about your involvement being made known. I don't understand why you—'

'Most of the older generation of Bassinger men and some of their sons died in the race to find the child—I killed them. All of the men who got close to me, who could recognize me, are dead. Surviving Bassingers still run the family businesses. If what I've just told you became known, I'd be in great danger.'

'You were instructed to kill these men?'

'I was assigned to recover the child. Finding him and protecting him were my only concerns. If I'd not killed the men, the Bassingers would have won the race to find him. If they'd found him, I daren't think what they might have done to him.'

Mrs Cosgrave pressed her lips together in a grim little smile. 'You hunt and kill like the Siberian wolves.'

'I wasn't driven by hunger, Mrs Cosgrave, just concern for the child.'

'And the child, this little boy, he'll be about seven now?'

Samantha nodded.

'What's his name?'

'Benjamin: Benjamin Hamilton.'

'And what were your impressions when you met him? What did you make of him?'

'A good-looking boy. Fair curly hair, wears spectacles, slightly built, perhaps a little small for his age. His real mother found him strange; said he was autistic. He was examined by psychiatrists after I'd recovered him. They said he was unusually intelligent, but otherwise normal. He was easily disturbed by disorder of any kind;

he didn't relate too well to other children, and he had difficulty distinguishing fantasy from reality, the inanimate from the animate, but at only five years old…'

'He was intelligent, you say?'

'Exceptionally. And sensitive and unusually intuitive for a child his age.'

Helen Cosgrave let out a bitter little laugh. 'That's more than I could say for the sons I gave my husband. Thirteen years of very expensive private education didn't do much to develop their minds. They excel at sport, they have perfect manners, they can make pleasant conversation, be very charming but neither of them could get a place in a decent university.'

'I don't think real intelligence, intelligence in the wider sense of the word, can be measured,' Samantha said gently. 'I'm sure your sons have their own very special qualities.'

Mrs Cosgrave felt a pang of guilt. Her treatment of this strange and rather exotic young woman had verged on the unpleasant, yet her only response had been to say something kind. Close to tears now, her chin trembled as she said, 'I want my sons to come home to me, Miss Grey. I want them with me. They're touring together, Central and Southern Spain, escaping the winter. I've tried to reach them on their mobile phones, but they don't answer. I hoped they'd contact me when Lawrence's death was announced. The authorities are searching for them, but so far…' Changing the subject from one she didn't dare think about to one she could hardly bear, she asked. 'Is there anything else you can tell me about Benjamin and his family?'

'He goes to the local Catholic school; Paula Hamilton and her husband were very devout. Paula's husband died while Benjamin was still a baby; she said their daughter's behaviour, all the shame and disgrace, had broken his heart. I found her a rather cold repressed woman who couldn't show affection, but she cared for Benjamin very well, loved him, was aggressively protective towards him.'

'She's alone then, a widow?'

Samantha nodded. 'After her husband died she became estranged from her daughter, then her daughter was murdered. But she still has Benjamin.'

Helen Cosgrave closed her eyes and allowed her head and shoulders to droop. 'I'm so alone, Miss Grey. I don't even have my sons with me. I want them to be found and brought to me. Then I want them to take me home.'

'The police are keeping you here for your protection.'

'I feel like a prisoner. And I hate the place. Too ancient, too much history, too many gloomy passageways. I dread the winter twilight. Sometimes I think I can see faces peering in at me through the windows, staring at me out of dark corners.'

Samantha reached for Helen Cosgrave's hand; it was thin and icily cold. Then she slid her arm around her shoulders and drew her close.'

'Are you married?' Helen Cosgrave was weeping now.

'I'm a widow.'

'So many widows. You're very young to be a widow.'

'My husband was killed by a Palestinian sniper. We'd been married six months. He was a doctor. He was attending a patient on a kibbutz near the Gaza strip.'

Helen Cosgrave sighed. 'We have things in common,' she said. Then, looking up, asked, 'Will you do something for me?'

'Of course.'

No wavering, no conditions; she'd just said, "Of

course". She was warming to this strange young woman. 'Will you visit Paula Hamilton, ask her for a photograph of Benjamin, a recent photograph? And will you bring it to me, tell me how they are?'

Samantha nodded. 'Regarding our conversation, Mrs Cosgrave, you must forget my involvement in this. What you do with the information about your husband, I can only leave to you. And when you return to your own home, you should have the place swept.'

'Swept?'

'For surveillance devices. Call in a private firm. And if you want to keep your secrets, be careful what you say over the telephone.' She released Helen Cosgrave's hand and rose to her feet. Then, keeping clear of the spray, turned off the shower and the taps. The radio was clearly audible now. A woman was reading the morning story.

Samantha returned to the bedroom with its pea-green carpet, its frills and delicate, flowered wallpaper. She gathered up her coat from the bed and was drawing it on when Mrs Cosgrave appeared in the doorway, dabbing her eyes with a towel.

Helen Cosgrave felt a renewed pang of remorse. She'd been cold and unpleasant, made offensive remarks about the young woman's furs when she'd taken great risks coming here and talking to her. Trying to make amends, she said, 'That's a very beautiful dress.'

Samantha smiled. 'Versace: winter collection. I bought it in Milan a few days ago. They have their main boutique along the Via Montenapoleone.' She drew on her gloves, picked up her bag, then concealed her eyes behind the dark glasses.

They made their way back down the long gallery, with its bookcases and sofas, reading lamps on polished tables and its dark Persian rugs.

'Will you have lunch before you go?'

'You're very kind, Mrs Cosgrave, but I have another appointment.'

They descended the ancient stairs and turned into the stone-flagged entrance hall. 'When will you bring me the photograph?' Mrs Cosgrave asked.

'Hopefully before the end of the week.' Samantha tugged off a glove and held out her hand.

'I may not be here. I may have returned home.'

'I'll find you.' Samantha squeezed the ice-cold fingers.

Mrs Cosgrave moved past her and pressed a button on a new-looking intercom mounted on the wall beside the outer door. She put her mouth close to the grille. 'My guest's leaving now.'

They heard a muffled voice say, 'Very good, ma'am,' and after a brief delay the lock clicked.

'See what I mean,' Helen Cosgrave muttered. 'They've made me a prisoner in this ghastly old place.' The door began to swing open. Helen put her mouth close to Samantha's ear and whispered, 'Tell the mother the payments will continue.'

Samantha emerged into bright sunlight, strode past the guard and lowered herself into the Ferrari. After drawing her furs around her, she slammed the door and keyed the ignition. She glanced back, intending to wave a goodbye to Helen Cosgrave, but the door to Chequers had already closed and the guard was watching her, sub-machine gun cradled in his arm, his finger hooked around the trigger.

She let out the clutch, circled the statue, then rolled to a stop at the gates. Blue-uniformed guards appeared beyond the courtyard walls and swung them open. She

negotiated the sharp bend at the head of the drive, then
roared off across sunlit winter parkland towards the
distant line of trees.

FOUR

'YOU OK, MRS BASSINGER?' James Cleaver's lean pock-marked face peered at her around the headrest.

'I'm fine, James, thank you.'

His thin lips stretched in a smile and he returned his gaze to the road.

It was the fourth time he'd asked, the umpteenth time he'd called her Mrs Bassinger. She wasn't Mrs Bassinger, he was just being respectful. Velma would be too familiar, and he'd probably feel uncomfortable calling her Miss Spellman. She'd have dearly liked to be Mrs Bassinger. It wouldn't happen now though: if Henry had wanted to make her his second wife, he'd have asked her a year ago.

She must have caught Henry's eye when she did the catering for his wife's funeral. There had been so many Bassinger funerals. They'd buried his son, Clifford, in the May of that year. His remains had been found on the moors, hidden beneath a pile of stones. He'd been shot. Henry's wife, Mona, had died a month later. Heart attack, grief and shock; you really can die from a broken heart.

Six months after the funeral, Henry had asked her to move in and, God help her, she'd agreed. She must have been crazy. The Bassingers were notorious, respected because they were feared; mad bad and dangerous to know, her mother would have said. And despite Henry's moans about the grasping government, the family was still wealthy. But it wasn't the money and the life-style, it was the man she was besotted with. She couldn't imagine life without him now. His big intensely masculine features, his height, his powerful shoulders, gave him enormous presence. And he was always kind to her, often surprisingly loving and tender, but she'd seen him be utterly ruthless in his business dealings. There was a dark undercurrent of violence in him. Deep down, he scared her, and somehow the fear excited and aroused her. She'd been crazy to say yes when he'd asked her to move in, but she couldn't have refused, not in a million years. When he held her and caressed her, when he moved his huge hands over her body, it was…God, she was worse than some infatuated girl.

Mark and Lewis, his surviving sons, seemed content with the arrangement, but their wives were cool. They were probably worried about the possibility of marriage and inheritance. They needn't have concerned themselves. It wouldn't happen now. And she was becoming more and more certain that if this woman they were going to see wasn't suitable, Henry would ask her to seduce the man. That would be the end. It would be over as far as she was concerned. She'd have to refuse; she'd lose every last bit of self-respect if she went along with that.

They were driving through Manchester's inner suburbs now, closing on the city. Big Victorian and Edwardian houses, most of them converted into offices and surgeries, had been in-filled with low-rise apartment blocks. 'That one', James pointed through the windscreen. 'The place with the balconies.'

Conrad swung the blue Bentley into the right-hand lane and parked it at the end of a short ungated path linking the block of flats with the street. Velma allowed her gaze to wander up from the recessed entrance with its bronze lamps and doors. Four storeys of biscuit-coloured bricks, corner-turning balconies and windows, ended in a grime-streaked parapet.

James climbed out of the car and glanced back at Conrad. 'I'll rouse Terry Gurdin and look the place over. If everything's OK, I'll give you a call and you can bring Mrs Bassinger in.' He slammed the door, strode off down the short path and stepped up into the entrance. After studying names on an intercom unit, he pressed a button. Velma lowered the window an inch and listened. She heard a click, then, 'That you, Terry? It's James Cleaver and Conrad Hartman with Mrs Bassinger. I phoned this morning.' There was a metallic, 'Come on up,' then James pushed open the heavy bronze and glass door and disappeared into a vestibule.

Velma said, 'This girl I'm going to see: what's her name?'

Conrad turned and looked at her through the gap between the seats. 'Terry Gurdin calls her Katie. That's all I know, Mrs Bassinger. James has met her once or twice, but I've never seen her. Mind if I smoke?'

'Not at all.' She did mind, really. She didn't want the smell to linger in her hair or on the grey and black suit she was wearing, but neither did she want to alienate Henry's minders. She teased a stray blond curl back in place. She'd taken a lot of trouble with her hair. Henry liked it this way: drawn tightly back from her face and gathered in a chignon. He said it made her look classy and sexy, like Grace Kelly, only she was lovelier than Grace Kelly. She smiled to herself. She didn't believe a word of it, but it was always pleasant to be complimented.

Velma lowered the window a little more to clear the

cigarette smoke and gazed out. A group of people, men and women of indeterminate ages, had emerged from the gate of a big old house and were heading towards them. Shepherded by carers, some of them holding hands, they appeared to be afflicted, or perhaps blessed, by a happy vagueness of mind. As they shuffled past the car one or two stared in and smiled, but most gazed blankly ahead, seemingly unaware of their surroundings.

A tune began to jingle out. Conrad reached inside his jacket, withdrew a gold-plated mobile and flicked it on. Velma heard a voice saying, 'Everything's OK. Terry says the girl's in the flat. You can bring Mrs Bassinger up now. First floor, door's on your right when you get to the top of the stairs.'

Dark-red carpet, coarse and hard-wearing, covered the entrance hall. Conrad carried Velma's attaché case, allowed her to walk head of him, enjoyed watching the gentle sway of her hips, the movement of her thighs beneath her tight skirt, as she climbed the stairs.

The murmur of male voices was escaping from an open door. Velma walked through, crossed a small hallway and entered a sitting-room that was stiflingly warm and misty with cigarette smoke. A hardwood floor, a huge wall-mounted television, a leather sofa and armchairs gave it a sparse, masculine look. There were no pictures on the pale-green walls; no ornaments, books or magazines. A small rug with a black and brown geometric pattern had been arranged in front of the sofa. Crimson Venetian blinds extended across a window that ran the full length of one wall; bright winter sunlight was making the slats cast hard shadows across the floor.

James Cleaver was relaxing in a chair. A bald thickset man with baby-blue eyes and a smooth pink face was standing behind a tiny bar, pressing a glass up to an optic. When he saw Velma his cupid's-bow mouth curved in an appreciative smile. 'Well now, the new Mrs Bassinger.' His Irish accent was Belfast, not Dublin. 'I can see old Henry's been looking after himself.' His smile widened. 'My name's Gurdin, Mrs Bassinger: Terry Gurdin. What can I get you to drink?'

'Thanks, Mr Gurdin, but not now. I've come to look at a girl. I understand she's here.'

'Terry; call me Terry. Sure you won't have one?' He glanced past her. 'What about you, Conrad? Vodka, Scotch, Belgian beer?'

'I'll give it a miss, thanks, Terry. I'm doing the driving.'

Terry Gurdin emerged from behind the bar with its bottles and optics, fairy lights and buttoned red-leather front. 'Got to drink on my own then.' He gulped at his glass then gestured towards the sofa. 'Sit down. Both of you, sit down.'

'We're short of time,' Velma said. 'Perhaps I could see the girl?'

Terry beamed. 'Let's all sit down, talk terms, then I'll call her in.'

'We can talk terms after I've seen her. She might not be what we're looking for. And I'd like to see her on her own.'

Terry's smile faded. He sniffed disapprovingly, took another sip at his drink, then nodded towards the hall. 'Front bedroom. She's in there.' His voice was curt.

Velma crossed the small hallway. As she reached out to open the door, she heard footsteps and turned. Conrad had followed her. 'I must see her on her own,' she whispered.

'I've been told to take care of you, Mrs Bassinger. If you don't mind, I'll just check the room, make sure it's all OK, then I'll leave you.' Moving past her, he opened the door.

The bedroom was fairly large. Built-in wardrobes with panelled mahogany doors lined the window-facing wall. A black silk counterpane covered the king-sized double bed. The carpet, curtains and walls were different tones of beige, and blue-shaded lamps stood on bedside cabinets. A slender girl was sitting on the edge of the bed. Her tawny hair, pale face and shabby clothes looked as if they needed washing. She was gazing up at Velma with hazel eyes that were wide and apprehensive.

Conrad checked the wardrobes, peered inside a tiny en-suite bathroom, then said, 'No problems, Mrs Bassinger. Call me if you want me.'

Velma heard the door close, then smiled at the girl and asked, 'Has Terry told you what this is all about?'

The girl shrugged. 'Not really.'

'It's Katie, isn't it?'

'Katarzina.'

'My name's Velma, Katarzina.' Velma sat beside her on the bed. 'I'll come straight to the point. We want to employ a young woman, someone attractive and presentable. We want her to seduce a man.'

'To seduce a man? What kind of man?' Katarzina folded her hands in her lap.

'An important man.'

'Young, old; attractive, ugly; refined or coarse?'

'He's middle-aged, distinguished-looking, intelligent, charming and well-to-do.'

'Well-to-do?'

'Reasonably wealthy.'

'Ah.'

Velma studied the girl. She looked dirty and unkempt. The broken zip of her flimsy white skirt had been secured with a safety pin. Her blue sweater was stained, her legs were bare, her white high-heeled shoes scuffed and worn. 'Would you be interested?'

'Maybe. What would be in it for me?'

'We'd take you away from Terry Gurdin.'

Katarzina grimaced and rolled her eyes towards the ceiling. 'You'd get me my passport and papers back?'

'We'd give them to you when you'd finished the job. And we'd pay you, of course.'

'How much would you pay me?'

'I really need to take a closer look at you before we talk about money. Would you mind?'

'What do you mean, take a closer look at me? Can't you see enough sitting there?'

'You'd have to captivate a powerful and influential man, a man who'd have no difficulty finding female company. I have to be sure you can be made to look the part.'

The girl began to blush. 'I'm filthy right now. I don't wash properly or take care of myself any more. I do this because I don't want Terry to bother me. I think that if I am not clean he will leave me alone.'

'And does he?'

Katarzina shook her head. 'He is an animal.'

'I'm sorry to have to ask you this, but I have to be sure about you. Could you just stand up and take off your jumper and skirt?'

Shrugging, the girl rose from the bed and did as Velma asked. Her once-white cotton knickers were grey and her thighs were covered in dark bruises, but she was quite shapely.

Velma gestured towards the bruises. 'Who did that to you?'

'Terry. He hits me and kicks me when I refuse to have sex with his friends.'

'Would you find it difficult to sleep with the kind of man I've described?'

'Not if he treated me properly and I was being rewarded.'

'Are your teeth OK?'

'I am not a horse!' Katarzina bared them angrily. 'Are they good enough for you? I have lost a filling, that is all. A back tooth. Sometimes I feel pain, but Terry will not let me leave the flat to get it fixed.'

'How old are you?' Velma asked.

'Twenty-seven.'

'You have a husband, a boyfriend?'

'I have never had a husband. My boyfriend deserted me.'

Velma reached out and took the girl's hands; she looked at the palms, then turned them over and examined the fingernails. She'd be suitable. A bath, some smart clothes, a visit to the hairdressers, a manicure and a few decent meals, and she'd be more than suitable; she'd be perfect.

'You've seen enough?' Katarzina's tone was scathing.

Velma nodded and said, 'Tell me a little about yourself. Where do you come from?'

The girl stepped into her skirt and drew it over her hips. She secured it with the safety pin, then reached for her jumper. 'Latvia,' she said, when she'd slid her arms into the sleeves and pulled it on. 'A little town called Sigulda, about fifty kilometres from Riga. It's a holiday resort.'

'And you've been educated? Your English sounds perfect.'

'I attended the Latvian Academy of Arts in Riga. I

was studying for a Bachelor's degree in the arts and humanities. I did two years of the four-year course.'

'Why only two years?'

'My boyfriend left me. He was supporting me.'

'You could talk convincingly about art, about painting?'

'Of course.'

Better and better, Velma mused, then asked, 'You have family in Latvia?'

'Brothers, sisters, a drunken father. My mother is dead.'

'No strong attachments?'

Katarzina shook her head.

'We would provide you with a flat and a job,' Velma said.

The girl sat down beside her again. 'A job? Terry said I am not allowed to work. I would go to prison.'

'We'd sort that out. All you need is a National Insurance number. The job would be with a firm that buys and exports fine-art and antiques. You'd be an appraiser.'

'An appraiser?'

'Someone who decides the worth, the value of things.'

'But I haven't the faintest idea…'

'Don't worry. It would be a pretence; something to give you a reason to go to certain places where this man would be. And we'd give you an allowance to cover your living expenses and pay you five-thousand pounds when you'd seduced the man and we had a video of your encounters.'

'A video? A movie of me making love? I don't like that. And what if he doesn't want to be seduced?'

'He's a man, Katarzina, and we've done some checking. The right kind of woman wouldn't find him difficult to seduce.'

'And when he's been seduced?'

'We'd pay you, give you your passport and papers, and book you on a flight to Latvia.'

'Why would I want to go back to Latvia? My drunken father and my brothers would take my money.'

'We're going to use the video to put pressure on the man. It would be best if you left the country, at least for a while, and you don't have to tell your father and brothers where you are. We'd expect you to complete the job within a month, six weeks at the most.'

'The clothes would be smart and expensive, like yours?'

Velma nodded. A natural refinement, a reluctance to be videoed while having sex, seemed to be making the girl hesitate, despite the situation she was in. But wasn't her own situation desperate, too? If she failed to persuade the girl, Henry would probably insist that she—

'And I could keep them?'

'Keep them?'

'The clothes; could I keep the clothes?'

'Of course. And the flat would be very comfortable; nicer than this. And we'd provide you with a driver, someone who'd watch over you and take you to and from the places where you'd meet this man.'

'Watch over me?'

'Make sure no one was unpleasant to you. You'd telephone him if you needed him.'

'What if Terry won't let me go?'

'He'll let you go.'

'He's got my passport, my papers. Every time he goes out I search the flat, look everywhere, but I can't find them.'

'We'll get your papers. Now, tell me, do you want the job, or don't you?'

'I come, I do it. I have nothing to lose.'

Velma made her voice stern. 'This is a serious business, Katarzina. I'm not your fairy godmother. We'd expect you to finish the job quickly, not drag it out if you began to like the man.'

'I understand.'

Velma rose from the bed. 'Collect together the things you want to take.'

'We are going now?'

'In ten minutes.'

CONRAD WAS DRIVING the Bentley limousine; Velma and Katarzina were riding in the back. Katarzina had pulled a shabby brown coat over her jumper and skirt. Her hair was still unkempt, her legs bare. She was holding a plastic carrier bag packed with a few personal things on her lap.

They were circling the inner ring road. Up ahead, separated from them by a car and a plumber's van, James was a passenger in Terry Gurdin's white Vauxhall Vectra. After a couple of miles the Vauxhall headed down an exit ramp. They followed, drove for a while past tall advertisement hoardings that hid railway sidings, then the Vauxhall's indicator began to flash. They turned over a bridge, swept down into an industrial estate and began to wind through a monotony of factory and warehouse units, all grey and windowless.

Velma stared out at the drab metal buildings. 'Gurdin has an office here; this is where he keeps the girls' papers and passports?'

'*Unit 17, Luxury Sauna and Massage.*'

'In a warehouse on an industrial estate?'

Conrad laughed. 'Nicely fitted out inside, good as a five-star hotel, it's well away from residential areas so the police leave it alone, plenty of parking, not over-looked. Every punter pays a room rent. Girls pay for support services, plus a percentage of their take. It's a nice little earner.'

The massage parlour was at the end of a row of iden-tical units, its entrance discreetly located to face a des-olate car and lorry park. Conrad swung the Bentley in a wide curve and pulled up beside the Vauxhall. James and Terry Gurdin were already passing through a yellow door set in a storey-high brick plinth beneath the metal sheeting. *Unit 17* had been spelled out in bright-yellow letters across the end of the building. Conrad drummed nicotine-stained fingers on the rim of the steering wheel and kept his eyes fixed on the yellow door.

Minutes later a tune began to jingle out. Conrad slid a hand inside his jacket, found his mobile phone and flicked it open. Velma could hear the thin sound of the caller's voice, but the words were indistinct. 'Now?' Conrad said. 'You want me to come now? He's being difficult…Do you want me to bring the cash? Just the sledge. OK.' He returned the phone to his pocket, then glanced between the seats.

'Henry said I had to stay with you, Mrs Bassinger. On no account was I to leave you alone. But there's a problem and James wants me to go in. I'll be about ten minutes, no more. If I'm any longer, you could just drive away and head back home. Are you happy with that?'

'Of course. Deal with it, Conrad. Henry wants this up and running, and so do I.'

Conrad climbed out of the car, slammed the door and walked round the back. Velma heard the boot lid open, then thud down. When he appeared again he was walking across to the windowless building, carrying a sledge hammer by the end of its shaft. It was hanging down beside his leg, its massive iron head almost scraping the tarmac.

'What's happening,' Katarzina whimpered. 'I'm not going back to that pig. I am not—'

Velma reached out and patted her hand. 'It's all under control, love. Conrad and James are sorting things out.'

'The hammer: why did your man take that great big hammer?'

'Gurdin's probably being difficult. Perhaps he wants too much money. Perhaps he wants to keep your passport and papers.'

'He'll come looking for me.' Katarzina's voice rose to a wail. 'He said if I ever ran away he'd find me, then there'd be no more fannying around. He'd lock me in a room and I'd have to go with many men—night and day—to pay for all the grief I'd caused him.'

Velma took hold of her hand and squeezed it tightly. 'You're safe now. We'll protect you. We won't allow Gurdin or anyone else to hurt you.'

'But the hammer; why the hammer?'

'They're probably going to break his legs, love. They might break his arms and crush his hands, too. By the time he's able to walk again, you'll be long gone.'

'He scares me. I hate him. Can you order them to kill him?'

'We'd have a body to dispose of then. Not easy to get rid of a body. And it's useful for the people we do business with to know what's likely to happen if they get too greedy or don't do as they're told.' Velma squeezed the girl's hand again. 'Stop worrying. I'm going to look after you, and when I'm not there you'll have a driver to make sure no one hurts you. Just do as I say, and you'll be out of the country with your nice new clothes and your money before Gurdin's left hospital.'

Velma loathed the violence. She'd forced herself to detach herself from it, to compartmentalize her mind, to separate the pleasures of life with Henry from the crime that funded it. He'd involved her in his affairs much more than he had his wife. He often asked for her advice. She sensed her usefulness to him, his dependence on her. It eased, but didn't dispel, her feelings of insecurity. And now they'd found a suitable girl she'd never know whether or not he'd have asked her to seduce the man. Or would she? The girl might become difficult; she might not be suitable. She was certainly educated and intelligent—perhaps too intelligent—educated people sometimes lacked common sense. She could only hope the girl was smart enough to realize that what was happening to Gurdin could happen to her if she didn't behave.

'Does this man have a name?'

'Man?' Velma brought her attention back to the girl.

'The man I am to seduce.'

'Farrell; Jeremy Farrell.'

'Is he important?'

'Very. He's a leading politician.'

'What does he do, this politician?'

'He's a member of the government. He was a close friend of the Prime Minister who was killed a few days ago.'

'Have you got a picture of him?'

Velma lifted the attache case on to her lap. Taking care not to expose the bundles of banknotes, she clicked it open, slid out a manilla folder and leafed through the contents until she found a page that had been torn from a magazine. It carried a portrait photograph that had been carefully posed and taken by someone skilled in the art. She handed it to Katarzina.

'Mmm…Rather mature, but very distinguished-looking and quite handsome. You say he is a refined and sensitive kind of man?'

'I would hope so. He's the Minister for Culture and the Arts.'

Katarzina handed back the image. 'If he treats me properly I do not think I will find it too unpleasant to allow him to seduce me.'

FIVE

PAULA HAMILTON AND her grandson, Benjamin, the child she'd passed off as her own, no longer lived in the tiny terrace house in Atherton Road. A woman wearing a black headscarf and a long black *abeya* had answered Samantha's knock. The small child she was carrying was crying and she was angry at having been disturbed. 'No one called Hamilton lives here. And no, I've no idea where they are.' She'd slammed the white plastic door. The old wooden door had gone, the stone step was no longer scrubbed, the snow-white nets had been replaced by curtains of a dark and uncertain hue. They were half-drawn.

Paula had been fervent in the faith: a daily mass attender. The old parish priest Samantha had met when she'd searched for Benjamin would know where they'd gone. She returned to her car and began to drive through the network of narrow streets lined with terraced houses, heading back to the dual carriageway. The Catholic church was on the other side, surrounded by detached houses and nineteen-thirties semis.

FATHER RYAN TRIED to ease the weight on his knees. They ached so now, especially in the cold weather, and the kneelers in the front pews desperately needed re-padding. He ought to get an upholsterer in, have them all…Heavens, the nonsense, the monkey chatter, that flowed like an unruly torrent through his mind whenever he tried to turn his thoughts to God. And the young woman was in such desperate need of prayer. Woman? Brenda Baxter was well into her twenties, but she still looked like a young girl. What did the men see in her? He'd baptised her, given her her first holy communion, presented her with prizes on school speech days. Now she was gone, vanished without a trace, and her mother, blinded by pride, fearful of the shame, had lied to the police; she'd told them her daughter'd gone to relatives in Ireland. He'd offered his masses for the girl and said prayers. It was all he could do, yet whenever he thought of her he had such feelings of desolation and dread.

He heard a movement behind him, made the sign of the cross, then rose to his feet and turned towards the back of the church. A woman was gazing at him out of the shadows; night-black hair with a deep fringe, green eyes in a pale and perfect face, blood-red lips. He felt a sudden and inexplicable unease. He knew her. She was removing a glove as she walked towards him, high-heels tap-tapping on the terrazzo floor.

'Father Ryan.' Her husky voice whispered around the empty church.

He grasped the proffered hand. 'Miss Grey! The woman who found little Benjamin.'

'That was quite a while ago, Father.'

'Paula was sure he was dead. She thought she'd never see him again, not even have his little body to bury.'

'I have to talk with her, Father. That's why I'm here. She's left the house in Atherton Road. I need her new address. I presume you have it?'

'She's quite close: Shelley Road, I can't remember the number, but I've got it somewhere. The house backs on to the school playing field. Will you have a cup of coffee? And a biscuit? I think I can find a biscuit.' He stepped out into the aisle, genuflected, then led her towards the sacristy.

She linked her arm in his, felt his body tense at the intimacy. 'Coffee would be pleasant, Father.' She gave his arm a squeeze. 'Tell me how you are?'

'Fine, Miss Grey. A few aches and pains, but apart from that, I'm fine.' They stepped into a narrow room lined with cupboards and shallow vestment drawers.

He didn't look fine. His white hair was thinner, his shoulders more stooped, his face even more lined and tired than she remembered. She squeezed his arm again. 'Is the bishop still banging on about poor collections and dwindling congregations?'

He chuckled. 'How did you know about that?'

'You told me, when I was searching for Benjamin, when I came to talk to you about the Hamiltons.'

'He's not so strident, but he still shows his displeasure.'

'Perhaps you should tell him to drive over in his big black limo and have a go himself.' She'd never understood the extreme deference priests displayed towards their bishops.

Father Ryan let out a shocked laugh. 'He'd be outraged, Miss Grey. He'd remind me of my vow of obedience.' The old priest opened a door that led into the hallway of the house, then turned his head and looked at her. Her face was very close. Dear God, those eyes and that soft red mouth: and she was so fragrant. She wouldn't be daunted by the bishop, and the bishop wouldn't dare complain about anything to her. He led her across a hallway and into a room at the rear of the house. 'Do you mind if we sit in the kitchen? I try to save on the heating and it's the place I keep warm.'

'Kitchen's fine.' Samantha drew a chair from beneath

a table covered with a yellow and white check cloth while he unhooked mugs hanging from a dresser, found coffee, sugar and a jug of milk. His movements were slow, his cheap black suit crumpled and shiny, but his grey shirt with its Roman collar was clean and freshly ironed. He filled a kettle and switched it on, then turned towards her.

'Paula still prays for you and has masses said for you.'

Samantha smiled.

Strange, he reflected, that this exotic creature, in her black roll-neck sweater and long herringbone-pattern coat, should suddenly appear. It was as if Our Blessed Lord had sent her. Could she be the answer to his prayers?

The kettle rumbled to the boil and he busied himself making coffee and finding biscuits, glad to be able to turn away for a moment from the woman's intimidating gaze. He carried steaming mugs and a plate of biscuits over to the table, then drew out a chair and sat facing her.

'Paula's been unwell,' he said, breaking a silence he was beginning to find embarrassing. 'Bronchitis. She suffers from it every winter, usually turns into pleurisy. It's particularly bad this year.'

Samantha sipped her coffee. 'How's she coping with Benjamin while she's ill?'

'They manage, and she has a good neighbour.'

'How is Benjamin?'

Father Ryan shrugged. 'Doing very well academically; they've put him in a higher class, with older children. He's exceptionally bright, but...'

Samantha raised an eyebrow.

'...but he's still a strange and unusual child. Doesn't relate very well to his classmates, he's reluctant to play games, can't cope with noise and confusion in the classroom or the playground. He has some very mature insights into things, but he still mixes up the real world with the world of his imagination. The teacher preparing him for his First Holy Communion wants to hold him back; she says he has some strange notions about angels and being visited by the dead.' Father Ryan reached for a biscuit and bit into it. 'But he's very loving and affectionate towards his mother.'

Samantha slid her mug on to the table. The coffee was bland and tasteless. 'Paula Hamilton's address, Father. You said you had it.'

'Of course.' The priest rose, scraped his chair over worn red tiles, and headed out into the hall. Cold air began to waft in through the open door. Samantha could hear him opening drawers and searching through papers. When he returned he was leafing through the pages of an address book. 'She lives quite close to the church now, Shelley Road, but I can never remember the… Ah, here we are, number thirty-six. Turn right after the school, then right again; that's Shelley Road.'

'Thanks, Father. And thanks for the coffee.' She reached for her black clutch bag.

'Please don't go, not yet. There's something I have to ask you.'

Samantha settled back in her chair.

'There's a girl—she's well into her twenties, so I suppose she's a woman, but she still looks like a girl—she used to be a parishioner. She's missing.' He glanced at Samantha. The green eyes were gazing at him, the glistening crimson mouth was smiling expectantly. He swallowed hard. 'Her friend reported it to the police, but the girl's mother said she was with relatives in Ireland. She was ashamed, you see.'

'Ashamed?'

'The girl works as a prostitute, shares a flat with the friend. The mother's very bitter. When I tackled her about it, she said she'd rather her daughter was dead than mired in sin. She meant it, too. They're from Galway. The old school. Hard as nails.' He sighed. 'Chastity without charity is a barren virtue, Miss Grey.'

'Did the mother tell you about this, Father?'

The priest shook his head. 'The friend came to see me when she realized what the mother had done, and now I can't stop worrying about the child.'

'Her mother could be telling the truth; perhaps she has gone to Ireland.'

'The family lives in a tiny little village on the west coast, just a pub and a shop, a few farms and a dozen cottages. I phoned the parish priest there. No one's visiting them.'

'She's a woman, Father, not a child. A woman who's chosen to earn her living in a precarious way.'

'I held her in my arms when I baptised her, Miss Grey. She'll always be a child to me.'

'What is it you're asking me, Father?'

'To find her.'

Samantha laughed softly. 'I have commitments, Father. And it's a job best left to the police. Can't you persuade the mother to be reasonable?'

'Her pride is stronger than her love for her child, and she's already lied to the police.' He frowned across the table at Samantha, disappointment etched on his face. He hadn't expected to be refused, not by an answer to his prayers. He made his voice coaxing. 'You found little Benjamin. After the police had given up, when they were certain he was dead, you found him and brought him home to Paula.'

'You don't know what you're asking, Father. Benjamin was special. The government might have fallen if he'd not been found. And I have duties and obligations. I can't drop everything and search when one of your parishioners goes missing.'

He gestured towards Samantha's coat, her bag with the big gold clasp, and there was a tremor in his voice as he said, 'God's been kind to you, Miss Grey; your fine clothes, your splendid car. Can't you give something back?'

'I'd walk barefoot and in rags if I could have back what's been taken from me,' Samantha hissed. 'You don't know a thing about me, Father. How dare you blackmail me like this. And you don't know the price that had to be paid to bring Benjamin home. Thirteen men died. I slaughtered my way to the boy.' She sat back. She'd said too much. Calming herself, she whispered softly, 'We're both keepers of secrets, Father. You must take that one with you to the grave.'

Dismayed by her anger, appalled by the revelation, he stared down at his cup. After a long silence, he mumbled, 'I'm sorry, Miss Grey. It was very wrong of me to say what I did.' He managed to look at her again. 'It's just that when you appeared in the church this morning, you seemed like an answer to prayer.'

'An answer to prayer!' Samantha laughed softly. 'I've been called a murdering whore, a sack of filth, the Daughter of Satan, but no one's ever called me an answer to prayer.' She laughed again. 'Give me the address of the flat, Father; and the name of the girl she shared it with.'

The old priest flicked through to the back of the notebook, took out a slip of paper and passed it over the table. 'The missing girl's called Brenda Baxter. The flat's in Manchester, decent area, Melton Court, High-grove Road. She shared with a girl called Laura Kirby. The telephone number's on there.'

'Do you have a photograph?'

Father Ryan shook his head. 'Might be able to get you an old photograph from the school, and I suppose there's a chance the mother would give me one.'

'Don't tell the mother. If she's as bitter as you say, she could cause problems. We'll keep this to ourselves.'

'If you give me your number, I'll call you if I find a photograph.'

Samantha slid the paper into her bag, then scribbled her mobile number on a square of card and handed it to him. 'I'll phone you, Father, when I have some information. But if there are no obvious leads, I'm going to forget it.'

Father Ryan led her through to the hall. 'Can I ask why you're visiting Paula?'

She gave him a knowing look. 'You know the family history, Father, you watch the news on television. You can guess why I have to talk to Paula Hamilton, and I'm sure she'll tell you what she wants you to know.'

'I'm worried about her. She's quite poorly. Illness has aged her dreadfully.'

'Are there any relatives?'

'Some in Ireland, her husband's family. They didn't keep in touch with her after he died.'

'And if she doesn't recover, what about Benjamin?'

'I daren't think about that, Miss Grey.' Father Ryan tugged open the front door.

Powdery white frost still lingered on trees and hedges, dusted spiders' webs lurking amongst ivy that covered a wall. On the drive, her red Ferrari Fiorano gleamed. Samantha stepped out into the cold misty air.

'You'll keep me informed about Brenda?' Father Ryan's tone was pleading.

'If I find her, Father, and if she's alive, I'll send her back to you for a blessing.'

SAMANTHA PRESSED HER thumb on the button. Tubular chimes ding-donged beyond the door. The house Paula Hamilton had moved to was small; a narrow path led down the side to a boarded gate, and a rectangular bay took up most of the frontage. Gravel had been laid where there had once been a table-cloth sized lawn, and plastic urns, arranged on either side of the porch, sprouted plastic bushes that seemed unnaturally green in the wintry gloom. She heard coughing, faint but coming closer. After what seemed a painfully long time, bolts were drawn, a key turned and the door opened.

Paula Hamilton froze, her eyes wide with shock, her wrinkled hand pressing a handkerchief to her mouth. 'Dear God, Miss Grey! I thought I'd never see you again. You never came back, and I wanted so desperately to thank you for finding Benjamin.' She opened the door wider. 'Come in. Please, come in.'

Samantha squeezed past her in the narrow hallway, heard the door close, more sounds of coughing and Paula Hamilton saying, 'Into the sitting room; it's the first door.'

'You've moved house. I had to ask Father Ryan for your new address.' The bay window made the stiflingly warm room seem larger than it was. Knitting and a prayerbook were lying on a sofa. Samantha unbuttoned her coat as she crossed a red and brown patterned carpet and sat on the edge of a chintzy armchair.

'There was only me and Benjamin left down Atherton Road. It filled up with Bangladeshis and Pakistanis.

I'd lived there for thirty years and in the end I felt like an intruder.'

'How is Benjamin?'

Paula's face brightened. 'Fine. Doing wonderfully well at school. They've moved him up a class, put him with the eight-year olds. He still talks about you—the lady with the green eyes.' Her face suddenly crumpled. She covered her mouth with the handkerchief and began to weep. 'God, I'm so grateful to you. I was certain he was dead. I never believed you when you said you'd bring him back. Why didn't you come into the house with him? I wanted to thank you. I wanted to—'

'It was best that no one saw me. I parked at the corner of the road, watched him walk over, then drove away when you opened the door.'

Paula blew her nose and tucked the soggy handkerchief in her pinafore pocket. 'I've been expecting a letter or a telephone call ever since I heard the news about Lawrence Cosgrave, but I never thought they'd send you.'

'His wife started looking through bank statements. She became curious about the monthly payments. I was asked to visit her and explain.'

'What must she be feeling; husband dead, sons dead, all within the space of a week. I hope God will help her bear—'

'Sons dead?'

'It was on the breakfast news. Their bodies were found in London. The police took Mrs Cosgrave to identify them last night. That's all they said. It was one of those breaking news things. Showed a picture of them. They were such fine handsome boys. I don't know how she'll...'

Samantha had stopped listening. She was trying to

absorb the news. It was transforming what had been no more than vague suspicions into a nagging fear. 'The news bulletin,' Samantha interrupted, 'there was no other information, just that the bodies had been found?'

'That's all; that and the picture of them. Will you have a cup of tea? Can I make you a bite to eat? Some toast, perhaps?'

'You're not well. I should be making you tea and toast.'

'It's the bronchitis; it affects me every year about this time.' Paula smiled. 'Anyway, when we first met you told me you didn't cook and didn't clean houses or wash dishes and clothes. You told me you had a man who did that for you.'

'He still does, but I could make you tea and toast.'

'Mrs Shepherd, next door, brings me something in. We sit and have lunch together. She's been good to me.'

Samantha returned Paula Hamilton's smile. Thick brown stockings were wrinkled over her scrawny calves, her face was sunken and pale, her hair lifeless and completely white, but her blue cardigan and grey skirt were spotlessly clean, her flowered pinafore freshly ironed. It was as if keeping herself neat and clean were part of the fight against illness and bodily decay. She couldn't pass herself off as Benjamin's mother now.

'Does the man who cooks and cleans for you still have a boyfriend?' Distaste sounded in Paula's wheezing voice.

'He's had several since we met. He's called Crispin. He's very kind and gentle, very handsome. If you met him, I'm sure you'd like him.'

Paula coughed and reached into her pinafore pocket for her handkerchief. 'I sometimes think I've lived too

long, Miss Grey. I don't understand the world any more.'
She covered her mouth and coughed again.

Samantha sensed that Paula was too tired and ill to
talk; that she ought to finish her business and leave.
'Mrs Cosgrave asked me to come and see you,' she said.

'I suppose she was shocked when you told her about
Rachel and her husband?'

'She was already struggling to come to terms with his
sudden death, but she was certainly shocked: shocked
and angry.'

'I saw her once or twice with her husband, at mass
in St Jude's in Stockport. When he became Prime Minister they didn't go there so much, but she still has the
big detached house up on Ludlow Hill. I suppose she'll
come back to it now.'

'She wanted me to ask you for a photograph of Benjamin, and to tell you that the payments will continue,
as before.'

Surprise registered on Paula's face. 'I didn't expect
that. I thought she'd sent you to tell me she was stopping
them. I've been dreading the money going. We'd have
managed somehow, but…' She frowned at Samantha.
'Why does she want a photograph?'

Samantha shrugged. 'Curiosity, perhaps. Benjamin is
her husband's child.' She saw Paula wince and rebuked
herself for being so insensitive. News of the deaths of
Mrs Cosgrave's sons had distracted her. Her thoughts
were elsewhere.

Paula pushed herself up from the sofa and shuffled
over to a sideboard. She rested her hand on its gleaming top while she recovered her breath, then slid open
a drawer. 'This one was taken at school, just before
Christmas. He never smiles for the camera, but at least
he's not scowling.'

Samantha rose and took it from her, a six-by-four in a red card folder. It was Benjamin, just as she remembered him: the fair curly hair, the dark eyes, intensely serious behind wire-rimmed spectacles, the unsmiling mouth and determined chin. The resemblance to Lawrence Cosgrave was striking. She glanced up. 'May I give her this?'

Paula nodded, then closed the drawer and shuffled back to the sofa. 'Tell her I'm sorry about her husband and her sons. Tell her I'll keep her in my prayers. And please thank her for not stopping the payments; tell her I'm very grateful.'

Samantha slid the photograph into her bag. 'You're not well. Why not let me make you a hot drink?'

'Don't worry yourself. It's the bronchitis. I'm like this every year. Mrs Shepherd will be round soon, and Benjamin gets home just after four. I wish he could have seen you. Will you come again?'

'Probably not. It's better that I don't.' Samantha clicked her bag shut, stepped over to the sofa and took Paula's hands in hers. They were clammy and cold. Paula's shoulders suddenly drooped. She lowered her head and began to weep. Samantha sat down beside her and drew her close. There was no flesh on her body, just skin and bones, and she was shivering, as if with a fever. Her breathing was laboured.

Paula pressed her handkerchief to her mouth, trying to control a bout of coughing, as she whimpered, 'I'm so afraid.'

'What are you afraid of?' Samantha held her tightly.

'Dying, Benjamin being left on his own. He's difficult with strangers. They frighten him, and his fear makes him tense and hostile. No one's going to want him when I've gone.'

'Then you'll have to look after yourself.'

'God might take me whether I look after myself or not.'

'If God takes you, He'll have to take care of Benjamin.'

THE SOUNDPROOFED OFFICE door suddenly swung open then crashed shut. Marcus glanced up, startled. Loretta Fallon was striding towards the desk. Today, her white silk blouse had a Mao collar and her navy-blue suit looked new. Unusually for her, the hem of its pencil skirt was an inch above the knee. She dropped her brief case and sank into a chair.

'Any developments, Marcus?'

'Nothing, ma'am. Quiet as the grave. Not much telephone or internet chatter, no news from the people in the field. How did the Emergency Committee go?'

'Deputy Prime Minister's finding her feet, developing quite a killer instinct, and the Home Secretary's egging her on. Metropolitan Police Commissioner's been told to consider his position.'

'Sir Nigel? He's been asked to resign?'

'More or less told to. Rather embarrassing; they shouldn't have done it in front of me. They're angry and scared, Marcus. There were a lot of raised voices. They're saying the Met's completely failed in its protection role. Seems that while Sir Nigel's people were floundering around in Spain, Cosgrave's boys were lying dead in London, and it wasn't the police who discovered the bodies.'

Marcus's wickedly blue eyes were twinkling. He'd never really cared for Sir Nigel. He gazed at Loretta for a long moment, then his lips slowly shaped themselves into a questioning smile.

'Rubbish skip at the back of a small art gallery in Pimlico,' she explained. 'Place was being refurbished and an exhibit got thrown away. Pile of rusty tins with numbers stencilled on called *Homage to the Gods of War*; been exhibited at the Tate Modern, quite valuable. Gallery owner went frantic, started searching in the skip and found the bodies amongst the tins. Media got hold of the story, so the Government haven't been able to control the release, but they've persuaded them to withhold the details.'

'Rusty tin cans?' Marcus's smile widened.

'This isn't funny, Marcus. The Met got a hammering today, it could be us tomorrow.'

'Just thinking about something Jeremy Farrell, our Minister for Culture and the Arts, said at the club the other night, but it's hardly fit for your ears, ma'am.'

Loretta scowled. 'Don't sit there grinning. Tell me, Marcus.'

'Farrell said, "If they wrapped dog shit in newspaper and painted the parcels pillar-box-red, they'd display it at the Tate Modern".'

Loretta fought back a smile. 'Jeremy Farrell has more feeling for art and culture than I imagined. Pity he confines his remarks to his friends at the club.'

'Surprised he became Culture Minister,' Marcus said thoughtfully. 'I'd have thought they'd have made him Home Secretary. Number two at the Home office in the last government, very close to Cosgrave, popular but feared; knows a lot of dark little secrets. Cosgrave used to call him his enforcer.'

Loretta crossed long and shapely legs; the hem of her skirt rose another inch above her knees. 'Quest's visited Cosgrave's widow.'

'I'm relieved. She was reluctant to go. Worried about the exposure.'

'It's ruffled Sir Nigel's feathers. I gather Quest took her into a bathroom and turned the taps and a radio on. They didn't pick up a thing.' Loretta laughed. 'He was livid. He thinks we're on to something. Kept going on about co-operation between the services; sharing information. I presume she'll let you have a report?'

'Probably not, ma'am. Private matter. And she did visit at the request of the widow. But I'll talk to her.'

'I think you should, Marcus. Would she renew her contract?'

'We've got good people working on this, ma'am; here and abroad. Would she be right? The politicians are going to want arrest and trial.' A red phone began to ring. Marcus snatched it up, listened for a moment, then said, 'The Chief's with me. She's just got back from Number 10...I'll tell her. And keep us both informed.' He cradled the handset and looked at Loretta. 'Mob have surrounded that big new mosque in Newham. Started to gather about an hour ago. Worshippers have barricaded themselves inside. Riot police are trying to disperse the crowd.'

'Probably the news about the Prime Minister's sons. Far Right's been rabble rousing. This is what the Home Secretary was afraid of.' She eyed Marcus for a moment, then said, 'Talk to Quest. Persuade her to renew, let her take a look at it.'

'Involve Quest and you could be throwing away any hope of arrest and trial. She's become paranoid about being exposed. She won't hesitate to kill if she thinks she's under any kind of threat.'

'Just instruct her to find out what she can and report back. The Met can gather the evidence.'

'Might not be any evidence to gather, ma'am. If you unleash Quest you might just have bodies.'

Loretta picked up her briefcase and rose to her feet. 'The Prime Minister's been assassinated and his sons have been murdered. I can't keep on telling the Emergency Committee I've nothing to report. I've got to have a result. And if it is Islamic terrorism or Dissident Irish Republicans, the politicians might not be too bothered about arrest and trial. Contact Quest, Marcus. Persuade her to find out what she can. When we know something, I'll talk to the Deputy PM and the Home Secretary. They can decide how robust they want our response to be.'

SIX

THE FEMALE VOICE rattling out of the intercom had a strong Liverpool accent. It sounded surprised and relieved. A remotely operated lock clicked, Samantha pushed open the panelled outer door and stepped into a dimly lit entrance hall. Another door opened beyond some concrete stairs and a smiling dark-haired girl called out, 'What did you say your name was?'

'I didn't.'

The girl beckoned her inside. 'But you did say Father Ryan sent you?'

'He asked me to come and see you.' Samantha entered a small hallway. Laura Kirby closed the door, led her into a sitting room and began to gather up magazines, a plate and a mug from a sofa with cream linen covers. 'Place is a bit of a mess. I didn't get in until after three, and I've—'

'It's fine,' Samantha said. It reminded her of her own sitting-room before Crispin had visited and given it what he called a thorough clean. She relaxed into the sofa and unbuttoned her coat. The girl dumped the magazines and crockery on the floor, then sat on an armchair beside a television and tucked her legs under her. Quite pretty, Samantha mused; glamorous with make-up on and her hair done and wearing a dress instead of the bathrobe and crumpled pyjamas.

'I suppose Father Ryan told you what's happened— told you what Brenda's mother did? Brenda wouldn't

go to Ireland. She hated the sanctimonious old buggers. It's the last place she'd go. Are you going to look
for her?' Dark and curious eyes swept over Samantha.
'That's a fabulous coat. I love the huge lapels and the
bold herring-bone pattern. And the boots and bag and
gloves are to-die-for.'

Samantha smiled. 'I need to talk with you. If you can
tell me something that's worth following up, I will. If
you can't, then I'll have to let it go.'

The girl's face clouded.

'When did you last see her?'

'Ten days ago. It was in the evening, about six, she
was having one of her regulars in and I was doing a call
out: dinner escort. Client took me back to his hotel, so I
didn't get home until after two. When I got up the next
morning, she wasn't here. I kept trying her mobile, but
all I got was the leave-a-message voice. I called the police around four in the afternoon. They didn't come until
nearly midnight. I had to cancel a booking; client got
very upset. The police had just got inside the door when
they had a message on their two-way radio. They'd sent
someone to see Brenda's mother and she'd told them
Brenda was visiting relatives in Ireland, so they just
left. Didn't ask me a thing. I could tell they thought I
was a time-waster. All I could do then was keep trying
her mobile, but I didn't get an answer. After a couple of
days I went to see the priest. She liked him. Nice to her
in confession, she said. He was really upset when I told
him. He phoned me after he'd been to see the mother
and told me he couldn't do anything.'

'You said you were doing a call out. Presumably that's
when you visit clients in their hotel rooms?'

'Homes or hotel rooms. Works better that way. Neighbours can get awkward if they see too many different

men coming to the flat. But Brenda used to see her regulars here.'

'Did she have many regulars?'

'They were mostly regulars; blokes who went for the little-girl look. She was small and slim; completely flat chested. When she tied her hair in bunches and wore kids' clothes she looked about twelve in a dim light.'

'And she'd entertained a regular on the evening she went missing?'

Laura Kirby nodded. 'He was OK. She liked him. Bloke in his late thirties, early forties. Very well spoken: Southerner, not from round here. I saw him once. I was coming in as he was leaving. Tall, good-looking, nice clothes.'

'And she dressed like a child for him?'

'Second visit he brought her the things he wanted her to wear. A blue-check gingham dress, white cotton knickers and some black patent-leather shoes: strapovers with rounded toes.'

'You have these things here?'

'They're in her bedroom. I'll take you through.'

Samantha rose from the sofa, followed the girl into the hall and through a door into a double bedroom. Pink curtains had been drawn across the window and the room was in semi-darkness. When Laura switched on the pink-shaded light, a warm glow illuminated pink candy-striped wallpaper, a pink carpet and the pink satin counterpane covering a double bed. Cuddly toys were piled up against the quilted headboard and along the top of a white chest of drawers and matching dressing-table. Samantha smiled at Laura Kirby. 'Brenda liked teddy bears and pink.'

'All part of the innocent-little-girl thing.' Laura stepped over to a wardrobe fitted across a recess and tugged open the doors. She lifted a hanger from a rail and held a faded blue gingham dress against her body. Its hem just reached the top of her thighs.

Samantha took it from her, felt in the side pockets and a breast pocket, then lifted up the white collar. A name tag had been cut away. Embroidered around a laurel wreath on the breast pocket were the words, *The Martha Hemmingway School for Girls. Educate, Enlighten, Empower.* She glanced at Laura. 'This was hanging here when you came in to look for her?'

'Thrown on the floor. I'd put it away, before I realized I ought to leave things alone.'

'And you remade the bed?'

Laura took Samantha's arm, led her further into the room and pointed towards the space between the bed and the dressing-table. A grass-green tufted rug had been unrolled there. White ankle-socks, shiny black shoes and some white cotton knickers were strewn on and around it. 'They never used the bed. He liked her to lie on this rug, on her back, put her legs in the air, then push her knickers down while she said, "Come and see what I've got, Edward." He asked her to call him Edward. She told me they never had proper sex.'

Samantha couldn't hold back a smile.

Laura laughed. 'You'd never believe the daft things some of them want you to do.'

'And they never had sex?'

'Not according to Brenda, and he was one of the few customers she really fancied. Poor bugger was probably impotent. After she'd asked him to come and look at her, he used to shuffle across the room on his hands and knees then stroke and fondle her while he said, "You're a bad girl, Nancy"—he called her Nancy—"you're a naughty, naughty girl." Brenda said he was very gentle.

He was never unpleasant. Once he started to cry. When she put her arm around him, he pushed her away, put his clothes on and dashed out without saying a word. She thought he'd never come back, but he did.'

'Have you got a clean bin-liner?'

'I think there're a few left on the roll.'

When Laura had left the room, Samantha reached into her bag, found a pair of latex gloves and snapped them on. She picked up the knickers. They were clean and unstained, with a brand and size tag sewn inside the waist. There was no maker's name on the shoes; just *Size 4* stamped inside the heel. Samantha heard a rustling and glanced up. Laura had returned with the bin-liner. Samantha said, 'Brenda had tiny feet.'

'Everything about her was tiny.'

'How did she meet this man?' Samantha folded the knickers and put them in the plastic bag, then gathered up the ankle-socks and shoes.

'We advertise, on the internet, with photographs and mobile numbers. I don't show my face, but Brenda does.'

Samantha knelt down and began to roll up the rug. 'He came in a car?' She slid the rug into the black bin liner, rose to her feet, then took the dress from the hanger.

'I never saw one. If he did, he parked it some distance away.'

'And you don't know his name?' Samantha folded the dress and put it with the other things.

'Only that he asked Brenda to call him Edward. But he did leave something once. At least, Brenda thought it was him that had left it—she'd had another client before she noticed it.' Laura went to the dressing-table, opened a mirrored casket and lifted out a tray of cheap trinkets. She peered inside, stirred things with her finger, then picked out a rectangle of white card. 'You make them pay before they get undressed. One time he dropped his wallet and she found this the next day, down the side of the chest of drawers.'

Samantha took the business card and read the words out loud. 'Zelda Unwin, Head of Criminal Law, Weinman Wallace and Webster, Devonshire Chambers, Grove Street, Manchester.' She turned the card over. Numbers had been written in pencil on the back: 3, 65, 42, 294, 39, and 196. 'Can I keep this?'

'Why not? Are you taking the other things?'

'They ought to be left here. Can they go in the wardrobe?'

Laura grabbed the plastic sack, settled it behind the hanging clothes and closed the doors.

'Did Brenda have any sort of appointment book?'

'Just a diary for the bookings. We note the names they give us, and times, and the places if it's a call-out, that's all. She kept hers in her handbag.'

'You have her bag?'

'I've looked for it, but I can't find it.'

'Did she take anything else?'

'A suitcase. I noticed it had gone a couple of days ago, when I went to get the hoover out of the store.'

'The store?'

'It's a little cubby-hole under the stairs to the other flats. We keep the ironing board and buckets and brushes in there. The case was at the back. She bought it to bring her stuff from her old flat when she moved in; big green canvas thing with wheels and a handle. Taxi driver could hardly lift it into the boot.'

'You're sure it went at the time Brenda left?'

'It must have done. Once a week I do my share of the cleaning and I'd hoovered through the day she disappeared. When I went for the hoover again, the things in the store were all over the place. That's how I realized the case had gone.' Dark eyes studied Samantha's face, then the girl's voice became plaintive. 'You're not very hopeful. I can tell.'

'I'll go and see this Zelda Unwin, but if that doesn't produce any leads, I'll have to let it go. It's a job for the police. They'd examine the rug and clothes for DNA traces then search their records for a match. And there might be street cameras they could check.'

'Police won't listen to me any more, not after her mother lied to them. As far as they're concerned, I'm just a stupid tart.'

Samantha turned towards the door.

'Will you come and see me and tell me what you find out?'

'I promised Father Ryan I'd keep him informed. Give him a call in a couple of days, but don't build your hopes up. If I were you, I'd look for another flatmate to share the rent. Get someone else in here so you can watch out for one another.'

THE YOUNG WOMAN on the reception desk put her hand over the mouthpiece of the phone. 'Miss Unwin says she's terribly busy, Miss Grey. She's asked me to make an appointment for you. When would be—'

Samantha opened her ID wallet, flicked through to the Serious Crime Unit card and held it up. 'This can't wait. Tell her I'll only take up a couple of minutes of her time.'

Still peering at the card, the woman uncovered the mouthpiece. 'Miss Grey's from the Serious Crime Unit, Miss Unwin. She says it's an urgent matter and she'll only keep you a…Very good, Miss Unwin. I'll ask her to take a seat.'

'Is anyone in there?'

The woman shook her head.

'Tell her I'm coming in. Where's her office?'

'Really! You can't just—'

'Where's her office?'

'It's the door facing you when you get to the top of the stairs, but…Miss Grey…Miss Grey…You can't just…'

The agitated voice faded as Samantha swept up the stairs. Without bothering to knock, she opened the door and stepped into a large room. Books lined one wall, filing cabinets another. A buxom woman with wavy shoulder-length dark hair was sitting behind a desk with her back to an uncurtained window.

'Whoever you are, and whatever your business is,' the woman snapped, 'this intrusion is completely unacceptable. I'm desperately busy, and I insist that you leave.'

'Just two minutes, no more.' Samantha gave Zelda Unwin a dazzling smile as she approached the desk across a square of red blue and green Turkish carpet. 'Do you know a girl called Brenda Baxter? She lives in Manchester.'

'Not that I recall. Should I know her?'

'She's a prostitute.' Samantha clicked open her bag, took out the business card, then leaned over ribbon-tied bundles of files and handed it to Zelda Unwin. 'This was found in her flat.'

'So?'

'She wasn't a client?'

'I don't remember the name, and I don't recall ever having been engaged by a prostitute. Perhaps a client of mine who was a client of hers left it there.'

'Thanks, Miss Unwin.' Samantha retrieved the card,

smiled, and flicked it over. 'Have you any idea what these pencilled numbers might mean?'

Zelda peered at the figures, then let out an exasperated snort. 'Of course not. Whoever had the card must have scribbled them there.'

Samantha allowed her smile to widen. 'I thought there was just a chance they might identify it for you.' She dropped the card back in her bag and clicked it shut.

'Miss…What did you say your name was?'

'Grey.'

'Miss Grey, I really am extremely busy. I must insist—'

'Of course.' Samantha retraced her steps to the door, tugged it open, then glanced back. 'Did you, by any chance, go to the Martha Hemmingway School for Girls?'

'How did you know that?'

'I remember you.'

'You were a pupil there?'

'Very briefly, perhaps a couple of months. I was taken away. Family problems.'

'It's quite a while ago. I'm amazed you remember me.'

'It was the name.'

'Unwin?'

'No, Zelda. I was a great fan of Scott Fitzgerald at the time.'

'Scott Fitzgerald?'

'*This Side of Paradise, Tender is the Night, The Great Gatsby.* His wife was called Zelda. When the girls told me someone in the upper school had the same unusual name, it made an impression.'

Zelda Unwin suddenly remembered her deadline and scowled. 'Miss Grey, I must ask you to go.'

Samantha stepped out on to the landing, then popped her face back around the edge of the door. 'Thanks for your time, Miss Unwin. You've been most kind.' Then, laughing, she made her voice schoolmarmishly brisk. 'Don't forget: Educate, Enlighten, Empower.'

MARCUS TOSSED HIS spectacles on to the blotter and sagged back in his chair. He was too tired to make any sense of the meaningless conversations in the transcripts. It was time he left. He shuffled the papers together and slid them into his briefcase. Beyond the circle of light from the desk lamp, the office was in darkness and, through the window, he could see the lights of an airliner winking as it drifted across the night sky. He wished he was on it, going somewhere where the sun shone and cold rain didn't drizzle down incessantly and he wasn't plagued by Dissident Republicans and Islamic fundamentalists.

The red phone began to ring. He snatched it up. 'Ma'am?'

'You're still here, Marcus.'

'Just about to leave.'

'Did you contact Quest?'

'She's agreed to extend, ma'am.'

'Did she take much persuading?'

'None at all. She surprised me. I think she wanted to be involved. The paperwork's gone off: another three months on the same terms. She asked for round-the-clock research back-up. I've laid it on. A small team working in three shifts. Quest's had them probing the Met's files already.'

'Keep your eye on it, Marcus.'

'I've told the back-up team to let me have copies of everything they send to Quest.'

'Where's Quest now?'

'Home, in Yorkshire. She contacted me about an hour ago, asked me to arrange another meeting with the Prime Minister's widow. Fixed it for tomorrow at ten.'

'Does she still have that manservant, the male model who owns a hairdressing salon? I can never remember his name.'

'Crispin. When she phoned me he was running her bath and they were having pre-dinner drinks. I understand he's quite a good cook.'

Laughter rustled in the earpiece. 'I've seen his photographs in magazines, Marcus. He can run my bath. Do you think he really is gay? I've always suspected Quest's been lying to us. I'm sure they sleep together.'

'Queer as a nine-pound note, ma'am. We checked him out when we were clearing Quest.'

'Such a pity. What are *you* doing tonight? Are you going home to Charlotte?'

'Dining at the club. I'm bunking down in an attic room there while the emergency's on.'

'Sign a car out of the pool and drive me home. I'll cook you a meal.'

'I'd like that, ma'am.'

'And you can stay over and bring me back to headquarters early in the morning.'

'Ten minutes: I'll park the car by the archway and wait for you.'

'And Marcus?'

'Yes, ma'am.'

'When are you going to stop calling me ma'am?'

Marcus chuckled softly. 'Just as soon as we're in the car.'

MOONLIGHT WAS ILLUMINATING the tower of St Michael and the Angels making the frost on the road and on the tops of gravestones glitter. The party had turned into a narrow lane that curved around the side of the churchyard. Jeremy Farrell and his local agent, Victor Norris, were walking in front. Their wives, Julia and Ruth, were a dozen paces behind. The two women were arm-in-arm, struggling to keep up in their high-heels. Jeremy had decided a brisk walk across the village to the vicarage would be a bit of exercise, build up an appetite. Julia Farrell was beginning to wish she'd insisted they'd come in the car.

'Pleasant change to see a bit of style at the vicarage,' Ruth said. 'The last vicar and his wife turned it into a tip with those great dogs peeing everywhere—place used to stink.'

'But Mrs Potter was kind and friendly; she was always visiting around the village. We don't see much of Mrs Leyton.' Julia glanced at her friend. Wrapped in a thick scarf and a rather dated mink coat, she'd gathered up her chestnut hair and clipped some large turquoise studs to her ears.

'Zelda? She's hard at work, earning the money. One of the women who does the flowers told me she'd contributed quite a bit towards the cost of the refurbishment. Ninian Comper vicarage, Grade One Listed: Diocesan Architect wanted varnished pine and William Morris wallpaper, Zelda wanted white paint and Laura Ashley. They had an almighty row. Zelda went to see the bishop, told him she'd pay for all the decorations and some of the improvements. He took the cash and told the architect he had to let her choose.'

Julia laughed. 'Good for her! And she was right. Gloomy old place wanted brightening up.'

'Victor fancies her.'

'I suppose she is rather attractive in a voluptuous kind of way,' Julia conceded.

'It doesn't bother me,' Ruth said airily. 'I quite fancy the vicar. I wouldn't complain if he was pressing me into the mattress every night. I'd moan, but I wouldn't complain.'

'Ruth!' Julia let out a shocked little laugh.

They'd progressed around the curving churchyard wall and the vicarage had come into view. Lights were shining behind every lancet window. Mrs Leyton hadn't bothered to draw her fabulous new curtains. It was as if she wanted the house to be on display.

'Do you think he says his prayers first?' Ruth went on. 'A sort of grace before sex. Bless me, oh Lord, and this my—'

'Stop it, Ruth,' Julia hissed. 'And when we get there, behave yourself. Remember you're the mayor's wife.'

'Mayor!' Ruth loaded the word with contempt. 'I should have been like Zelda Leyton. Had the good sense to get an education and have a career; marry someone intelligent and refined, not that pompous old bore who couldn't wait for his turn to wear the silly hat and drape the gold chain round his neck.'

'God, you're so cynical, Ruth. I don't know what's got into you lately. Victor brings dignity to the Borough, and he gives a lot of pleasure to people when he attends functions. And he's worked hard for Jeremy at more elections than I can remember. He's a very decent man and a loyal friend.'

'He's a pompous old bore,' Ruth muttered.

Their husbands were passing through the vicarage gate and moving on down the path. A door opened to reveal a brightly-lit hall and a tall fair-haired man wearing a smart black suit, grey silk stock and clerical collar stepped out to greet them. 'Jeremy, Victor…' he peered past them, into the shadows between the bushes that lined the path, '…and Julia and Ruth. Wonderful to see you. Come in, come in.'

A woman appeared beside him, her bust and narrow waist, the emphatic sweep of her hips and thighs, subtly emphasized by the elegant plainness of her dress. She shook hands with the men, ushered them in, then stepped out into the frosty night to greet their wives.

'She's displaying her assets,' Ruth whispered. 'If the neckline of that little black dress were any lower she might as well go topless. A couple of drinks and Victor's going to be drooling.'

'Shush,' Julia hissed. 'Don't you dare embarrass me.'

She held back, allowed Ruth to move on ahead. Zelda, serene and smiling, kissed Ruth on the cheek, urged her into the warmth of the house, then turned to Julia and took her hands in hers.

'Lovely to see you, Julia.' She drew her close, kissed her on both cheeks, then followed her up the steps.

A sudden pain stabbed through Julia's ankle. She gasped, swayed, then stumbled back against Zelda.

Zelda slid her arm around Julia's waist and held her steady. 'It's your stiletto heel. It caught against the edge of the mat well.' She called down the hall: 'Take everyone's coat, Andrew, and go through to the sitting-room. Julia's hurt her ankle. I'm just going to attend to it. We won't be a minute.'

Julia heard Jeremy saying, 'Can't understand how she can walk in those ridiculous shoes.' Then, as if dismissing her from his thoughts, he announced breezily, 'Freezing out there. Must be the coldest night of the year.'

'Take your coat off,' Zelda murmured, 'and lean on

me while we cross over to the cloakroom.' She took Julia
into a room lined with white tiles and mirrors, lowered
the lid of the WC and helped her to sit down. Kneeling
beside her, she eased off her shoes. 'It's this one, isn't
it?' She lifted Julia's right ankle.

'It's not too bad. Just a sprain. It—'

'I'll go and fetch a bag of frozen peas. We'll wrap it
round it for a few minutes. If we catch it early, it won't
swell so much.'

Julia gazed around the dazzlingly bright cloak room.
The mirrors, the chrome, the black borders in the til-
ing, the big pedestal wash basin, were very Art Deco.
She smiled to herself; the diocesan architect must have
been absolutely livid.

Zelda returned, a bath towel and a bag from the
freezer in one hand, two glasses balanced on a tiny tray
in the other. 'Mulled wine. Just the thing for a night like
this.' She offered the tray to Julia, then took the other
glass herself. 'It's quite hot.' She dragged a low stool
over, sat in front of Julia and spread the bath-towel over
her lap. Reaching down, she lifted Julia's leg, rested her
foot on the towel and covered her ankle with the bag of
frozen peas. 'There,' she said. 'That should do the trick.'
Her eyes found Julia's. 'How's the world of Westminster?' She sipped her wine.

Julia laughed. 'I've no idea.'

'You don't get involved?'

'I look through correspondence that comes to the
house and the constituency office, send urgent items on
to Jeremy, and I hang on his arm at functions. That's
about all.' She tasted the mulled wine. It was hot and
spicy. After a few sips it began to drive away the shiv-
ery cold and calm her.

'You don't stay with Jeremy in London?' Zelda seemed surprised.

'We have a flat there. Jeremy uses it during the week; I don't go down very often.'

Zelda was holding Julia's gaze. 'And your daughter's just started university. Must be lonely up at The Grange. It's a beautiful house, but Old Forge Lane's a bit isolated.'

Julia's lips tightened in a bleak smile. Loneliness was something she didn't want to think about tonight. She made her voice bright. 'What about your husband? The days must seem long for him with you working in Manchester.'

'Andrew and I have an understanding.'

Julia finished her wine. 'An understanding?'

'Please, have this one, too.' Zelda held out her glass. 'I've only taken a tiny sip. It'll help you get over the shock.' They exchanged glasses, then Zelda explained, 'Being escorted by a handsome and affable husband can sometimes be useful to a woman professionally. His stipend's pathetic, so the money I earn is essential. And having a wife is a big advantage to him; congregations are more comfortable with clergymen who have wives and preferment's usually given to the married man.'

'Preferment?'

'Dean, bishop, archbishop; Andrew's clever and ambitious. It's a very satisfactory arrangement.' She laughed. 'Surely that's the secret of all successful marriages. What about yours? I bet Jeremy wouldn't be a Government Minister if you hadn't been there for him, supporting him, telling him when he was being a bit stupid.'

Surprised by the frankness and not sure how to respond, Julia remained silent and sipped her wine.

Zelda lifted the ice-cold bag and checked Julia's ankle. 'Swelling hasn't developed; in fact, it seems to have gone down a little.'

'It's not painful any more, but that could be the wine.' Zelda was massaging her ankle. Julia felt her hand move up her leg and begin to stroke her calf. Two large glasses of hot wine had blurred her instinct to be shocked, and she was finding the sensation rather pleasant.

'You have beautiful legs. So slender and shapely.'

Julia blushed.

'And your blue dress is simply gorgeous; I think strong colours suit blondes.'

'You look pretty eye-catching yourself,' Julia said, and drained her glass.

Zelda laughed. 'Andrew's a bit outraged. Showed his displeasure before you all arrived. Neckline too low, hem too high and much too body-hugging for a vicar's wife. Said I looked like a chorus girl.' She lowered Julia's foot to the floor and tossed the bag of peas into the hand basin. 'How does it feel?'

'It seems OK. It doesn't hurt.' The wine had made Julia's head swim and her cheeks burn.

'Leave your shoes in here and hold on to my arm. We'll go through to the others. The caterers are waiting to serve dinner.'

A STRIP OF light gleamed beneath Andrew's study door. Nightdress brushing her ankles, Zelda descended the last flight of stairs, crossed the hall and pushed it open. He was frowning down at the books and papers strewn across his desk. His hair was tousled and his shirt-sleeves were rolled up, exposing muscular arms.

'It's late, Andrew. I think you should finish now.'

He smiled at her, then tapped the papers with his

pen. 'Sermon. Tomorrow's Sunday.' He watched her approach across the new red carpet. Her movements held the folds of her nightdress against her body, and there was darkness where the thin cotton brushed her nipples and at the meeting of her thighs. Couldn't she have put on a dressing gown, or at least worn some underwear? She knew how he felt. It was almost as if she were deliberately taunting him, displaying herself in this way.

Zelda rounded the desk and rested her arm on the back of his chair. A brass lamp with a green glass shade was illuminating the pages of a well-worn Bible, a copy of *Blake's Commentary on the New Testament* and several sheets of paper covered with his spiky handwriting. 'I thought the dinner party went well,' she said.

'I enjoyed it. I think they did, too. The media vilifies politicians too much. Jeremy and Victor give a lot to the community.'

'They don't give as much as you do to the ungrateful buggers. You're looking tired, and you've been very preoccupied recently. What's the theme?'

'Theme?'

'Of your sermon?'

'Parable of the talents. It's in tomorrow's readings.' He ran a finger around his clerical collar. Zelda kept the heating running full-blast, day and night, and the entire house was stiflingly warm. She was obsessed with what she called drying the place out. He frowned up at her. 'I do wish you wouldn't talk like that about the parishioners, Zelda. They're mostly kind and decent people.'

She shoved his papers aside, perched on the desk and rested her foot on the edge of his chair. 'Do you think they ever listen—to your sermons, I mean?'

'Some do. I can see the attention in their faces.' His gaze rested fleetingly on breasts that were faintly visible beneath the thin cotton nightdress, then flicked down to his bible.

'It's mostly adoration your female followers feel, Andrew. They don't give a damn what you spout from the pulpit.'

'Nonsense. They're committed to the life of faith, to the Church and the parish. It's the most important part of their lives. It has nothing to do with me.'

'The song not the singer?'

Andrew laughed. 'I couldn't have put it better.'

She rose from the desk. 'I'll leave you to get on, but don't be much longer, it's after midnight.'

He watched her walk towards the door, hips swaying, arms and shoulders smooth and pale in the shadows beyond the light of the lamp. 'Be careful, Zelda,' he said softly.

She paused and looked back. 'Careful? I can't think what you mean.'

'Julia Farrell: I can always tell when someone's taken your fancy. Conference flings, discreet little liaisons in the city, are one thing, but this is too close to home. And she's the wife of a government minister.'

'Exactly, Andrew. She's a wife to him, a mother to her daughter, and she'll probably be no more than a pleasant friend to me.'

THE SERMON WASN'T one of Andrew's finest. If his congregation were listening they wouldn't be much wiser, probably more confused, about the meaning of the parable of the talents. And his delivery wasn't up to scratch; he seemed worried and preoccupied about something. Zelda knew she neglected him, but didn't they have their understanding? Being a senior associate at Weinman

Wallace and Webster demanded most of her time and energy, and he had his flock to minister to.

His ardent female following, his groupies she called them, were packing out the front pews, gazing up at him, resplendent in his lace-trimmed surplice. Julia Farrell was sitting with her MP husband on the other side of the aisle, picking invisible specks of lint from the lapels and sleeves of her very smart peacock-blue suit. Her blonde hair was gathered up under a tiny blue hat that sported a short veil and an explosion of black feathers; probably something she'd bought for a trip to the races.

Zelda recalled Julia's slender calves, the occasional glimpse of inner thigh when she'd nursed her ankle on her lap. She shivered with pleasure. It might come to something. She worked so hard, earning the money that supplemented Andrew's pathetic stipend, she deserved the occasional distraction. She'd invite Julia over to the vicarage for a light lunch and a tour of the newly decorated rooms—ask her to come on a day when Andrew would be at the Deanery meeting.

Winter sunlight slanted through mullioned windows, setting fire to saints imprisoned in crazy spider-webs of lead, spilling over the heads of the congregation in a blazing benediction. Brass-work gleamed, Ninian Comper's decorations were a riot of red and blue and gold on delicately carved oak. The church had fallen silent. She glanced up at the pulpit. Andrew had stopped preaching. He nodded gently towards old Miss Spry at the organ. She began to play; he began to lead the singing. 'Rejoice my soul, the splendour of the Lord. His countless mercies fill my heart with joy.' Miss Spry's fingers fluttered over the consoles, her feet danced over the pedals, her wavering contralto joined Andrew's fine baritone voice. The congregation rose and sang.

It was a rousing hymn. Zelda sang along softly, her lips shaping the words, keeping up appearances. Her husband was offering them a little hope, giving them a little joy, in a sad, shabby, sinful world. He deserved more than the mindless adulation of the women, the indifference of the men. He deserved more than her disbelief.

SEVEN

SPEARS OF ICY rain were hurtling down, bouncing off roofs and pavings, swirling along gutters and into gratings. Blue-uniformed police guards, stoical in their waterproofs, were standing in the narrow pedestrian gateways, gazing across the parkland that surrounded the big Elizabethan house. The heavy door opened and the portly grey-haired man who'd welcomed Samantha on her first visit was standing on the threshold. He unfurled a large black umbrella and strode over to the Ferrari. She climbed out.

'Dreadful weather, Miss Grey. May I escort you into the house?' They made a dash for the entrance, climbed steps and passed into the panelled hallway, their footsteps clattering over the stone floor.

'Mrs Cosgrave asked me to show you up to her bedroom.' The attendant slid the dripping umbrella into a stand then led her through an opening and up the ancient flight of stairs. 'She asked me to bring coffee; coffee and cinnamon toast. Do you care for cinnamon toast, or would you prefer—'

'Cinnamon toast is fine.' Samantha unbuttoned her long coat with the big lapels as they strode on past the white-painted bookcases that lined the upper gallery. The reading lamps hadn't been switched on and dark shadows lurked in the spaces between sofas and tables and armchairs. Walking through the house, Samantha could hear the rain pelting down relentlessly beyond the tall windows; she understood why Mrs Cosgrave felt so uneasy about living there with only the servants for company, understood what she'd meant by too many dark corners and too much history.

They turned into a passageway and paused beside a door. The man knocked gently. At the muffled sound of a woman's voice, he led Samantha inside. 'Miss Grey to see you, Mrs Cosgrave. You instructed me to bring her straight up.'

'Thank you, Angus.'

Samantha heard the door close behind her as she strode on into the room with the pea-green carpet. Mrs Cosgrave was standing at the foot of the four-poster bed, looking rather chic in a long-sleeved black dress that had padded shoulders and a narrow V neck. Her brown hair had been expertly cut and styled, and she'd clipped pearl studs to her ears. Carefully applied make-up wasn't hiding the grief and anguish that ravaged her face. She was a woman clinging to her dignity; a woman fighting hard to maintain her self-control.

'Thank you for coming back, Miss Grey. I'm very grateful to you.' Her voice was flat and emotionless. Samantha wondered if she'd been prescribed sedatives. 'You've heard about my sons, I suppose?'

'Yes. I'm very sorry.'

'Do you want to…' Mrs Cosgrave gestured towards the door to the en-suite bathroom.

Samantha nodded and they went through. The radio was resting on the toilet cistern. Mrs Cosgrave switched it on while Samantha turned on the shower and taps.

'Is this really necessary?' Helen Cosgrave asked, when they were perched, side-by-side, on the rim of the bath.

'It's already been commented on,' Samantha said. 'I

gather the police have complained about not being able to record our last conversation.'

'I'm amazed they should want to. I feel as if I'm invisible now, a mere nuisance to them. I keep on asking when I'll be allowed to return home, but they just give me evasive answers.'

'They're concerned for your safety. Chequers is surrounded by open parkland. They can watch and guard the approaches.'

Helen Cosgrave sighed. 'The staff are very attentive. I can tell they're sympathetic, but I feel as if I've become an embarrassment.'

'They probably don't know what to say,' Samantha murmured softly. 'I don't know what to say. Saying one's sorry is so inadequate it's almost offensive. Words are useless.'

'You told me terrorists murdered your husband.' Helen Cosgrave's voice was tearful now. She was staring down at her hands, her thin fingers restlessly twisting her wedding ring.

'And my half-sister and her husband and their little girl.'

'Does the pain ever go away?'

'No.'

They were sitting very close so they could hear each other's whispers above the hiss and splash of flowing water and the voices on the radio. When Mrs Cosgrave glanced up she found herself caught in Samantha's steady gaze. She shuddered. Dear God, those eyes! So calm and remote, yet always watchful, like an animal stalking its prey. She was suddenly beset by the notion that this strange young woman could read her thoughts. What thoughts? Her mind was in a daze. She wasn't thinking, just endlessly revisiting her agony and pain.

'I've lost everything,' she whispered bleakly. 'My husband, my belief in his fidelity, my tall handsome sons.'

'You still have your life and your health, and you don't fear poverty.'

'True, Miss Grey, but what am I to do with them now?' Helen Cosgrave sighed. 'How is little Benjamin?'

'I understand he's well. Still unusual and showing his intelligence; they've put him in a class with older children.' Samantha clicked open her bag and took out the photograph Paula Hamilton had given her.

Mrs Cosgrave studied it for a while, then said, 'He looks rather intense and very determined. And he's very much like Lawrence; the eyes and nose and the firm little chin.' She looked at Samantha. 'Is he very strange?'

'His intelligence makes him unusual. And he has difficulty separating fantasy from reality, the animate and the inanimate, the living and the dead.'

Helen Cosgrave gave Samantha a questioning look.

'He stayed in Cheltenham for a while. There's a massive bronze at the end of the Promenade, of a minotaur and a hare. He was convinced the hare had escaped and the minotaur was chasing it. I had to tell him I'd killed the minotaur. And classical statues decorate some shop fronts there. He was afraid the shops would collapse if the Greek maidens walked away.'

'And the living and the dead?'

'Benjamin thinks that everyone can come back from the dead, not just Jesus; the teacher preparing him for his First Holy Communion wants to hold him back because of his strange ideas. What the teacher doesn't know is that the man who married his birth mother gave evidence at the Bassinger trial. The police had to protect him. After the trial, they faked his death and gave him a new identity. The man came back to Stockport and took Benjamin to Cheltenham. That's why Benjamin believes that people return from the dead. He's not being stupid or fanciful, he's basing his belief on personal experience.'

'And his grandmother,' Mrs Cosgrave said, 'the woman who's pretended to be his mother, how is she?'

'Paula's unwell. Severe chest infection; bronchitis, pleurisy. I understand it recurs every winter.'

'And who cares for Benjamin when she's ill?'

'A neighbour helps, but I suspect he mostly cares for himself and does his best to care for Paula.'

'Does Paula have any relatives?'

'Only by marriage; her late husband's family. They live in Ireland. They've kept themselves scarce since her husband died.'

Helen Cosgrave held up the photograph. 'May I keep this?'

'Of course. Paula said it was taken just before Christmas. And she asked me to tell you she's sorry about your husband and sons, that she's very grateful to you for not stopping the allowance. She's keeping you in her prayers.'

'Will you be going to visit her again?'

'I've no plans to.'

Mrs Cosgrave gazed for a while at the image of the curly-haired boy with wire-rimmed spectacles that were slightly askew, then turned to Samantha. 'Do you know how my son's died?'

Samantha nodded.

'Armed men took me to identify them, in the early hours of the morning. They were on steel tables in the mortuary of a London hospital; I don't remember which one. They'd bandaged their throats so I couldn't see...' She pushed back her head and closed her eyes, fighting back tears. When she spoke again her voice was barely audible. 'I keep asking them when I can arrange a funeral, but they won't tell me. They don't know whether there should be separate funerals for Lawrence and the boys, or whether there should be a joint service; they can't decide whether or not Lawrence's death should be marked by a public ceremony. The Home Secretary was even suggesting they should all be buried secretly, at night. He's concerned about public disorder. You know there's been rioting, that they've set fire to mosques?'

Samantha nodded again.

'I suppose I can understand Muslim extremists being angry with Lawrence, but I can't imagine why they'd want to hurt my boys.' She held up her hands in a despairing gesture. 'The police didn't even know they were back in England. An art gallery owner found them when he was searching in a skip for some tins.'

'They were probably murdered in Spain,' Samantha said. 'Perhaps on the day or not long after your husband died. Their bodies would have been hidden in a truck, brought back to England and left where they could be found.'

'Are you searching for the killers?'

'Yes.'

'Will you come and see me again; keep me informed?'

'If you wish.'

'How can I contact you?'

'Do you have Marcus Soames's number?'

Mrs Cosgrave nodded. 'He gave it to me when he told me you were going to visit me. He asked me to contact him if I felt he could help me in any way. Such a charming man.'

'Phone Marcus. Tell him you want to see me. He'll get a message to me, and I'll come.'

'Angus will have brought up the coffee and toast by now.' Helen Cosgrave rose to her feet.

Samantha turned off the shower and the taps, then reached for the radio. 'When we go out there, just talk about the weather and the coffee and toast.'

JULIA FARRELL DROPPED the mail on the kitchen table, took a sip of coffee, then dragged the waste bin closer. She flicked through the bundle, dumped circulars, then began to slit open envelopes and sort the letters into three piles: the ones that had to be faxed or sent to Jeremy in Westminster, the ones she could send standard replies to, and the ones that could wait until he arrived back home at the weekend.

She heard the thud and rattle of a ladder being leaned against the house and glanced through the window. Gavin had come to unblock the gutters. About time. She was tired of the drip, drip, drip on her head when she unlocked the back door. Jeans skin tight over muscular thighs, brown boots huge on the ladder rungs, he began to climb. A thick sweater was making his chest and shoulders seem even broader. He was holding on with one hand, the other was clutching a bucket and a long scraper.

There was something about Gavin that made Julia a little edgy. He was always polite, extravagantly so by today's standards, but he seemed to possess a kind of secretive watchfulness that made her uncomfortable. Bartlett and Bryden, Jeremy's building contractor friends, sent him whenever work needed doing on the house. Plumbing, small joinery repairs, replacing tiles on the high, steeply sloping roof. The youth was quick, efficient, didn't make a mess. That's probably why Arthur Bryden sent him. He could rely on him to be respectful and do a good job for a friend. And it was all charged to Parliamentary allowances or constituency expenses. She often wondered how Jeremy continued to get away with it, especially after all that hullabaloo in the media. And he still paid her a handsome salary, just for sorting the mail; called her his constituency secre-tary. The salary went into their joint bank account. She didn't keep it. Still, she couldn't say Jeremy had ever been mean. If she wanted something she always got it, and he never quibbled about clothes.

Julia slit open the last envelope. *Strictly Private and Confidential* had been printed across the top, followed by *The Rt Hon Jeremy Farrell, MP., Minister for Culture and the Arts*. She smiled to herself. Jeremy knew even less about culture and the arts than she did. When she unfolded the letter, she realized someone was accusing Bartlett and Bryden of giving Vincent Norris and half the members of the local council cash inducements to secure planning permissions. She read: *I am able to support these allegations with documentary and other proof and, as we are all members of the same political party, which we would not wish to see tarnished, I am giving you this opportunity to arrange for Central Office to carry out a discreet, but thorough, local investigation.* The name scrawled at the bottom and the address at the top meant nothing to her. Rising from the table, she crossed over to the wall phone by the refrigerator and dialled Jeremy's direct line.

'Mr Farrell's office.' The young female voice was re-fined and welcoming.

'I'd like to speak to Mr Farrell, please.'

'May I ask who's calling?'

'His wife.' Julia's tone became icy.

A laugh tinkled out of the earpiece. 'It's Nicole here,

Mrs Farrell. I'm sorry I didn't recognize your voice. Jeremy has someone from the Treasury with him. Can I—'

'It's urgent,' Julia snapped. 'He'd want you to put me through.'

'One second, please, Mrs Farrell.'

The line clicked, then went dead while the girl conferred with Jeremy. Another mini-skirted researcher. Or maybe this one was his secretary, someone to keep him company while he waited for the division bell. And she was on Christian name terms! Bloody Westminster. It was one big bed, and Jeremy was—

'Hullo, love. What's the problem?'

Reining in her imagination, resisting the urge to make caustic comments about his staff, she said, 'You've had a letter in this morning's post. It's very sensitive. I daren't fax it, and I'm reluctant to put it in the post, but you ought to see it; today if possible.'

'Sensitive? What makes it sensitive?'

'The writer makes allegations.'

'About me?' His voice had dropped to a whisper.

'About people we know.'

She heard his sigh of relief. 'Was it sent up from the constituency office?'

'It was delivered here. Whoever sent it knows your home address. Can't read the signature, looks like Arthur something or other, but it's come from Manchester.'

'The people he's complaining about: do we know them well?'

'Very. I think you should come home this evening and take it back with you tomorrow.'

'Can't. I'm bogged down. I'm opening an exhibition of East European painting tomorrow; strange stuff they had to hide from the Nazis and then the Communists. Representatives of three countries are going to be there.

It's politically sensitive. I've got to go over some notes with the researcher and put a speech together.' There was a silence, then a thoughtful voice said, 'I wonder why the letter was sent to our private address? Why not the constituency office, or straight here to me at Westminster?'

'Probably being cautious, like I'm being cautious,' she said.

'Could you bring it to me?'

Take it to him! That was the last thing she was expecting. 'I've got a very full diary,' she protested.

'Full of what? You're always moaning about how lonely you are. Come down to London. Stay in the flat for a few days; we can charge the fare to expenses. You can do some shopping; we can dine out together.'

Julia began to feel interested. 'It's only coffee with friends, the bridge club, an Inner Wheel meeting. I suppose I could phone round and cancel. What time will you finish tonight? If I catch a train this afternoon I could be in Westminster by six.'

'I'll probably be later than that. Why not go straight to the flat. There's food in the fridge. I should be there about eight. We could open a bottle of wine; have supper together.'

'All right,' she said, still rather taken aback. 'I'll see you later this evening.' The line clicked and she cradled the phone. His invitation had surprised her; made her suspicious. Maybe he was feeling guilty about something, or maybe he was laying smoke screens.

She slid the incriminating letter back in its envelope, then went through to the sitting-room and put it in her bag. Rain began to pepper the French windows. When she returned to the kitchen she heard boots scraping on ladder rungs and saw Gavin racing for shelter in an outhouse. She couldn't leave him out there in the freezing cold. She opened the back door. 'Come into the house, Gavin. I'll make you a mug of coffee. Or would you prefer tea.'

'Tea would do nicely, thanks, Mrs Farrell.' His Welsh voice had a musical lilt that Julia found rather pleasant. He stepped inside, then crouched down, unlaced his boots and tugged them off before walking over the grey marble tiles.

'Sit down, Gavin.' Julia pointed towards a chrome and leather chair beside a glass-topped table. She began to open cupboard doors, gathering tea things together. Hand-made solid oak units, granite work tops, gold-plated taps: she'd thought the kitchen sumptuous when it was first installed, but she'd soon become tired of it, especially when she'd discovered the layout didn't work very well. When she was in London, she'd talk to Jeremy about changing it. It was usually just a matter of finding an expenses heading to charge the cost to.

'You get a lot of letters, Mrs Farrell.'

'They're my husband's. They're not for me. I look through them when they arrive, then send the urgent ones on to him.'

She smiled at Gavin. He was sitting very straight in the chair, his arm resting on the glass top of the table, his dark hair arranged in that short spiky style that seemed fashionable amongst young men. He returned her smile. He looked quite boyish when he smiled, and his height and physique seemed less intimidating. He needed a shave; black stubble covered his cheeks and chin and throat. Fashion, she reminded herself. The unshaven look went with the spiky hair. His brown eyes were alert and wary; he seemed unsure of himself, uncertain what to make of her.

The kettle seethed to the boil. As she poured water

over the tea bag she caught him gazing at her black skirt. It was rather short and probably a size too small. His eyes rested for a moment on her crimson sweater, then flicked up to her face. He began to blush when he realized she'd seen him looking at her.

'Do you like your tea strong?'

'Just as it comes, Mrs Farrell.'

She squeezed the tea bag with a spoon a few times, then tossed it into the waste bin and carried the mug over to him. 'Milk and sugar's there, Gavin. Help yourself to the biscuits.' Moving back to her end of the table, she put the letters she intended to take to London in a big manilla envelope, the rest in a folder for Jeremy to read at the weekend. She glanced up. Gavin was gazing at her over the rim of the blue-striped mug. She hoped he wouldn't linger. Phone calls had to be made, meetings cancelled, and she had to pack and get ready. She smiled at him. 'Tea all right, Gavin?'

'Perfect, Mrs Farrell.' He lowered the mug to the table and stared down at it while he mumbled something she couldn't hear.

'I'm sorry, Gavin. I didn't quite catch that.'

Brown eyes, bright and wary, looked up at her. He made his voice more distinct. 'I think about you, Mrs Farrell.'

She frowned and gave him a puzzled smile. 'Think about me? Why do you think about me?'

'Because you're lovely.' His cheeks and throat had turned bright pink beneath the stubble.

Julia laughed, then wished she hadn't when she saw the hurt on his face. 'That's very kind of you, Gavin. I don't think I've ever been paid such a nice compliment.' He was still studying her. She sensed that deep thought and the words to express it didn't come easily to him and he was finding his inability to communicate with her frustrating.

'I don't mean lovely nice,' his embarrassment was making his Welsh accent more pronounced, 'I mean lovely beautiful. I think you're very nice as well, of course,' he added hastily, then lifted his mug and hid his face behind it while he sipped the hot tea. Unable to meet her eyes, he mumbled, 'That's why I think about you, Mrs Farrell. I think about you a lot. Fact is, I think about you most of the time.'

Stunned, Julia gazed at the tall, dark-haired young man with the hard muscular shoulders and powerful thighs. She had to say something, but she didn't know what. Taking a deep breath, she made her voice serious, almost severe. 'You really oughtn't to be thinking about me in that way, Gavin. I'm old enough to be your mother.' Then, suddenly regretting the excess of honesty, she let out a little laugh and added, 'Well, perhaps not quite as old as that, but I am a good deal older than you. Certainly much too mature for you to be having thoughts like that about me.'

'Can't help it.' His blush had deepened. He was staring down at the glass top of the table. Julia wondered if he was looking at her legs and tucked them under her chair. 'I've felt this way from the very first time I saw you—that day I came to fit a new seat on the downstairs loo.'

She sucked in her cheeks to hide a smile. The inappropriateness of the event that marked his sudden awareness of her seemed lost on him. Moving the conversation on to less personal things, she said, 'I've been expecting you for more than a week. Mr Bartlett promised to send you to do the gutters days ago.'

'Police arrested me. Spent three days in custody.'

'Arrested you! What on earth for?'

'The murder; the assassination.'

'Of the Prime Minister? That's preposterous, Gavin. Whatever possessed them?'

'I've got licences, for a shot gun and a rifle. I shoot ducks down on the marshes beyond Howden Woods, and I sometimes bag a few rabbits. Cosgrave's car was ambushed where the road goes across on an embankment. The police were scary. They kept going on and on at me about knowing the woods and the marshes like the back of my hand. They must have known it wasn't one of my guns that killed old Cosgrave, but they wouldn't let me go. My mam got me a solicitor. He said they'd no right to keep me in custody, said they had to charge me or let me go. He had a real rant, but it didn't do any good. They said they were acting under emergency powers and they could do whatever they wanted. He went to see a magistrate or a judge or something. They let me out after that; told me to hand in my passport, but I couldn't because I've not got one. They kept my guns.'

'Good heavens,' Julia breathed. Armed police had been stationed outside the Grange for almost a week after the assassination, supposedly guarding her. She'd found that tiresome enough, but to be dragged off and locked up…

'So, you didn't get your gutters unblocked,' Gavin went on, 'and old Daniel worked himself up into a right state.'

'Old Daniel?'

'Daniel Shoesmith, the Sexton. I dig the graves at Saint Michael and the Angels. There's a standing order from the vicar. Mr Bartlett charges me out at cost because it's the Church. Old Daniel's a bit past it now. He does the shuttering and gives me a hand barrowing the

earth and backfilling, but that's about all. There was a
grave waiting to be dug when they came and arrested
me. Mam was so upset she forgot to tell anybody I was
in jail and Daniel got in a right lather.'

The indignation suddenly faded from his voice and
his tone became contrite. 'I'm sorry if I've upset you,
Mrs Farrell, saying what I did, the last thing I'd want
to do is upset you.'

'You haven't upset me, Gavin, but you've shocked
me. I'm a married woman. You should be trying to find
a nice single girl, someone your own age.'

'There aren't any nice girls on the estate.'

'Which estate is that, Gavin?'

'Dunmoor; it's in Mosgrove, this side of Stockport.'

Julia shuddered. The council was using Dunmoor
as a dumping ground for addicts and problem families.
She'd heard Jeremy complaining to the chairman of the
housing committee about it. 'But surely you meet nice
girls when you're in town at dances and things?'

'I don't know any girls like you.'

'Of course not.' Julia tried to sound firm. 'It's because they're girls; fresh and lovely young girls, not
mature women.'

'I mean, they're not as beautiful as you.' A note of
plaintive desperation sounded in his voice. 'Your eyes
and mouth and hair and everything. And you always
dress so smart and smell so nice. I don't know any girls
who—'

'Stop it, Gavin! You really will upset me if you go
on like this.'

'Sorry, Mrs Farrell,' he mumbled. 'I never wanted
to make you mad.' He glanced out of the window, then
rose to his feet. 'Rain's stopped. I'll make sure the fall
pipes at the front are clear before I go, but I'll have to

come back. Some joints need sealing and I've not got the stuff with me.' He moved over to the door, impatient to be outside where he could hide his embarrassment. After stepping into his boots, he knelt down, first on one knee, then on the other, while he laced them up. When he'd opened the door he looked back. 'I'm really sorry, Mrs Farrell. I'm stupid. I should have kept my thoughts to myself. The last thing I wanted was to upset you.'

'Stop apologizing, Gavin. Just forget our conversation. I won't tell anyone what you've said, and I hope you won't either.'

The door closed. He was gone, back to his buckets and ladders.

Julia took a deep breath. Gavin was little more than a boy; a tall, handsome, muscular boy; and his shyness made him very sweet. And how flattering! A smile touched her lips. He probably thought she was very much the fine lady, but she'd more in common with the girls on the Dunmoor estate than he could possibly imagine: born in a back-to-back down Sidings Lane, went to Rufford Road Comprehensive and left without a certificate to her name. Her face and figure had got her her first job. Dentist's receptionist. Dirty old sod. Hand up her skirts one minute; in the patients' mouths the next. But she'd always used her assets and dressed as well as she could afford. And she'd been lucky. No matter how smart you are, no matter how hard you work, you've got to be lucky. She'd decided the Young Conservatives was a good place to find a husband. That's where she'd met Jeremy. He was ambitious, his own insurance business, local politics for ten years, then elected MP for Stockport. She'd had to run to keep up. Went to Manchester for elocution lessons from an old actress; didn't want to go to someone in Stockport who'd tell every-

one what she was doing. Even spent a couple of afternoons with a head waiter at a big hotel: which knife,
fork spoon; which plate; lefts and rights. She'd like to
think she'd pass for quality in any company now. But
educated women, women like the vicar's wife, still un-
settled her. Their refined voices, their poise and charm,
were natural, not acquired. And Zelda was educated, a
successful lawyer. Educated people made her uneasy.
She sometimes felt they might be secretly mocking her.

London: she had to choose some smart things to wear
and pack a suitcase. She pushed herself up from the table
and headed for the stairs.

'ANY DEVELOPMENTS?'

Marcus glanced up at the tall slender figure standing in the doorway. 'None, ma'am. Two teams at GCHQ
have trawled back over the past eighteen months, sifted
through every intercept, every piece of intelligence.
There's no warning of a possible assassination; no trace
of likely suspects entering or leaving the country.'

Loretta Fallon closed the door, sauntered across drab
brown carpet and settled herself in the visitor's chair.
'Anything from Quest?'

'Nothing. She visited the PM's widow this morning.
Our people intercepted the Met's exchanges about it.'

'And?'

Marcus smiled. 'Same as last time: anger and frus-
tration at not being able to record what was being said.
They think we're on to something.'

'I hope we are *on to something*, Marcus. Any feedback from the researchers you've given her?'

He groped beneath papers and charts, found a blue
wallet file and began to leaf through the contents. 'Not
what one would expect, ma'am. So far she's asked for

details of a man the police arrested on the day of the assassination. He's called…' Marcus struggled to read the hand-written notes. '…Gavin Jones, employed by a Stockport building firm, Bartlett and Bryden. They occasionally supply him as a gravedigger to the Anglican church in Enderley; Saint Michael and the Angels. She wanted a transcript of the police interviews. Researchers had the devil of a job getting that. And she's requested details of a Manchester solicitor, a woman called Zelda Unwin. She's married to the vicar of Saint Michael and the Angels, a man called Andrew Leyton.'

'Nothing on the half-dozen extremists we'd picked out?'

'No, ma'am, but she's asked for fullest possible details of surviving Bassinger males.'

'Did any Bassinger males survive the search for little Benjamin? I remember showing Quest's event log to Cosgrave. His face turned grey.'

Marcus flicked through the papers. 'One brother, Henry, and his sons, Mark and Lewis; and there are the four surviving sons of the brothers Quest killed, but they're no longer resident in the UK. She's also asked for the search to include male cousins who don't carry the Bassinger surname; they're having a little more difficulty with that one.'

'It's shown us the lines she's thinking along.'

'Her instincts could be right, ma'am.'

'I can't believe it, Marcus. The ragged remnants of a criminal family taking its revenge on the political establishment? Surely not.'

'They were a very close family, ma'am. Rich, powerful, utterly ruthless. And the sequestration of Ronald's assets was vicious. Cosgrave demanded it.' Marcus gazed across the desk at Loretta. She was frowning, showing her disagreement. He smiled, kept his voice respectful, as he reminded her, 'The Mafia didn't hesitate to take on the Kennedys, ma'am.'

'This is England, Marcus, not America. And the Bassingers might have been bloody awful, but they weren't the Mafia.'

He slid the papers back in the folder. 'What did you tell the Emergency Committee?'

'That we're taking urgent and exceptional measures to identify and locate the killers, but I couldn't report in detail as it might prejudice the outcome of the operation. I won't get away with that for long. Quest's got to come up with something soon, but after listening to you, I'm not very confident. Who else have we got working on it?'

'In the field?'

Loretta nodded.

'A dozen of our best, plus about a hundred on round-the-clock surveillance. And we've got people in the radical mosques and religious study centres, plus operatives in the Dissident Republican movement. If they uncover anything promising, I'll pass it on to Quest.'

Loretta picked up her briefcase and rose to her feet. 'Still staying in London?'

'Until this is over. Charlotte understands.'

'Book a car out of the pool and drive me home. You can give me your thoughts about it over dinner. Marks and Spencer microwave meals, I'm afraid, but I've got a couple of bottles of decent red.'

JULIA FARRELL HAD never been happy with her face. She'd always thought her chin too long, her nose too large, her mouth a little on the small side. Her eyes, grey and large and serious looking, were its only redeeming feature. Sighing, she leaned over gleaming-white porcelain, brought her face closer to the mirror and applied lipstick, deftly making her mouth larger.

She much preferred this bathroom in their London flat to the en-suite at the Grange. The young designer had been inspired: gold-veined green marble walls, floor like black glass, recessed lighting in the lowered ceiling, an unbroken line of mirror-fronted cabinets above the his-and-hers wash basins.

Having arrived on an early train she'd been able to shop in Harrods before taking a taxi to the flat. She'd spent the next two hours searching it for evidence of another woman's presence: the kitchen, tiny hall, sitting room, master bedroom, the second bedroom Jeremy used as an office. She'd been painstaking; she checked under beds and furniture for buttons, hair grips, lost earrings; she'd searched for feminine items in the fitted wardrobes, the drawers and cupboards in the kitchen, even on the shelves behind the sliding mirrors in the bathroom. She'd found nothing: no clothes, no underwear, no jewellery, no medicines; just an abundance of House of Commons stationery in the office and half-a-dozen bottles of whisky with the House of Commons portcullis printed on the labels—small gifts Jeremy offered as tokens of appreciation for favours rendered, or to create a sense of obligation so a favour might be asked.

Perhaps Jeremy had been telling her the truth. Perhaps he didn't have a dalliance with every compliant little secretary or nubile researcher who came within arm's reach. The possibility that he might be faithful to her after all made her feel the trip to Harrods, the hamper of supper things, the time spent in the lingerie department, hadn't been a waste of time.

She took a black negligee from a hanger and drew it

on. When she stepped into her flimsy high-heeled slippers its hem just cleared the floor. She studied her reflection. Gently waved bottle-blonde hair tumbling around her shoulders, eyes and face rather heavily made up; with her all-over sun-bed tan she looked a teeny bit tarty, but pretty good for her age. Jeremy ought to be grateful. He should feel pleased he'd invited her to spend a few days at the flat. Fragrant with perfume, she crossed the hall and swirled into the bedroom.

Jeremy was already in bed, propped up by pillows piled against the maple headboard. A lamp with a black and gold shade illuminated the papers he was reading. He didn't look up, so she began to hang clothes in wardrobes that had maple doors inlaid with ebony and silk linings decorated with Japanese scenes. She really did like this flat. The young designer had transformed it. Whenever she came here she was tempted to suggest they sell the Grange, buy a larger flat in London and hire him to organize a complete refurbishment.

She picked up Jeremy's shirt and draped it over the back of a chair. 'Who's Nicole?' She watched him closely.

'Mmm?' He was engrossed in his papers. 'Who's who?'

'Nicole: the girl in your Westminster office?'

'Nicole Roberts. You've met her. She's Ted and Betty's daughter. Ted asked me if I'd find her a job while she decides whether or not to stay on at university and do a masters. She's supposed to prepare notes on events in the arts for me, but she spends most of her time answering the phone and shifting correspondence. She's very bright.'

'I thought that sexy little redhead answered the phone and typed letters?'

'She's on her honeymoon. Got married on Saturday to a bloke who works in the City. Rupert or Roland or something. Very well heeled.'

A feeling of shame at having been frosty with the girl on the phone, at having suspected Jeremy of staffing his office with nubile little concubines, was mingling with a feeling of relief. Perhaps he did deserve all the trouble she'd taken. She picked up his tie. 'What are you reading?'

'Nicole's notes on the exhibition I'm opening tomorrow.'

'What do you make of that letter I brought you, accusing Vincent and half the planning committee of taking back-handers.' She put his suit on a hanger and drifted over to the wardrobe. He still hadn't looked at her. Her efforts were being ignored.

'I'll have a word with Alan Bailey in the Whip's Office. If he agrees, I'm going to pass it on to the police.'

'We know most of these people, Jeremy. Some of them are old friends. Don't we at least owe them a warning? And what if some of the mud sticks on you?'

'If the allegations are true, they've been stupid and careless, and if I give them a warning, I'll be implicated. I'm not risking everything we've worked and struggled for. And no mud's going to stick on me. I'm as pure as the driven snow.' He chuckled. 'Well, put it this way, I've always been careful not to leave any footprints in the snow.' He dropped his papers on the floor, yawned and looked up. 'Jesus! How long have you had that?'

'Had what?'

'The Baby-Doll and the négligé?'

'About six hours. I bought them this afternoon. For you.'

'You wore a Baby-Doll nightie on our honeymoon.'

His voice had become huskily affectionate. 'Baby-Doll and no knickers.'

'That was a rather tasteless thing to say, Jeremy.' She moved closer to the bed and posed herself with her hands on her hips, slender fingers with crimson nails fanning out over black silk. She shaped her mouth in a reproachful smile. 'I didn't wear a Baby-Doll on our honeymoon. I wore a white satin nightdress. The Baby-Doll was in Benidorm, our first holiday abroad. And I did wear the frilly knickers.'

She pulled at a ribbon, let the negligee slide over her shoulders and fall to the floor.

'Bloody hell, Julia! You'd give a corpse a hard-on.'

She kicked off her tiny gold slippers. 'Is that the most romantic thing you can think of, Jeremy: "You'd give a corpse a hard-on"?'

He drew back the covers and patted the sheet. 'Just get into bed, love. You want romantic? I can do romantic.' His weathered hands and face and neck contrasted with pallid flesh normally concealed, fuzzy grey hair frosted his chest, and the elastic top of his boxer shorts had slid beneath his paunch. Julia caught a faint odour of stale perspiration. He hadn't bothered to take a shower. She slid her legs beneath the covers, felt his arm snake around her waist and draw her close. After giving her a rather wet kiss he murmured, 'If you were on the game, Julia, you'd make a bloody fortune.'

Her smudged lips hardened. Angry now, she turned her back on him. 'That's vile, Jeremy. Take your hand away.'

His silent laughter was making the mattress shake. He began to fondle her breasts.

'I said, take your hand away,' she snapped, then dug

her nails into his arm. 'Hard-ons and corpses and being on the game: I wish I hadn't come.'

He made his voice tender. 'I was only joking, love.' He kissed her shoulder, then her neck. There was a time when she'd have laughed, when she'd have enjoyed a little earthy humour, but the working-class girl who'd escaped from Sidings Lane was the lady of Enderley Grange now. Sometimes he wished the transformation hadn't been quite so complete. 'We've come a long way, Julia.'

'So you keep telling me,' she snapped frostily.

'Don't you like it: the Grange, this flat, the cottage in the Dales, the life we have?'

'Of course I like it. It's just that I'm on my own in Enderley most of the time. And when I come down to London and make you a special supper and take a lot of trouble with the way I look, you're just coarse and vulgar. And it's not as if you can't say nice things in a cultivated way. You're very clever when you're making speeches, wooing the electorate, but you never say anything nice to me.'

'I love you,' he whispered, then kissed her ear. Her perfume had a bitter taste. She rolled on to her back and gazed up at him. He lowered his head and kissed her lips. 'You made it all possible, Julia. The journey wouldn't have been worth the fare without you riding beside me. If I had to choose between you and all this, I'd take you back to our little semi in Crowther Road like a shot.'

Julia felt him tugging at her knickers. She lifted her haunches so he could ease them down. He was so predictable. It was as if he made love by numbers: one, kiss lips; two, fondle breasts; three, caress thighs. Nothing had changed in almost twenty-five years. His body was softer, flabbier, heavier; lovemaking left him short of breath, but nothing had really changed.

When he began to snore, she rose from the bed, drew on her négligé, then crossed the darkened hall. After closing the bathroom door, she switched on the lights. The woman gazing at her from the mirrors had tousled bottle-blonde hair, and what was left of her lipstick was smudged around her mouth. She washed away powder and eye-shadow, dabbed her face with a towel, then began to apply cream. Her face looked older without the make-up, and startled. It was as if the wide eyes were shocked by what they saw.

Coming here hadn't been a good idea. She'd cut her stay short, return home tomorrow and resume the solitary routine of her life in Enderley.

EIGHT

JEREMY FARRELL'S GLEAMING black shoes trod quietly over the parquet floor. He settled the jacket of his dark-blue pinstripe suit more comfortably on his shoulders, adjusted his wine-red tie, then tugged at the matching display handkerchief to expose a little more of it. No one could see him preening himself. Apart from a solitary woman engrossed in one of the paintings, the galleries set aside for the exhibition were deserted. Representatives of three governments and the press were gathering in the lecture room where he was to make his speech. The young civil servant they'd sent from the Ministry was checking the buffet and putting together a list of names of the people he ought to chat to. Things were running smoothly.

Bloody paintings! Three-million unemployed, cuts across the board, no sign of the recession ending, and all these arty-farty fuckers could think about were these meaningless daubs. Still, he reflected, got to wave the flag, maintain cultural links, strengthen the bonds of trade and friendship with our partners in Europe. He strolled on. Better take a final look at Nicole's notes, try to memorize the speech prompts he'd scribbled in the margins. He drew a fold of papers from an inside pocket.

Shit! He'd picked up the letter about Bartlett and Bryden's and left the exhibition notes by the bed. It was Julia's fault, going all huffy and silent on him, saying she was returning home, distracting him. He glanced at his watch. Twenty minutes to the opening. There was no way they could get the notes to him in twenty-minutes. He had to recall some of the things Nicole had written, scribble a few thoughts in the catalogue. He could re-member most of the comments he was going to make in his speech, but…

A feeling of panic was creeping over him. He stared at the pictures on the wall, then flicked through the cat-alogue, frantically trying to identify which was which: Czech, Polish, Lithuanian. He couldn't even—'

'Have you lost your bearings? The catalogue is very confusing.'

Jeremy glanced up. The soft voice with its faint gut-tural accent suited the more than pretty young woman. He let out an exasperated sigh. 'I've not even found my bearings.'

'May I?' She gave him a radiant smile, took his cata-logue and leafed through it. 'The paintings are arranged in date order, not by country. This section is 1920 to 1940. Polish, Czech and Lithuanian; all displayed to-gether. We are standing by…' She ran a slender finger with a polished and perfectly manicured nail down the page. 'This one.'

'You know about paintings?' Jeremy gazed at the woman in the crimson winter coat. Her hazel eyes, her smile, her short and casually styled hair, were quite be-guiling.

'I know a little.'

'Talk to me.' There was a note of desperation in his voice. 'Tell me something about the paintings; one from each country.'

The girl's laughter was soft and enticing. 'I'm OK on Polish and Lithuanian, but not so good on Czech, but I'll do my best.' Beckoning with her hand, she said, 'Shall we look at them together?' then led him along the display and paused by a large and gloomy canvas. 'This one is Polish. *The Resurrection*, by Artur Modjeska. It is considered to be a masterpiece of twentieth-century Polish realist art. It depicts the dead, rising from their graves in a dark pine forest and striding towards a blinding light. In Poland there was much killing in forests. The drawing of the figures is deliberately naïve, almost grotesque, rather like your own artist, Stanley Spencer.'

'Stanley who?' Jeremy was scribbling furiously on the back of the catalogue.

'Stanley Spencer. He painted *The Resurrection in Cookham Churchyard*, but his work is happy and serene, while Modjeska's is dark and sinister. Modjeska's was commissioned as an altarpiece for a church in Krakow, but the bishop would not allow it to be hung. Spencer also intended his painting to be an altarpiece, but it was never used in that way. The two pictures are strikingly different in appearance, but almost identical in subject and style.'

'Talk to me about another,' Jeremy urged, still scribbling. 'A Czech painting.' He followed her as she strolled on.

She paused and frowned. 'Mmm…This one, I think. *The Red Cafe*, by Mirek Nicas. A brightly lit cafe viewed from a dark street. Just four figures, a man, a woman, and the proprietor and his waitress. If we're still making comparisons with the art of the West, we could say it is similar in theme and content to Edward Hopper's *The Nighthawks*.'

'Edward Hopper?'

'The American realist painter who depicted urban loneliness and melancholy. *The Nighthawks* also has four figures in a brightly lit restaurant, but Nicas's painting is more formal in its composition.' She pointed with her finger. 'See, the tables, some with cloths, some with their red tops exposed, form a zig-zag pattern that leads the eye slowly towards the rather sad looking couple sitting by the back wall. Now, a Lithuanian painter.' The girl studied the catalogue, then crossed the gallery to a large abstract and began to explain it.

'Minister…Minister…'

Jeremy glanced up from his note-taking. The bright young civil servant was standing in a doorway, tapping his watch. 'They're ready. Shall we go through? The Director of the Tate's waiting to introduce you.'

'I'm coming.' Jeremy scribbled frantically for a few seconds more, then glanced up. 'This is Miss…' He looked at the young woman and smiled.

'Liegis; Katarzina Liegis.'

'Will you escort Miss Liegis through for me as my guest, Damien, and take care of her at the buffet. I must thank her when the ceremony's over.'

Katarzina was intrigued. Jeremy Farrell's features were pleasant and the flecks of grey in his hair made him appear quite distinguished, but he was shorter and a little heavier than she'd expected, and he looked older than he did in the magazine photograph. But her disappointment in his appearance had been more than compensated by his flawless performance on the podium. It had impressed her. Her comments on the paintings had been woven seamlessly into words of welcome for the visitors and praise for the exhibits. Successful politicians, she reflected, were actors playing different roles, always eloquent, always confident; minister for this one year, minister for that another, deftly concealing the fact that they lacked any real knowledge or experience to fit them for a particular appointment.

That chance conversation about the paintings had left him indebted to her, and she'd probably have an opportunity to talk to him again after the opening ceremony. Things were moving more quickly than she'd expected, perhaps more quickly than she'd hoped. The flat they'd given her was quite splendid, and beautifully furnished. The woman called Velma had urged her to choose the most expensive clothes, and her driver was old and pleasant and not over-friendly. She sensed his main job was to keep an eye on her for Velma. Chauffeuring her and minding her were secondary duties. Still, it was all unbelievably grand and it would be a pity if it were to end too soon. Suddenly recalling the man with the sledge hammer, she shuddered. Better do what she'd been hired for, get her papers back, collect the five-thousand pounds, take the clothes and return to Riga, perhaps go back to university and finish her degree. And she wouldn't tell her father or her brothers that she was in Latvia.

It was so warm in here. The charming fresh-faced young man who'd been instructed to escort her had relieved her of her heavy winter coat and taken it to a cloakroom. If Jeremy Farrell were able to detach himself from the crowd and come over and talk to her, he'd see her in her red silk dress. Obviously expensive and very elegant, it fitted like a glove. It gave her confidence, made her feel incredibly sexy, gave her a feeling of empowerment.

LIGHTS CHANGED. THE dark-green Jaguar pulled away, turned on to Victoria Embankment, then merged with the traffic heading towards Parliament Square.

'That went exceptionally well, Minister.'

'Nearly a bloody disaster, Damien. I left my notes

in the flat. The Liegis woman saved me; talked to me about the paintings for ten minutes before it all started.'

'She seemed very knowledgeable,' Damien said. 'Employed by some art importers and exporters. Must say, I thought she was rather attractive.'

Jeremy relaxed back on the cream leather and smiled at Damien's gentlemanly understatement. Katarzina was more than *rather attractive*. Perky tits and a fabulous arse—in that red dress with the skin-tight skirt she was bloody mesmerizing. His smile widened. She'd declined his invitation to lunch, but she'd agreed to have dinner with him. A thank you, he'd murmured. He'd insisted on thanking her properly.

'The Polish Cultural Attache was rather overwhelmed,' Damien chattered on. 'She said it was so refreshing to visit a country where the Minister for Culture had such a profound feeling for the visual arts. She said it was obvious you'd read her book on the Soviet repression; she said drawing a comparison between Modjeska and Spencer was inspired.'

Jeremy glanced at his aide. 'You mean the short plump woman, greasy skin, specs and untidy hair?'

'That's her; Helena Wajda. If you approve, Minister, I think we should send notes on the opening to the Foreign Office. They'll be more than interested in the favourable impression you've created.'

'Do it, Damien. Of course I approve.'

Big Ben and the Palace of Westminster loomed up ahead. As the Ministerial car turned on to Bridge Street, Jeremy leaned towards the driver and said, 'Sorry to mess you about, Chris. Could you take me to my flat. I've left papers there.'

'No trouble, Mr Farrell. You want me to wait?'

'No. Just drop me off, then take Damien back to the

Ministry. I'll find the papers, make a few phone calls, then catch a cab back to Westminster.'

He had to make sure Julia really had buggered off home to Enderley. And he had to change the bed and tidy the flat; the mood she was in, Julia would have left it the way it was and the cleaning woman wasn't due until Friday. And he had to choose a restaurant and make a reservation; somewhere decent and discreet, somewhere not too far from the flat.

St Michael and the Angels stood on a gentle rise. From her vantage point beside a huge buttress, Samantha could see the vicarage at the end of a narrow lane that curved around the churchyard. Its blue slate roofs were steep and fretted barge boards, freshly painted white, decorated the gable peaks. Lancet windows, arranged in groups of three, had dressed stone surrounds that contrasted with the rough-hewn stone of the walls. Very pretty in a solid kind of way, Samantha decided, and in an idyllic setting. Utterly unlike her own modest house on a nondescript estate in a grimy Yorkshire town.

She brought her gaze back to the churchyard. Slabs of weathered limestone marked the graves close to the church. Lower down the slope, an invasion of black and white Italian marble looked tacky and out of place. Holly bushes lined the enclosing wall, and beyond the lane that led to the vicarage, ploughed fields, their furrows white with frost, stretched away to a misty horizon.

The tall dark-haired man had almost finished. She watched him tip earth from a wicker basket into a wheelbarrow, then push it to a mound concealed amongst the bushes beside the wall. When he returned, he dragged a heavy sheet of plywood over the newly dug grave. His movements were effortless and practised; he'd obviously done this many times before. He unrolled plastic grass over the board, smoothed it, then weighted it down with planks. After laying his pick and shovel in the wheelbarrow, he gathered up the basket, a length of rope and a short ladder before heading up the rise to the church.

When he reached the path he turned and walked on down the side of the nave. He hadn't noticed her, standing behind the buttress. Samantha drew her lapels across her throat and followed him. The cold had seeped into her. Her Ralph Lauren coat was stylish, but she wished now that she'd worn her furs. He paused by an iron gate at the top of a fenced-off flight of steps. He must have heard her boots crunching on the gravel because he turned and stared at her, a startled expression on his handsome young face.

'Mr Jones; Mr Gavin Jones?'

'That's me.' He lowered the wheelbarrow.

Samantha unfolded her ID wallet and showed him one of the windows.

'Not the police again. What do you want this time?' Alarm and irritation sounded in his Welsh voice.

'I'm not from the police, Gavin. I just want to talk to you.'

'There's nothing I can say. I don't know anything about that Cosgrave business. I was putting tiles on a roof when he was killed. Half the village must have seen me. I've told them that, over and over.'

'I know you don't know anything about it, Gavin. May I call you Gavin? I just want to talk to you about the woods and the marshes. Let me buy you lunch.'

His body began to relax, but his eyes were still wary. 'I'm not dressed for fancy places.'

'I don't care how you're dressed. And I'm sure you

know a quiet little country pub where we can have a steak. You can talk to me while we're eating.'

'Foreman's going to go barmy. They paid me for the three days I was in custody, but they'll not—'

'I'll pay you for the afternoon. Would a hundred pounds cover it?'

'Suppose so.' He managed a smile. 'What do you want to know?'

'Everything about the pathways through the woods and across the marshes.'

'That shouldn't be a problem.' He pushed at the iron gate. It swung open and banged against the church wall. A steep flight of steps led down to a door that was unusually tall and wide. 'I'll just put the gear away.' He hoisted the short aluminium ladder over his shoulder and gathered up the rope and basket. Glancing at her, he said, 'These go down into the crypt. Won't be a minute.'

'Can I come and take a look?'

'I wouldn't mind if you did. I don't like being in there on my own.'

Samantha followed him down the worn stone steps. 'I should think it's a bit awkward, keeping your equipment down here.'

'It is. Used to store things in an old laundry at the back of the vicarage, but we had to move out when the new vicar's wife had the place done up. Dragging the wheelbarrow up and down the steps is the worst.'

'She's called Zelda, isn't she?'

'You know her?'

Samantha smiled. Her little research team had found out what they could about Zelda Leyton nee Unwin. 'I know of her, but I don't know her. She's a lawyer, her office is in Manchester. What's she like?'

Gavin opened the heavy door and flicked a switch.

Unshaded bulbs illuminated a labyrinth of pillars and vaulting. 'Never spoken to her. Only seen her a couple of times, and then from a distance. She's not like the old vicar's wife. She used to bring us a flask of coffee with a tot of rum in it when we were digging graves in winter.' He scraped the ladder along the wall as he manoeuvred it inside, then dropped it, together with the basket and rope, on to the stone flagged floor.

Her curiosity aroused by the strangeness of the place, Samantha strolled off beneath the vaulting, peering into shadows. She could make out an old brass lectern, a pile of broken chairs, an ornate canopy that had once been a sounding board above a pulpit.

'Are we walking?' Gavin's voice echoed after her. 'It's a fair way: a mile to the woods, then perhaps a couple of miles through the woods to the marshes?'

'We'll go by car. I'll get as close as I can to the entrance to the woods, then we'll walk a little way inside and you can explain the pathways. We'll drive back through the village and you can direct me to the road where Cosgrave was killed.'

He flicked earth from his jeans and baggy argyle sweater. 'I'll fetch the rest of the stuff and get the wheelbarrow down. Then I'd better take these boots off if we're going in your car. Do you mind if I leave you on your own?'

'Not at all.'

When he'd clumped back up the steps, she walked on through the gloom, found herself in a short passageway that ended in a massive door. Its iron handle turned, but the door wouldn't open. Unable to explore further, she strolled back, past dusty hymn books stacked on sagging shelves, a pile of rusty collection tins, discarded benches, a large and new-looking central-heating boiler.

Unsold copies of the Parish Magazine were piled on
a rickety old table. Taking a recent one, she flicked
through to the editorial. A fair-haired vicar, attired in
dog-collar and stock, smiled out at her from a photograph at the top of the page. She tore it out and slipped
it into her bag.

When she returned to the entrance, Gavin was sitting on a chair that had lost its back. He'd removed
his boots and was sliding his huge feet into a pair of
trainers.

'What's through the door at the end of the passage?'

'Lots of dead bodies in dusty old coffins: that's what
Daniel the sexton told me. Lords and ladies of the manor,
landed gentry and such like. Daniel's never been inside,
and I don't even go near the door. New vicar asked me
if I'd take the sexton's job over when Daniel retires, but
I said no. I don't mind digging the graves for old Daniel, but this place gives me the creeps. I'm really glad
you're here.'

GAVIN RAISED HIS glass and drank deeply at an amber-
coloured brew called *Bishop's Finger*. Four pints of the
strong ale, a large and surprisingly tender steak, together
with the warmth of the fire burning in the pub lounge,
had brought a glow to his cheeks.

They'd visited Howden Woods and he'd shown her
the path that circled Enderley, the path used by dog
walkers and mountain bikers and pony-riders. Before
leaving, they'd walked a short distance through the leaf-
less trees and he'd pointed out the vague track that led
over the hill to the flood plain and the marshes. Then
they'd driven back through the village and he'd guided
her to the road that crossed the valley. They'd parked
there and leaned over the highway fence while he'd

pointed down to the culvert hidden beneath overhanging bushes and trees. Across flat meadows, on the distant hillside, fluttering bands of yellow tape marked the spot where the gun had been placed.

'Do you think the killer escaped through Howden Wood to Enderley?' Samantha asked.

'He'd have come out by the old gamekeeper's house and Mrs Smeaton would have seen him. She was watching us when we parked the car. It's a lonely place and she's scared; forever looking through the window at people coming and going. He could have taken the path that curves round the village, but there's always someone walking or riding along it at that time and he'd have been seen. And there's no clear path through the wood to the marshes. Unless he really knew the place he'd have been ages trying to find his way.'

Samantha clicked open her bag, took out an Ordnance Survey map, unfolded it, then re-folded it, exposing the part she wanted to study. 'He could have moved round the hill, heading away from the spot where he'd located the gun, then doubled back and escaped this way.' She ran her finger along the line of the stream and let it come to rest in the marshes beyond the elevated road. 'Where could he have gone from here?'

Gavin shrugged. 'Could have hidden in the plantation that covers the hill,' Samantha unfolded the sheet so they could see more of the terrain, 'or he could have continued on through the trees and across these fields to the motorway.'

'What's this?' Samantha pointed at a tiny rectangle.

He leaned over. 'Tillbrook Farm. It's derelict. I shelter there sometimes when I'm out shooting and do a brew-up.'

She judged the distance. 'It's about two miles from the marshes to the motorway.'

'Probably. I've never walked further than Tillbrook Farm.'

Samantha studied the map, saw a tiny circular shape near the highway. 'What's this?'

Gavin peered at it. 'An old windmill. Just the tower; no sails, no roof. You can see it from the road. It's near the contractor's compound. They're putting another lane in on both carriageways. Been doing it for months.'

The Ordnance Survey sheet refused to be folded back to its original size. Eventually it surrendered, and she dropped it back in her bag. She dipped her fingers into her wallet, plucked out five twenties, and slid them across the table.

'It's OK, miss. You don't have to pay me. I'll tell the foreman frost made the digging bad. He can charge the time to the church.'

Samantha smiled at him. 'Let's call it a cold-weather bonus.'

'You've bought me lunch. It's OK.' He was blushing.

She slid the fold of notes under his hand. 'It's been worth it to me; you saved me a lot of time. You've been a great help.'

Calloused fingers closed over the money. 'Thanks, miss…I'm sorry, I can't remember your name.'

Samantha smiled. 'I didn't tell you what it was.'

They rose, left the warmth of the inn and stepped out into the freezing car park. The sky was overcast. It would soon be dusk. When they were cocooned in the Ferrari, Samantha asked, 'What's the vicar like?'

'He's all right, I suppose. Popular in the village, especially with the women. Good cricketer; plays for the village team. Someone told me he'd played for Oxford University and rowed in the boat race.'

'I sense you don't really care for Mr Leyton?' She keyed the ignition. The low-slung car rumbled into life.

Gavin sniffed. 'Well, if he sees you he'll say hello and pass the time of day, but you can tell he thinks he's doing you a big favour.'

MARCUS SNATCHED UP the red phone, tapped in a number and sank back in his chair.

The line clicked open and a curt voice said, 'Fallon.'

'Just had a call from Villiers at the Home Office, ma'am. Edward Ashton's dead. His cleaner found him this morning, on a sofa, fully clothed, a Fortnum and Mason's carrier bag over his head.'

'It would have to be a Fortnum and Mason's bag. You're telling me it was suicide?'

'Gin and methadone. Lot of empty blister packs on the floor; must have been a massive overdose. Editor of one of the tabloids has been sent a video of a party attended by Ashton. He's put the Home Office on warning; he's going to publish the details.'

'Rent boys?'

'Bit more than rent boys, ma'am. Rent boys and coprophilia.'

Laughter rustled in the earpiece. 'The darkness in the hearts of men, Marcus. This is all on the video?'

'Very clear images, I gather, ma'am.'

'They couldn't possibly use them.'

'They're the proof they need before they publish, and they can describe what's going on. Villiers is sending a copy of the disk and some stills over. He wants us to try to identify the location. I gather one of the items of furniture in the room is rather unusual in an oriental kind of way.'

'One of the items?'

'The low glass-topped table they used.'

'I'm not following you, Marcus.'

'Perhaps we should leave it there, ma'am.'

'Marcus,' Loretta's tone was reproachful, 'I've spent twenty-five years in the service. Do you think there's anything that could possibly shock me. What did they need a glass-topped table for?'

'Ashton gets his kit off and stretches out underneath it while the boy squats on top and—'

'With you, Marcus.' She said hurriedly. 'How very strange, and quite revolting. How do they cope with the mess? How can they stand the smell?'

'With some difficulty, I should think, ma'am. It's not without precedent. There was that Cabinet Minister, years ago, quite famous, always on television, they elevated him to the peerage: he indulged in that sort of thing. I can't recall his name?'

'Presumably Edward Ashton was sent a copy, too?'

'Police found one in the DVD player under the TV.'

'Mmm…Have we had any feedback from Quest?'

'Nothing. Her research team have been feeding her information on companies that organize pilgrimages to Catholic shrines in Spain.'

'Thought she was a Jew. She was trained by the Israelis.'

'Her father was Jewish; mother an Irish Catholic. Quest was convent educated.'

'That's all we need, Quest disappearing on a bloody pilgrimage.'

Marcus laughed. 'I don't think she'll be touring the

holy shrines, ma'am.' There was a silence, then he said softly, 'She may be right.'

'Right about what?'

'About the Cosgrave assassination. It might not be terrorism, Islamic or Dissident Republicans. Think about it: the politician who caused so much trouble for the Bassingers was Cosgrave, with Edward Ashton soothing the lawyers at the Home Office and Jeremy Farrell dealing with reluctant party members in the Commons. The government sequestered a fortune, and Quest killed fathers and sons in the hunt for the boy. So, Cosgrave and his sons are killed, and the lesser players are ruined. It could be retribution.'

'What about Farrell? Nothing's happened to him. He's never been touched by scandal; there was some talk of him being involved in paybacks for hospital contracts, but he shook that off, and I gather he's devoted to his wife.'

'Perhaps they haven't got round to him yet. As you said yourself, ma'am, there's a darkness in the hearts of men. They'll find something. Do you think we should warn him?'

'I think we should leave it alone, Marcus. Just watch and wait. But if something happens to Farrell, I'll start to believe Quest might be right.'

KATARZINA WANDERED OUT of the sitting-room with its soft cushions and Regency stripes, and crossed the tiny hall. She could hear Jeremy Farrell in the kitchen, sliding drawers open, rattling spoons and arranging crockery on a tray.

'Milk or cream?' he called out.

'Cream.' She pushed open a door, felt for a switch and clicked it on. She caught her breath. Bright lights in the low ceiling gleamed on great slabs of white porcelain and sparkled on chrome. The bathroom, with its glassy black floor, was a shrine to opulence.

'You'll have a brandy?' Jeremy called from the kitchen.

'Just a little, in the coffee.' She switched off the lights and closed the door, then opened another on the opposite side of the hall. Bedside lamps with black and gold shades were already on, casting their brightness over the blue counterpane on the double bed, bathing the rest of the room in a softer light. She stepped inside, ran envious fingers over furniture made from some honey-coloured wood, opened a wardrobe door and was captivated by the silk linings decorated with oriental scenes. Four dresses, a summer coat and a couple of skirts were hanging from a rail. She flicked through them. They'd have been expensive, but looked a little dated now. They were probably things his wife had left behind.

She caught sight of her reflection in a dressing-table mirror and decided her arms and shoulders were too pale for the emerald-green halter-neck dress; a summer tan was needed to really show it off. She teased a stray curl back in place. Her lipstick ought to be repaired, but her bag was in the...

'Shall we have it in the sitting-room?' Jeremy called.

Where else would they have coffee and brandy? 'That would be nice,' she called back, then returned to the hall and opened the one remaining door. When the fluorescent light had flickered on, she saw a printer and some papers in trays on a small table beneath the window. A filing cabinet stood in the far corner, behind an antique mahogany desk. There were no papers on the desk, just a telephone and a photograph in a silver frame. She stepped inside the room and studied the image of a smiling blonde woman standing arm-in-arm with a sullen looking girl.

'It's all ready. I'm taking it through.'

Katarzina switched off the light and followed the rattle of crockery into the sitting-room, still holding the photograph.

Jeremy Farrell was sitting on the sofa, a tray of coffee things on a low table in front of him. He'd removed his jacket and loosened his tie.

She held up the photograph. 'Your wife is most attractive and your daughter very pretty. She's going to be quite a beauty.'

Jeremy dropped spoons into saucers and smiled up at her. 'Just like you. She's a clever girl. She's at St Andrews.'

'St Andrews?' Katarzina stood the photograph on the table and sank into the other end of the sofa.

'University, in Scotland.' He handed her a green and gold cup. The coffee was black and fragrant. 'Cream?'

She took the jug. His face was flushed and he seemed tense. She poured cream, added sugar, then stirred the mixture and took a sip. The taste of brandy was overpowering.

'You're breathtakingly lovely, Katarzina.'

She smiled. 'Thank you, Jeremy. You're being very sweet to me, and the meal was delightful. Do they always have a pianist there?'

'Not every night. We were lucky.' His voice had thickened, become a little breathless. He could feel his heart pounding. Must be the brandy, or those fabulous tits trying to burst out of the dress. He shouldn't stare at them like this, but he simply couldn't help himself. Somehow he managed to wrench his eyes away and look up into her face. He swallowed hard. 'Coffee OK?'

'Perfect.' It was lukewarm and unusually bitter. The cream and the brandy had cooled it excessively. She leaned forward and slid her cup on the table.

Jeremy shuffled along the sofa, sat beside her, close enough for his thigh to press against hers, and inhaled her perfume. He studied the flecks of gold in her hazel eyes. She gazed back at him without blinking, a faint smile shaping her rather full lips. She knows what this is all about, he decided, then lowered his head and kissed her, very gently. When he drew away her eyes were closed. He laid his hand on her thigh and whispered, 'We'd be more comfortable in the bedroom.'

Katarzina concentrated her thoughts. She didn't want to suffer this humiliation again. She had to persuade him to take her back to the flat with the hidden cameras. She laid her hand over his and gently moved it down towards her knee. 'I'm sorry, Jeremy, but I'm not comfortable here.'

'Not comfortable? It's a pleasant flat, warm, nicely—'

'It's not the flat…Well, it is the flat, I suppose. It's just that I can sense your wife's presence here. I get the crazy feeling she's watching us.'

Jeremy laughed. 'Watching us? She's not been here for more than a year. We hardly see one another.'

'Some of her things are hanging in the wardrobe; I can smell her perfume on them. Her photograph was on your desk.' She gave him an imploring look. 'I can't, Jeremy. Not here. I won't be able to relax.' When she tried to rise to her feet, she felt his hand on her arm, holding her back. 'Please, Jeremy…'

That damned photograph. He'd been careless. He should have remembered and shoved it in a drawer, but he hadn't expected her to wander all over the place. 'I don't think you realize how unbelievably lovely you are.'

He breathed the words into her ear. 'And you can't possibly imagine the effect you're having on me.'

'Take me to my flat. It's not late and it's not far away.'

'It's wet and freezing cold out there.'

'You can stay the night.' She stared pointedly at the photograph of his wife and daughter. 'Please, Jeremy, I can't. Not here.' When she pressed her hands into the sofa again, he allowed her to rise.

Jeremy gave a resigned sigh. 'If it'll make you more comfortable.' He rose and stood beside her. 'I'll call a cab and get our coats.' He suddenly slid an arm around her waist, drew her close and tried to kiss her.

She closed her lips against his and turned her face away. 'Please be patient, Jeremy. Don't rush me. I've not been with a man since my boyfriend left me, and that's more than three years ago. I'm not accustomed to…'

He kissed her neck, her shoulder, then made his voice tender as he whispered, 'Don't worry, Katarzina. You've no need to be afraid. You're so sweet, so lovely, I'd die rather than distress you.'

His heart was pounding. He could feel the blood throbbing in his temples. He'd not been this aroused for years. He moved his body away. She was gazing at him, her lips parted, her eyes wide and apprehensive.

'I'll go and phone a cab,' he said breathlessly. 'We'll put our coats on, then go down and wait for it in the lobby.'

NINE

VELMA BEGAN TO stack the breakfast things on to a tray;
the small dish she'd used for her grapefruit segments,
the large egg-smeared plate that had been heaped with
Henry's full English. She envied him. No matter how
much he ate, he never put on weight. Perhaps it was because he was so tall and big-boned. Some men needed
a lot of food. 'More coffee?'

'Please, love.'

When she reached for his cup he lowered his newspaper an inch and looked at her. She could only see his
eyes, but they seemed gentle. She gave him a nervous
smile.

'What's the matter, love?' The words rustled up
through the gravel in his throat.

'Nothing's the matter.' She held the lid of the pot
while she emptied the last of the coffee into his cup.
'Anything in the paper?'

He chuckled. 'Edward Ashton. Front page and cen-
tre spread. Bloke who's written the article's a bit of a
craftsman: doesn't leave much to the imagination. Plenty
of pictures, too. They've fogged out the boys' faces,
but that fat bastard Ashton's in there, large as life and
twice as ugly.'

Velma added milk and sugar, then slid the cup towards him. 'I can't understand that sort of thing.'

'Each to his own.' He was still gazing at her over
his paper. 'What's the matter, love?' he repeated softly.

Velma suddenly wanted to cry. 'I've told you, nothing's the matter.'

He tossed the newspaper on the table and pushed his chair back. 'Come over here.'

She picked up the tray. 'I've got things to do, Henry. I can't—'

'I said, come over here.'

Feigning exasperation, she lowered the tray and walked around the table.

'Closer.'

She took another step. Their legs were almost touching. In his white shower robe he looked for all the world like a heavyweight boxer waiting to step into the ring. He leaned forward, huge hands circled her waist and he drew her down on to his knee. When she slid an arm around his neck to steady herself she felt that shiver of excitement ripple through her.

He kissed her cheek. 'What's the matter, love?'

'I've told you, twice already, nothing's the matter.' Her chin began to tremble. She turned her head, unable to look him in the eye, felt him drawing her closer, heard his deep voice whispering:

'I've never known a woman who looked as lovely as you over a breakfast table, Velma. And you're wise and witty and smart, but I can always tell when you're fobbing me off. What's the matter?'

She sniffed. 'Well, I…I sometimes think you don't love me or want me any more.'

'And what's made you think that?' He whispered the words in a voice so deep it made her body shake.

'You've been very distant this past few months, you don't talk to me the way you used to, and you don't seem to…'

'Don't seem to what?'

'Need me any more.' Her voice lowered to a whisper, 'Especially in the bedroom.'

He lifted her hand and pressed the palm against his lips.

'Business, love. Serious business. I've been preoccupied, dealing with something I should have dealt with a year ago. But it's almost over now. Everything's coming together nicely. The dead can rest in peace.'

'What do you mean, "the dead can rest in peace"?'

'Family business, love. Something that had to be done. Something it's best you don't know anything about.' He kissed the palm of her hand again, squeezed her, then, with his mouth close to her ear, murmured, 'Have you ever seen women staring at babies in prams, coo-cooing and saying, "You're so lovely, I could eat you"?'

She gave him a questioning look.

'I used to think they were stupid, Velma, but that's just how I feel about you. You're so lovely, I could eat you.' He held her gaze for a dozen heartbeats, then said softly, 'Marry me, Velma. I want you to marry me.'

'Marry you?' She couldn't believe what she was hearing.

'Would it be so terrible? I know I'm older, I know—'

'Of course I'll marry you. I'd love to marry you.' She flung her other arm around his neck and kissed him.

He eased her away. 'Soon. As soon as possible. And a small wedding, very quiet, just close family. Don't want to attract attention at the moment. Then we'll go abroad: Spain, Greece, Italy, wherever you fancy. We'll buy a villa; you can choose it. The boys can take over the business.'

She pressed her cheek against his and hugged him. Tears were running down her cheeks. 'I love you, Henry. God, I do love you,' was all she could say.

'How's the Katie woman getting on with Farrell?'

'Katarzina?' Velma sniffed back happy tears. 'She's finished the job, night before last.'

'Didn't take her long.'

'She's very attractive.'

'What's the video like?'

'Well…'

'Well what?' He pushed her away so he could look into her face. 'Tell me.'

'It's rather explicit.'

'Wouldn't be any use if it wasn't explicit.' He grinned. 'What do you mean, "explicit"?'

Velma laughed. 'It's the things he does to her. And he was insatiable. Went on for ages. After a while, she got off the bed, fetched him a whisky and made him talk. She was probably hoping he'd go to sleep, but he started all over again. You can tell she's getting sick and tired of it at the end.'

'What did they talk about?'

'He kept going on about his wife being frigid, called her a scrawny nagging bitch, said she'd never been interested in him or his political career, that she was so stupid and uneducated she embarrassed him. And he had quite a lot to say about politics and politicians, especially the woman who's acting as Prime Minister. It was all dreadfully malicious.'

'Picture's clear?'

'Perfect. And so is the sound. You can hear them breathing, every tiny noise. It's embarrassing. The man Conrad knows—the one who worked in film studios—is editing it. I told him to cut it down to less than an hour, but leave in all the incriminating talk. I'll collect the disks this afternoon, then I'll pay the girl off and hand over her passport and papers.'

'Where is she now?'

'I moved her into a small hotel. Farrell sent her flowers and kept phoning her, demanding to see her again. She was becoming frightened. And I didn't want her to become too attached to the flat.'

'Tell Conrad to contact the blokes who installed the gear and have them strip it out, today if possible.'

'And you want me to pay the girl off?'

'Yeah. Give her a bonus. Give her another grand. But find out where she wants to fly to, buy her a first-class single, book her on a flight, and hand everything over in the departure lounge. Tell her she could be in big trouble if the press or the police start looking for her here.'

'I'll deal with it, love. What date were you thinking about for the wedding?'

'Next week if you can. I want us to be married and away on honeymoon before the end of the month.'

'Next week!' Velma laughed. 'We can't arrange it for next week!'

'Try. Bung the registrar. Mark's the eldest, so he can give you away. Lewis can be my best man, and their kids can be bridesmaids and a pageboy. Got to keep it small. Just close family. Can't afford to attract attention right now.'

'But I'll need a wedding outfit, and I'll have to—'

He squeezed her into silence, made his voice urgent: 'We're doing a runner, Velma. I need to get out of the country for a while. Do what you want, buy whatever you want, but keep the party small, keep it quiet, and for God's sake, do it quick.'

JULIA FARRELL UNFOLDED the letter and scanned the contents. She could tell at a glance which category the correspondence fell into. This one could wait until

Jeremy came home at the weekend. She was wishing now that she'd stayed on at the flat; not been so hasty and so unpleasant to Jeremy. She could have done a little shopping, enjoyed the London bustle, persuaded him to take her to a show. He could always get tickets for shows; it was a perk of the job. There seemed to be so many perks. She heard a ladder banging against the wall. Gavin had come back to seal the gutter. She put the paper knife down, trotted over to the door and pulled it open.

'Mrs Farrell! Thought you said you were going to London?' He was holding a white tube that had a plunger and a long nozzle.

'Decided to come home early.' She opened the door wider. 'It's freezing out there, Gavin. Come inside and I'll make you a cup of tea before you start; or would you prefer coffee?'

'Tea would do nicely, thanks, Mrs Farrell. I've got my trainers on. Do you mind if I walk on your floor in trainers?'

'Not at all. Come into the warm.'

He laid the sealant gun on the window-sill and followed her inside.

'Sit down.' She nodded towards the table, then switched the kettle on and began to assemble tea things: two mugs—there was something she wanted to tease him about today.

'You're sorting the mail again, Mrs Farrell. You've got a big pile.'

'There's always a big pile, Gavin.' She dropped tea bags into the delicate china mugs, then smiled at him over her shoulder. He seemed to be admiring her blue and white high-heeled shoes, her white dress. Her smile widened. 'You're the talk of the village, Gavin.'

'Me?'

'Taking women into the woods; very attractive women, so I hear. Women with stylish hair and fashionable clothes.'

His face relaxed and he laughed. 'She was from the police.'

'Don't tell me the police are pestering you again?'

'She was from a special kind of police.' He tried to remember what was printed on the card in the wallet. 'Serious Crime Unit. She never told me her name. She wanted to talk to me about the woods and the marshes. She bought me a meal.'

'Bought you a meal! You must have been very helpful.'

'Who told you?'

'Mrs Smeaton, the widow who has the gamekeeper's cottage.'

'Thought so. I could see her curtains twitching when we drove up.'

'She was telling everyone in the village shop. It was the woman's coat that caught her eye. She kept going on and on about how stylish and unusual it was.' The kettle came to the boil. Julia poured hot water over the tea bags, squeezed them a few times with a spoon, then flicked them out and carried the mugs over to the table. She smiled at Gavin. He was blushing. 'Was it a nice coat?'

'Didn't really notice. It had a sort of black and white pattern.'

'Herringbone?' Mrs Smeaton had described it in great detail.

'That's it, herringbone. It was long, with big lapels. Tight around the waist, then it seemed to flare out.'

Julia laughed. 'I think you noticed much more than you'd care to admit, Gavin.'

His blush deepened.

'Did you go for your walk in the woods before or after your meal?'

'Before,' he muttered gruffly, then reached for his mug. He could hear the amusement in Mrs Farrell's voice.

'I suppose you were working up an appetite?' She gave him a teasing smile. 'And where did she take you for this meal?'

'Bricklayer's Arms in Welby.'

'Not what you'd call an expensive place.'

'I told her I wasn't dressed for posh. She came looking for me in the churchyard, see. I'd just finished digging a grave. And the food at the Bricklayer's is OK, and the room's nice and warm; they keep a fire burning in the lounge.'

'That must have been very cosy for you both, Gavin. Did she take her coat off?'

'She unbuttoned it.'

'And what was she wearing underneath?'

'Don't remember.' He sipped noisily at the tea. Embarrassed by her teasing, he was trying hard not to smile.

'Think, Gavin. Mrs Smeaton and half the women in the village would like to know.'

'Just a black sweater with a roll neck, and a black skirt.' Then he added irritably: 'And she wore black boots and long black leather gloves that had rows of buttons at the wrists.'

Julia laughed. 'You really were taking notice, Gavin. The sweater and skirt; were they loose or tight?'

'Tight.' He blushed crimson. She'd tricked him. The word had slipped out before he'd remembered to feign ignorance.

'And did you tell her how lovely she looked?'

'No I didn't. I didn't know her, and even if I had known her I wouldn't have said it, because she wasn't that kind of person.' He hid his face behind his mug. 'I've only ever said things like that to you.'

Julia dunked a biscuit in her tea. 'Not that kind of person?'

'She was a bit strange, didn't say much, just asked a question now and then. And she had green eyes that sort of looked right inside you, and she'd darkened her eyelids, and there was all this bright red lipstick.' His Welsh accent made the words dance.

Julia laughed. 'You were *very* observant, Gavin. She must have made quite an impression.'

Gavin spooned more sugar into his tea, stirred it, then took another sip. 'She knows the vicar's wife.'

'Zelda Leyton?'

He nodded. 'She was asking me about her and the vicar.'

Julia began to sort the mail again. Strange, someone from the police asking about Zelda and Andrew. Perhaps the woman had become acquainted with Zelda during a court case.

'She had a nice car.'

Julia hadn't been listening. 'A nice what, Gavin?'

'Car. A Ferrari Fiorano. Flame red.'

'Aren't Ferraris awfully expensive?'

'Really expensive, Mrs Farrell.'

Curious, Julia mused. A police woman, even a plain-clothes police woman, wouldn't have a car like that. And by all accounts, her clothes were far from plain. Suddenly aware of a silence, she glanced at Gavin.

He was frowning at her, his face serious. 'Can I say something to you, Mrs Farrell?'

'That depends what it is, Gavin.' She gave him a warning look.

'It won't upset you, Mrs Farrell, honest. It's something I want to tell you, something from my past, something I've never told a living soul.'

Julia became apprehensive. Gavin took her silence as permission to speak.

'It was before I left Pontypridd and came here with my mam. I'd be seventeen. My dad had always had a temper, but that year things got very bad. He and my mam used to have these dreadful rows about nothing at all. Shouting and swearing was so bad the neighbours complained to the Council. And they usually ended with him knocking her about. I used to try to stop him, but he'd lay into me and he'd a lot of weight and he was quick with his fists and all it got me was a right battering.'

Julia stared at him, a little surprised. Reliving this as he recounted it to her, was clearly distressing him.

'I used to cry; seventeen, and I was crying my eyes out. It wasn't the pain, it wasn't the humiliation, it was because I was upset for my mam. I couldn't do anything to help her, see. When we came up here, I started going to a gym, got myself in shape, did some boxing, some judo. My dad wouldn't be able to give me a beating now, Mrs Farrell.'

'Your mother left him?'

Gavin nodded. 'They're divorced.' He gulped at his tea.

Making her voice gentle, Julia said, 'I'm sorry, Gavin. It must have been awful for you.'

He nodded. His face was gaunt. Julia sensed he was on the verge of tears. Not wanting to embarrass him, she gathered up the piles of letters and began to rise from the table.

'That's only part of what I wanted to tell you, Mrs Farrell, and not the important part.' He watched her sit down again, then went on, 'That last year in Pontypridd it got to the point where I couldn't stand it any more. When they started rowing, I used to run out and go across to some allotments by the railway tracks. A big rambling place it was: tatty sheds and water butts, mostly overgrown with weeds, with the one or two decent gardens fenced off with old railway sleepers and wire netting.

'One day I walked the length of the path that wound through it, came to a thick hedge, so thick you couldn't see what was on the other side. Don't know why, but I kept on going down the side of this hedge, through long grass and garden rubbish and gooseberry bushes, until I found a gap behind a ramshackle old greenhouse. When I squeezed through, there was this meadow, all fresh green grass and wild flowers, hidden behind tall hedges. It was so quiet and peaceful, no shouting and screaming, just flowers and sunshine. After I'd found it, I used to go there every day, stay out of the house until it was dark.' He sniffed and looked down at the table. He was clearly embarrassed now.

Julia gazed at him across the silence, more than a little embarrassed herself. She wasn't accustomed to dealing with the emotional outpourings of young men. Perhaps if he'd been smaller, if he'd looked vulnerable, she'd have been more comfortable with the conversation. The refrigerator clicked and began to hum. The sound of a tractor droning along the lane at the front of the house grew louder, then faded. She had to say something. 'I'm sorry, Gavin,' she murmured softly.

'So sorry you had such a hard time. But it's over now. It's all behind you, and—'

Bright brown eyes swept up and met hers. 'That wasn't what I wanted to tell you, Mrs Farrell. I wanted to tell you that when I saw you in that white dress, with your brown arms and golden hair, it was like being back in my meadow, in the sunshine, amongst the grass and the flowers, all calm and peaceful. That's what I really wanted to tell you.'

Julia stared at him, appalled. He was completely infatuated with her. She had to put a stop to it. She drew in a breath. 'That was by far the sweetest thing anyone's ever said to me, Gavin, but I wish you hadn't.'

'I was just telling you how I felt. Telling you the other stuff, about my mam and dad, was just so I could explain how I felt.'

'I didn't mind you telling me about your parents, Gavin. What I'm trying to say is, you shouldn't be having those kind of feelings about me.'

He frowned down at the table. 'I can't help the way I feel.'

'I'm old enough to be your mother.'

'But you're not my mother.' He looked up, a triumphant little smile on his face. 'And anyway, what's age got to do with it; you're lovelier than any girl I've ever known.'

'I'm a married woman, Gavin.' Julia made her voice stern. 'I've been married for more than twenty years. I love my husband and my husband loves me. It's not appropriate for you to say things like that to me.'

'But they're true.'

'That has nothing to do with it.'

He sighed, gave her a shy smile and rose to his feet. 'I'd better get that gutter fixed.'

Julia followed him to the door. When he'd stepped outside, he turned towards her, his face painfully serious, 'I don't accept what you say about age, Mrs Farrell. If you don't mind my saying so, it's a load of rubbish. All you've got to do is look in a mirror. But I do understand when you say you're a married woman. I'll keep my thoughts to myself in future.' He began to climb the ladder, then paused and looked down. 'If anyone ever hurt you, Mrs Farrell, I'd sort them for you. Anyone bothers you, you just tell me. I'd kill anyone who hurt you.'

'No one's going to hurt me, Gavin. Don't say things like that. Don't even think them.'

She closed the door, went through to the sitting-room, poured herself a large gin and tonic and flopped down on the sofa. This young man: this tall, strong, handsome young man; this fixer of toilet seats and digger of graves and sealer of gutters had just said the sweetest thing to her. She thought of Jeremy, remembered his vulgarity, his tasteless remarks about hard-ons and corpses and women on the game, and was suddenly glad she'd returned home to Enderley.

TEN

Traffic was flowing slowly. Spied on by cameras, drivers were being obedient to an instruction to reduce their speed along the stretch of road where the carriageway was being widened. Samantha stayed in the left-hand lane, occasionally glancing towards the rising ground that bordered the motorway, searching for the landmark. Eventually she saw it, up ahead; a derelict brick tower, without roof or sails, standing dark against the grey winter sky. After another half-mile a gap opened in the line of cones and a sign announced *Motorway Maintenance Traffic Only*. Samantha slowed, eased the Ferrari on to the fenced-off hard shoulder and cruised past a compound stacked with concrete blocks and pipes, steel barrier rails and posts.

A collection of huge yellow machines separated the compound from a cluster of pre-fabricated huts. She turned through a gap between the low buildings, swept past fuel containers and allowed the car to roll to a stop on an area of rough concrete. A storage hut and a latrine block had been erected close to the rocky face of the motorway cutting. On the other side of the parking area, with their backs to the motorway, were two more of the long huts; one appeared to be a canteen, the other a site office. Samantha circled the enclosure, parked the car facing the exit, then headed for the office.

Fluorescent lighting was bright beyond the windows. Without bothering to knock, she pushed open the door and stepped inside. Heaters, fed from squat red gas cylinders, were making the long space uncomfortably warm, sucking the oxygen from the air, leaving it stale and smelling of cement and tar and oil. At the far end, a man in a hard hat and yellow visibility jacket was poring over a plan on a drawing board. He looked up, watched her making her way towards him, past a desk, filing cabinets, a table, shelves stacked with surveying equipment.

Stepping around one of the heaters, she paused by a plan chest and said, 'I'd like to see the foreman.'

He stared at her for a long moment, sniffed, then growled, 'There is no foreman. There's a site manager.'

Samantha gave him her sweetest smile. 'Then may I see the site manager?'

He looked her up and down again. He was making it obvious he didn't want a woman on his site or in his hut. The collar of his green check shirt was open, exposing a weather-beaten neck, and the back and sides of his head were closely shaved. Not a man to waste words, he snapped, 'I'm the site manager.'

Samantha plucked the wallet of ID cards from her bag and held up the one that said Serious Crime. Fleshy lips pursed and small sloe-black eyes left her face and studied it.

He glanced up. 'So?'

'I'd like to know who worked on the site on Tuesday the third.'

'Lot of men work on the site. Sub-contractors work on the site. They come and go.'

'You keep a log-book, a diary, Mr...'

'Pearson. I keep a site diary.'

'May I look at your site diary, Mr Pearson?' She managed another smile.

He stared at her for a while without speaking, then pushed himself off the drawing board, edged her out of the way and headed down the office. He planted himself in a spindly chair behind the desk, pulled open a drawer and took out a blue leather-bound book. 'What's special about February the third?'

'Benefit cheat. We've had a tip-off he's working on a motorway maintenance unit. He was claiming benefit on February the third.'

Stubby fingers tufted with black hair flicked through the pages.

'What's his name?'

'Can't reveal his name; allegation could be malicious.'

He spun the book around so she could read it, then sagged back. Spindles creaked. He stared up at her, his expression dour. He hadn't offered her a chair.

The diary was two pages to a day. About thirty names had been listed on the left hand page. On the right, written in the same careful hand, were notes on the weather, plant and progress. Samantha studied the list, looking for a name she could recognise. She really needed a copy she could take away and compare with the list of names the researchers had sent her.

He cleared his throat. 'Is it worth it?'

Samantha looked up. 'Is what worth it?'

'Sending someone like you to check on a benefit cheat.'

'He's been cheating in a very big way.' She turned to the day before February the third, folded the page over so she could compare both lists, then did the same for the day after. The three lists appeared to be identical and none of the names struck a chord. 'What does this mean?' She turned back to the third and pointed to a note on the right hand sheet. 'Tar spreader and big shovel cylinder seals to be replaced by BC.'

'What it says.' There was a sneer in his voice. 'Most of the machines we use have hydraulic systems; when the seals fail they have to be replaced. I usually call in Barry Clovis, Express Hydraulics.'

Something stirred in her memory. 'Do they always send the same man?'

'There is only one man: Barry Clovis. He owns the firm. And he's no benefit cheat, he's a right grafter. Worked on the spreader for me during the night; electricians rigged lights up for him. Then he fitted new seals on the shovel cylinders early the next morning.'

'You saw him?'

He scowled up at her. 'Course I saw him. Had a word with him just before he left.'

'What time would that be?'

He snatched the diary and spun it round. 'It's here.' He stabbed the page with a hairy finger. 'Left site at 10.20 hours.'

'And when did he arrive?'

The site manager turned back to the previous day and pointed to an entry on the right hand sheet. 'Express Hydraulics. Tarmacadam spreader and big shovel. B C signed in 13.10.'

'So, this hydraulics man…What did you say his name was?'

'Barry; Barry Clovis.' The site manager turned in his chair and studied a memo board fixed to the wall behind the desk. Business cards were tucked into a gap under the frame. He tugged one out and handed it to her.

'So he stayed in the compound from around one in the afternoon on the second to ten-twenty on the morning of the third?'

The site manager gave her an exasperated look. 'That's what it says.'

'Was he here all the time? Could he have slipped off to do another job, perhaps?'

'How would I know? I knocked off at four, started the next day at seven.' There was a rising note of irritation in his voice. 'These are seriously big machines, love. He had to disconnect the arms and dismantle the cylinder ends. There's four cylinders on the spreader; two on the shovel. It would have been a three-day job for most blokes. He was doing me a favour. We're running behind and I can't afford any down-time. I've got to keep shifting earth on the embankments, spreading tarmac on the new lanes. He might have snatched an hour's kip in his van. He might have had a cuppa in the canteen, but there's no way he could have slipped off to do another job.'

'Was this a one-off, or has he been here before?'

'Lot of machines here. Been coming regular over the past twelve months; he doesn't just do hydraulics.'

'Emergency call, was it?'

The site manager sighed out his irritation. 'He's busy. Got to book him.' He licked his thumb and flicked back through the diary. 'December: December the nineteenth, that's when I phoned and arranged the visit. Machines hadn't broken down. Operator told me he was topping the fluid up too often, so I called Barry and arranged to get the seals renewed. Costly if the machines break down; men standing around, job slipping further behind.'

'Could you photocopy me these sheets?' She nodded towards a copier by the door.

'Copier won't work; out of toner.' He gave her a smug little smile. 'And I'm widening a motorway here, not nancying around, chasing benefit cheats. I've got more to do with my—'

The phone began to shrill. He snatched it up and listened. 'I'll check it, Martin. I was checking it when I got interrupted. Invert level, manhole sixty-three. Hang on a sec.' He tossed the phone down, heaved himself out of the chair and strode back to the drawing board.

Samantha opened her bag, took out a pad and pen, and scribbled: *Taken for examination, one site diary in blue-leather binding.* She scrawled an illegible signature, then tore out the sheet and laid it on the desk. She called down the long office, 'You're obviously busy. I'll leave you in peace. But thanks for talking to me.'

He didn't look up, just grunted and gave a dismissive wave. She slid the diary under her coat. On her way to the door, she glanced at the photocopier. The *ready-to-print* symbol was gleaming on its control panel.

Glad to be out of the stuffy office, she climbed into the Ferrari and made her way back to the motorway. At the first junction she turned off, drove for a couple of miles, then parked in a lay-by. She dragged a folder from behind the seats and began to look through the notes her researchers had prepared. The information she wanted was on the second page: *Barry Clovis. Mother, Fay Clovis, nee Bassinger (sister of Morris Bassinger, deceased).*

Samantha searched in her bag, took out the encrypted phone and keyed in a number. Almost immediately a male voice said, 'Selfridges Department Store.'

'Give me Judy Garland in fine china and glassware.'

'And your name is?'

'Temple; Shirley Temple.'

The line hummed, clicked open, and a female voice said, 'What can I do for you, Miss Temple?'

'Second sheet of the list of names you sent me: half way down. There's a Barry Clovis.' She slid the business card from her glove. 'He has an engineering firm, Express Hydraulics, probably works out of a private address, 14 Bankside Villas, Brentwood, Essex. I'd like you to find out all you can about him: education, employment, marriage, medical records, everything. And I want his phone calls monitored, and his email and paper mail intercepted.'

'Have to get clearance for the phones and the mail.'

'Talk to Marcus Soames. If you can't get him, go to Fallon. Any problems, get back to me within the hour. The monitoring's important.'

THE OLD IRON gate clanged shut, its latch clicked, and Julia Farrell headed down the path. A sudden and unseasonal mildness had thawed the frost and water was dripping from the holly bushes that bordered the lawns. Zelda must have been watching for her through one of the mullioned windows, because the front door opened and she stepped out, smiling, brown hair gently waved, breasts shaping her green jumper, her tweed skirt tight around her hips. 'I'm so glad you remembered our little get-together, Julia. How's the ankle?'

'Fine. The pain had gone the next day. The frozen-pea compress did the trick.'

'Coffee?' Zelda took her coat. The house was stiflingly warm. 'Come and see the new kitchen.'

As she followed Zelda down the red-carpeted hall, Julia stared up the lofty stair-well. The ornate newel posts and fretted balusters were icing-sugar white now, and an ivory paper with a powder-blue pattern decorated the walls. 'I see you've got rid of all the dark wood and that tatty old Turkish carpet.'

'Only after a blazing row.'

'Row?

'With the diocesan architect. Arrogant, twitchy little man with a great beak of a nose. He was terribly upset; couldn't bear to be challenged; wanted to do all the rooms with those gloomy William Morris wallpapers and have the pine re-varnished. When I said I wasn't having it, he almost foamed at the mouth. I went to see the bishop. Told him I'd pay. That decided it.' Zelda laughed. 'Architect said I was a vulgar little Philistine intent on vandalising a Ninian Comper gem.'

Julia turned and gazed up the stairs again. 'I think it's wonderful, Zelda. You've transformed the place.'

'You saw the dining-room and sitting-room when we had the dinner party. When we've had coffee, I'll show you the bedrooms.'

They entered a dark passageway beyond the stairs, Zelda pushed through a door at the end and they stepped into a gleaming new kitchen. 'Kettle's just boiled.' She waved towards a circular table set in a bay window. 'Sit down. I'll bring everything over. You don't mind instant?'

'Not at all.'

Zelda glanced across at Julia from an island work-top. 'How was London?'

'Can't say I enjoyed it. Waste of time, really.'

'I thought you were looking forward to it.'

'I was, but it was a disappointment. I wish I hadn't gone.'

Julia watched Zelda carry the tray over. She felt drawn to this voluptuous woman with the soft brown eyes, felt that she could confide in her. She needed someone to talk to. Her daughter was completely absorbed in herself, Ruth Norris was a dreadful gossip, and even when Jeremy was there he never listened.

'I did a bit of shopping,' Julia went on. 'I quite like shopping in London; spent a night at the flat, then came home on an early train.'

Zelda smiled. 'I take it Jeremy was the disappointment?'

'How did you guess?'

'It was your tone of voice when you said, "Spent a night at the flat." Help yourself to sugar.' Zelda pulled out a chair and sat down. 'That's a beautiful suit, such a gorgeous peacock blue. I saw you wearing it in church, with that cheeky little hat with the black feathers.'

Julia wanted to unburden herself, not chatter about clothes. Ignoring the compliment, she went on, 'He's become so insensitive, so coarse. He doesn't seem to respect me any more. I thought he might be having affairs; London, the flat, all those nubile little researchers.'

Zelda bit into a biscuit with her white and rather too-perfect-looking teeth. 'And is he?' She began to chew.

'Don't think so. I searched the flat from end to end. Didn't find anything incriminating. And I discovered his secretary's just got married and his researcher's the daughter of friends.' She sighed. 'I suppose that's something you don't have to worry about, being the wife of a vicar.'

Zelda held Julia's gaze for a moment, then said, 'Deep down, men are all pretty much the same, don't you think? Bit like shoddily constructed androids, cobbled together from left-over parts, their brains wrongly wired.'

Julia burst out laughing. 'Not all men, surely?'

'No, I mean it,' Julia insisted. 'Barristers, bishops, builders, bus drivers: it's genetic. They're all the prod-

uct of unfinished evolution, programmed for brief pair-
ings—no longer than gestation and weaning—strutting
around, spreading their genes, gratifying their monu-
mental egos.'

Julia was still laughing. 'Rather like chimpanzees?'

'Very much like chimpanzees. And they don't know
the first thing about us, about the way we think, about
our feelings.' Her voice lowered, became gentle again,
as she added softly, 'About our needs.' She took two sips
at her coffee, then said, 'Only another woman can really
understand a woman's physical and emotional needs.'

Julia returned Zelda's smile. She was enjoying this
heart-to-heart. 'Can I tell you something?' she said.
'Something that must stay with you.'

'People tell me their confidences each and every day.
Of course it will stay with me.'

'A boy, a young man really, seems to be infatuated
with me. I'm finding it a little worrying.'

'Why on earth should it worry you? And why
shouldn't a young man be infatuated with you? You're
very attractive.'

'Obsessed might be a better word.' Julia decided to
tell all. 'It's Gavin Jones, the tall young man who helps
the sexton. Bartlett and Bryden send him to the Grange
sometimes to do repairs. He's said some very flattering things to me. I've told him I'm old enough to be his
mother and he's got to stop it.'

'And has he?'

'I suppose I'll have to wait and see.' She took a biscuit. 'The police arrested him after the assassination; he
has guns and goes duck shooting on the marshes. Then
a policewoman came to see him a few days ago; she
talked about the woods and the marshes. He said she'd
asked after you and Andrew.'

'Asked after me?'

'Gavin didn't get her name, but he said she had black hair and bright-red lipstick and was very well dressed. Mrs Smeaton saw her. She couldn't stop talking about her coat in the village shop.'

Black hair, bright-red lipstick…Zelda suddenly recalled the woman who'd burst into her office and asked about a missing person. She'd been too busy to take much notice of her clothes, but the woman did have black hair, and she'd mentioned going to school with her. 'Sounds like someone who came to see me at the office; she reminded me we were at boarding-school together.'

'You went to boarding-school?' Julia suddenly felt a little less comfortable.

'Martha Hemmingway School for Girls. They had a sixth-form, so I went straight from there to Oxford.'

The feeling intensified. No matter how pleasant they were, people like this always revived her insecurities. Making her voice bright, Julia asked, 'How did you cope with being sent away from home like that?'

Zelda sighed, remembered Agnes with her hard little breasts and slender thighs, pink-faced Belinda with her plump legs and unusually… She pushed herself to her feet. 'My last two years there were the happiest of my life. Come on, I'll show you the rest of the house. The bathroom's quite grand and my bedroom's turned out rather well. We'll not bother with Andrew's study; it's a bit cluttered. And his bedroom's not much better. We'll start with…' She paused. Julia was giving her a questioning look. Zelda's lips parted in a smile. 'I think I told you,' she said softly, 'Andrew and I have an understanding: I do my thing, and he does his. It works rather well.'

SAMANTHA HEARD A faint bleeping, slowed, then pulled over to the kerb. She opened her bag, pushed aside the gun, then rummaged around in the clutter until she found the encrypted phone.

'That you, Sam?'

'Who else would it be, Marcus?'

'Where are you?'

'Driving into Manchester.'

'We have to meet and talk.'

'Tomorrow?'

'Tonight,' he insisted.

'Not tonight. I have to check something out.'

'You know about Edward Ashton?'

'Who doesn't? Papers are full of it.'

'Similar thing's happened to the Culture Minister, Jeremy Farrell. Newspaper that exposed Ashton's been sent a video. Editor's put the Home Office on warning, just as he did with the Ashton story. They've tried to persuade him to delay publication, but he's refused.'

'Does Farrell know yet?'

'We think not. He flew to Rome this morning—a conference on world heritage sites.'

'And what's on this video?'

'Usual thing. He's in a bedroom with a woman. Worst part is, he stops for a breather and makes some very un-flattering comments about the Deputy Prime Minister and members of the cabinet. Some of the things he says are downright incriminating. After Cosgrave's assassi-nation, the murder of his sons, and the Ashton exposé, this could bring the government down.'

Samantha listened to the hiss of traffic speeding along the rain-swept road, the faint chirps and bleeps of the encryption in the earpiece of the phone. A lorry roared past and she could hardly hear Marcus saying:

'I think you were right, Sam. This isn't terrorism.'

'Do we know the woman?'

'The woman?'

'The woman Farrell was in bed with?'

'A civil servant who went with him to open an exhibition at the Tate recognized her on the video. Katarzina Liegis. Latvian, supposed to work for some fine art exporters.'

'Does it look as if she knows she's being videoed?'

'She doesn't seem to, but one can't really tell.'

'You're pulling her in?'

'She's not broken the law.'

'Have you located her?'

'She's booked on a flight out of Heathrow, going to Riga. Departure's scheduled for 17.50 this evening.'

'And you're not going to question her?'

'Lorreta's discussed it with the Deputy PM and Macefield at the Home Office. They think it would be better if she's out of the country when the story breaks. Our instructions are not to intervene in any way, just let her go.'

'Do the Met know about this?'

'No.'

'You can buy me dinner, Marcus. Tonight. Eight o'clock.'

'Where?'

'Somewhere near Heathrow.'

He laughed softly. 'I know a decent place just outside Chertsey. That close enough?'

'Chertsey's fine.'

'Connaught Hotel; it's a couple of miles along the road to Shepperton.'

ELEVEN

HEELS DRUMMING ON wooden decking, Samantha ran across the dimly lit passenger bridge. Two stewardesses, a tall redhead and a petite brunette, smart in their tiny hats and sky-blue uniforms, were standing by the aircraft door, poring over a clipboard. The redhead glanced up.

Samantha opened her ID wallet. 'You have a passenger on board. Katarzina Liegis. I want to speak to her.'

'We're about to move out on to the runway. I can't—'

Samantha brought the wallet closer to her face. 'Two minutes. Just two minutes.'

'The bridge is going to be removed. I've been instructed to close—'

'See the captain. Tell him two minutes; two minutes or I'll call the control tower and have the flight stopped.'

The dark-haired woman said, 'I'll go through and tell Peter.' The red-head took the clipboard and frowned at Samantha. 'Did you say Katarzina Liegis?'

'Just take me to her; walk down the aisle ahead of me, don't speak, just indicate where she's sitting, then leave us.'

The stewardess studied the schedule, then led her down the half-empty plane, pausing by a seat before walking on.

When Samantha sat down the young woman turned from the window and took a sideways look at her.

'Katarzina? Katarzina Liegis?'

The woman's eyes became apprehensive. When she saw the ID wallet, her body tensed. 'What is it? What do you want?'

'Nothing to worry about, Katarzina. Just answer a couple of questions, then you'll be on your way home.'

'Questions? I haven't done—'

'Who was the tall blonde woman who came with you to the airport?'

'The tall blonde woman? That was Velma.'

'Does she have another name?'

'Men who work for her partner call her Mrs Bassinger, but Dennis told me she isn't married to the boss, they're just living together.'

'Dennis?'

'The man who used to drive me around: my minder.'

'Have you ever met the boss, this Mr Bassinger?'

'No, never. I dealt only with Velma. Things between Velma and the Bassinger man could be changing, though. She was always so serious, a little sad perhaps. Tonight she was laughing and happy. When we parted, I asked her if she had had good news and she told me she was going to be married, very soon.'

'To this man called Bassinger?'

'I presume so.'

'What was his first name, his Christian name?'

'When she spoke to employees she used to say Henry says you must do this and Henry says you must do that.'

'She engaged you?'

'Engaged me?'

'Employed you to liaise with Jeremy Farrell?'

'Liaise!' Katarzina smiled, grateful for the delicacy. 'Yes, she engaged me.'

'She provided the flat?'

'Yes.'

'Where is it?'

'In Knightsbridge—flat 6, Westgate House, Queen's Gardens. Why are you asking me all these things? Have I done something that is against your laws?'

Samantha rose and stepped out into the aisle. 'Thank you, Miss Liegis, have a pleasant journey.' Leaning forward, she whispered, 'And if I were you, I wouldn't come back to the United Kingdom, no matter how much the newspapers offer you.'

THE STILLS TAKEN from the video recordings were sharp and clear. Samantha leafed through the glossy images. 'Edward Ashton looks positively ecstatic, lying there under his glass table. And our beloved Minister for Culture and the Arts is being...' she rotated the picture '...rather athletic.' She glanced up at Marcus. 'Perhaps he's working his way through the Kamasutra. It's interesting that both videos were made in the same suite of rooms.'

'Different places, surely?'

'Just redecorated and with new furnishings.' Samantha held up two of the stills. 'Central heating pipe's in the same position, down the corner of the room, although it's been painted to match the wallpaper and partly covered by the armchair in this image. Both show the slight break where the cornice has been extended after a chimney breast was taken out.' She passed the prints across the table.

Marcus shuffled them into a tidier bundle and slid them back into the file. 'You were saying this Barry Clovis, Henry Bassinger's nephew, could be Cosgrave's assassin? It's a bit tenuous, Sam.'

'Had a call from the researchers an hour ago. Clovis was a corporal in the army—deployed as a sniper in Iraq and Afghanistan. He won regimental cups for target shooting, was decorated for bravery. And he was working on machines in the motorway maintenance compound on the morning of the assassination.'

'Makes it a bit easier to swallow, but it's still very circumstantial.'

'Did you authorize the phone taps and the mail intercepts?'

'Loretta sanctioned the phone taps, they should be in place now, but not the mail: not so easy to set up a covert mail intercept.'

'Phone taps are better than nothing, I suppose.'

'If Clovis killed Cosgrave,' Marcus mused, 'who killed Cosgrave's sons?'

'According to their mother, they were travelling in Spain, escaping the winter. I'm pretty sure they were murdered there—their bodies shipped back to England and then dumped where there was a good chance they'd be found. The Bassingers wanted to make a statement.'

'Evidence, Sam; where's the evidence? Every step the boys took through Spain has been meticulously checked. The trail ends in Madrid. They returned a car they'd hired to a depot at the airport. After that, nothing, no record of their having boarded a plane or booked into a hotel. And the Spanish police and security people have been thorough.'

Samantha glanced out of their isolated alcove, across a crowded dining-room that was noisy with talk and laughter. The meal had been more than pleasant; the Connaught deserved its reputation. She returned her gaze to Marcus. Despite the soft lighting he was looking his age, and he seemed tired to the point of exhaustion. Evening stubble darkened his cheeks and chin, his grey suit could have done with a press and his shirt needed changing.

Deciding to make one more attempt to persuade him, she said, 'Carl, Clovis's cousin, was the first of the Bassingers to die. I left his body in a cellar in Stockport. I killed Carl's father, Morris, a few days later. Morris's widow is called Elaine. She went with her surviving son, Trevor, to live in Spain; they have a villa there. They run a fleet of buses, a tour company, they specialize in pilgrimages to religious shrines: Fatima, Garaban-del, Avila, Compostela, places like that. The business is based in Santander, but they maintain a depot in Lon-don; in Stepney, off the Mile End Road. I think Trevor Bassinger killed, or hired someone else to kill, the Cos-grave boys. Their bodies were probably brought back to England in the luggage bay of a bus and off-loaded at the Stepney depot. The luggage bays on tour coaches are quite big, Marcus. They could have made a small compartment at one end and hidden the bodies in that.'

'Conjecture, Sam.'

'Around the time the boys were killed, one of the firm's buses returned to London after touring Spain.' Sa-mantha passed a slip of paper over the table. 'That's the registration number. It's worth getting Customs to use some pretext to look it over when it next passes through.'

Marcus picked up the note and frowned at it. 'Got to tread carefully. We don't want to put the Bassingers on their guard if we're going to search for evidence. And the Crown Prosecution Service won't move without it, espe-cially after that courtroom fiasco a couple of years ago.'

'They had cast-iron evidence then, but they still made an utter mess of it.'

'Precisely.' He slid the paper into his wallet.

'How's Mrs Cosgrave?' Samantha asked. 'Have they fixed dates for the funerals?'

'Held a joint funeral in the early hours of Monday morning. The service was at St Jude's, Stockport, followed by burial in Stockport Cemetery. She's agreed to forget the headstones until things have calmed down.'

'You kept that quiet.'

'Vital that we did. If the funeral of an assassinated Prime Minister and his murdered sons had been splashed across the front pages, we'd have had to bring in troops to protect the mosques.'

Samantha folded her napkin and laid it on the table. 'How did Mrs Cosgrave cope?'

'Macefield from the Home Office attended. Said she was dignified and composed; behaved in exactly the way one would expect the wife of a British Prime Minister to behave. She's had a while to get used to the situation, I suppose.'

'She'll never get used to it,' Samantha snapped, reproaching his callousness. 'Is she still at Chequers?'

'She is, and she's restless. She's demanding to go back to her own home. Metropolitan Police want her to stay put, but they realize they're going to have to give in. The house is in her husband's constituency: Stockport side of Manchester. Security's being improved before she returns.' Marcus frowned and brought his attention back to the crisis that was exhausting him. 'I take it you're quite convinced this whole thing's been orchestrated by the Bassingers?'

'I'm certain of it. It's retribution: an eye for an eye. Cosgrave and his sons are dead. The two people who played a big supporting role in the sequestration have been destroyed; one of them's taken his own life.'

'Don't forget your involvement, Sam. How many Bassingers did you kill? Seven, eight, plus hangers on?'

'I was the government's agent, Marcus, and it was agreed that I could take any measures, no matter how extreme, to recover the child.' She paused for a moment, then said softly, 'And I made sure no one would come looking for me afterwards. Anyone who could recognize me died.'

'You're completely sure?'

'Dangerous to be complacent. One can never be completely sure, of course. They got a picture of me from a security system. It was grainy and indistinct, but…' She let her words hang in the air. Her fears had eased with the passing of time.

'The Bassingers, Sam, remind me again how many adult males survived?'

'From the older generation, what you might call the fathers, only Henry. Then there are his sons, Mark and Lewis; and five nephews, including Barry Clovis and Trevor. Trevor and his mother run the bus tour company in Spain.'

'If your take on this is correct, they're a serious threat, to Cosgrave's widow and to you. I'll get the DPP's comments, then have a word with Loretta. We need guidance from the politicians, and I think they're going to have to be told that due process may be out of the question. Unless the DPP advises otherwise, I don't see much chance of a trial and conviction.'

'There's going to be a wedding.'

Marcus grinned from ear to ear. 'Sam! I'm absolutely delighted. Who's the lucky—'

'Not me, Marcus. Velma and Henry Bassinger. Velma gave Katarzina Liegis the news when they parted at Heathrow.'

'Is that relevant?'

'We might have all the people we're interested in gathered here. I think we should monitor Henry and Velma's calls. By the way, the address of the place they used to make the videos is Flat 6, Westgate House, Queen's Gardens, Knightsbridge.'

Marcus scribbled in a notebook. 'I'll have the ownership and any letting details checked. If we could link the place to the Bassingers... Where are you heading now?'

'Back north. Home, relax in a hot bath and have a whisky while Crispin regales me with tales of the daily dramas at his hairdressing salon. Something soothing and normal for a change.'

Marcus began to laugh softly.

'What's funny?'

'Nothing normal about you lying in a bath and drinking whisky while you chat to your gay manservant about hairdressing.'

'He's my dearest friend, Marcus, not my manservant. He's very sweet and caring. And where might you be heading?'

Still laughing, he said, 'Think I'd better head home, too. Spend a few days with Charlotte. Not been home for ages. Thank God she understands.'

'She's a bishop's daughter, Marcus.' Samantha's tone was faintly mocking. 'One would expect her to understand about service and dedication. And she has the farm to run and all those sheep to care for.'

His wickedly blue eyes were twinkling. 'A sheep-rearing bishop's daughter and a gay hairdresser; we both have rather unusual partners, Sam.'

'Crispin's very caring and tender towards me, Marcus.'

'Can't say Charlotte's ever been anything else to me.'

ZELDA PUT HER book down, untucked her legs from under her and walked over to the window. She parted the curtains and peered into the darkness. A sudden gust of wind rattled the sash and peppered the glass with rain. She shivered. She could just make out the tower and nave of the church, and the tops of the taller gravestones. Enderley vicarage wasn't a house she cared to be alone in, especially in winter.

Spending the morning in the company of Julia Farrell had been more than pleasant. Julia hadn't responded to any of her gentle and not so gentle hints, but then, she hadn't shied away, either. And she seemed to be developing a strong antipathy towards Jeremy; children leaving home didn't necessarily bring couples closer together. Zelda sighed and her breath misted the glass. She'd have to be patient, proceed carefully, cultivate a deeper affection before trying to make Julia more than a friend.

Rain lashed the window again. Zelda allowed the curtains to fall back. She'd go and see what Andrew was doing, ask him if he wanted a drink, perhaps torment him a little. She left the sitting-room, crossed the hall and pushed open the door to his study.

'Isn't it time you gave up, Andrew?' She strolled over to his desk, enjoying the sensation of the deep pile of the carpet beneath her stockinged feet.

He glanced up and gave her a tight-lipped little smile. 'It's something I have to finish, and I'm not the only one who burns the midnight oil.'

'But at least my clients pay me, Andrew; the church pays you next to nothing.' Perching on the edge of the desk, she raised a knee and rested her foot on his chair, aware that this would irritate him. She wriggled her toes under his thigh. 'What are you working on tonight?'

'Trying to put a few words together for the funeral

tomorrow, but I'm not making much progress—there've been so many funerals this past few weeks; must be the winter. Man called Matthew Dalton; treated his wife rather badly, drank to excess, kept her short of money, didn't bother to conceal his involvement with other women. She's cared for him while he's been dying, but she's very bitter. Thin, gaunt-looking woman. You'll have seen her with her eldest daughter. They usually sit at the back of the church on the font side.'

'What's the problem?'

'How do I say something remotely kind about the deceased without offending the widow?'

Zelda pondered for a moment, then said, 'How about: we that are strong must bear the transgressions and infirmities of the weak, but it takes a big and a loving heart. Most of us manage to conceal our faults, our sins, even from ourselves. They're hidden things, secret, known only to God. Matthew's life was an open book. His failings were exposed for all to see. Then you could enthuse about how devoted and caring his wife's been, censor the biographical bit and go easy on thanking God for a wonderful human being at the end.'

Andrew smiled. 'You're every inch the cynical lawyer, Zelda, but that's pretty good. I've been trying for an hour and I haven't got very far.'

She wriggled her toes under his thigh again and almost laughed at his frown of annoyance. 'Want me to make you a drink?'

He finished noting down her words. 'Don't think so, Zelda. I ought to make a fair copy before I turn in.'

'Wind's moaning through the big trees and the house is making all sorts of funny noises. Don't be long before you come upstairs. I'd rather not be alone up there tonight.'

'Fifteen minutes. By the time you get out of the bathroom, I'll be up. And I'll wedge my bedroom door open.'

'Thanks.' She removed her foot from his chair and rose from the desk.

Andrew watched her walk towards the door. Strange the way unbelievers could be afraid of the dark; the way they found some places sinister. When the door had clicked shut he glanced down at his scribbled notes. *We manage to conceal our sins, even from ourselves. They're secret things, known only to God.*

Known only to God. He tossed his pen down and put his head in his hands. He had a secret, a terrible secret, that he hoped was known only to God. The recollection of it, vivid and ugly, was suddenly lurching along the dark alleyways of his mind. What had possessed her? She'd never behaved like that before. She'd always done just as he'd asked; said the rehearsed words of invitation, mimicking the talk of little girls, then been silent and passive. But that last time she'd started whispering things to him, lewd things; and she'd touched him, fondled him, done things to him. He'd had to…

Andrew dragged in a shuddering breath. It wasn't wise to think about this. It had been weeks now. The worry and fear were less intense, but that old restlessness, that nagging need that stalked him like the hound of hell, were growing. He'd have to find someone else to relieve the unbearable tension that was building up inside him, but until he did…He'd leave his homily for now, take a whisky up to bed with him, let Zelda know he was in his room, just across the corridor from hers.

Zelda stood by her bedroom window. From up here she could see the dark branches of trees swaying in the wind, hear rainwater rushing and gurgling along the huge gutters that crossed the attics above her head, conveying the torrent to gargoyle-headed hoppers on the outer walls.

Feet thudded on the stairs. She heard Andrew calling, 'I've decided to come up, Zelda. I'll leave my door open.'

Despite all her taunting and teasing, her complete indifference to his vocation, he continued to be patient and kind, even loving, towards her. But then, he was the vicar of Enderley, and weren't vicars supposed to be patient and kind? If her sexual appetites had been different, if Andrew had desired her body, their life together could have been everything outsiders perceived it to be. Before they'd married, they'd been very open with one another, made their positions quite plain. He was determined to give his life to God and his ministry; men held no sexual attraction for her. A while ago she'd discovered a photograph of his parents—they'd died a few years before she and Andrew met. His father had been tall and handsome, the image of his son, his mother dark-haired, with an hour-glass figure and a pretty face. She'd realized then that Andrew had been attracted to her because she looked so much like his mother. Perhaps that was why her body seemed to disturb him so.

TWELVE

JULIA TOSSED CIRCULARS and junk mail into the bin, then drew the pile of envelopes towards her. It was still raining. It had rained all night and it was so dark outside. God, she hated the winter, and the winters in Enderley seemed endless and were so gloomy.

Ruth and Vincent were on vacation in Florida. They'd rented a house with its own private beach; they were probably paying for it with back-handers from Bartlett and Brydens, blissfully unaware that the police were about to become involved. Jeremy was vile. He could have given them some sort of warning. And if Jeremy had developed his insurance business instead of wasting his time in politics, they'd have been free to take winter breaks together. Still, she really had enjoyed spending a few hours with Zelda yesterday. She liked her. She was smart in a worldly kind of way, affectionate as well as attractive. Despite the many differences in their backgrounds, they understood one another.

An envelope caught her eye. Small and square, it was made from heavy cream-coloured paper, the sort of thing that usually contained a wedding invitation. She plucked it from the pile. A London postmark, and someone had typed on it, *Personal. For the attention of Mrs Julia Farrell, The Grange, Enderley, Nr Stockport, Lancashire.* It was for her.

She reached for the paper knife and slit it open, took out a plain cardboard wallet and looked inside. It held a silvery video disk. There was no letter, no clue to the sender. She turned the wallet over. A typed label had been stuck to the white card. She read: *The Rt Hon Jeremy Farrell, Minister for Culture and the Arts, and companion. Courtesy copy for Mrs Julia Farrell.*

Julia felt a shiver of alarm. She rose from the table, went through to the sitting room, switched on the television and slid the disk into the DVD player. Seconds later, a girl appeared on the screen, a very attractive girl, her short hair beautifully styled, her face carefully made up. The girl was looking over her shoulder. She was smiling, but her eyes were wide and apprehensive. Jeremy suddenly came into view, his face flushed, his expression intense. He reached out, took the girl by the shoulders and turned her towards him.

Julia's heart was pounding. In spite of all her suspicions, the revelation was coming as quite a shock. It was making her breathless. What was that he'd just said to the girl? *You're ravishing, you're so unbearably lovely.* Unbearably lovely! The miserable old goat. He'd never said things like that to... The girl had stopped smiling now. Julia watched her husband reach behind her back and tug at the zip of her dress. He was having trouble with the halter neck, but the girl freed it for him and he pulled the green satin down to her waist, lowered his head and began to nuzzle...

Mouth dry, mind numb, Julia sagged back on the cushions and gazed, appalled, at the drama being enacted on the screen. The moving images were sharp and clear, the colours vivid despite the soft lighting in the bedroom. After almost an hour, Julia ejected the disk, crossed over to the sideboard and poured herself a large gin and tonic. Her shaking hand made the glass rattle against her teeth as she drained it. She shivered and poured herself another. She felt icily cold. It was shock, of course. The alcohol began to blur her anger, her sense of outrage, and feelings of fear and bewilderment took their place. Her head was starting to spin. She must make the call now, while she still could. She snatched up the phone and keyed in his number.

A breezy female voice announced, 'Jeremy Farrell's office.'

'Get Mr Farrell for me will you. It's his wife.'

'He may have gone to see the Chief Whip. One moment please, Mrs Farrell.' The line went dead, then clicked open and the voice said, 'He's still in his office, Mrs Farrell. I'm putting you through.'

'Julia, love. What's—'

'You've got to come home. Now.'

'Why? What's the problem?'

'Something in the post. About you.'

'About me?' His voice had dropped to a whisper.

'I can't talk about it over the phone. You must come home.'

'I've just arrived at the House; Chief Whip's left a message; he wants to see me urgently. I can't just—'

'Don't bother going to see the Chief Whip. He probably wants to talk to you about the thing that's been sent here. Just put your coat on and catch the first train home.'

ZELDA SIPPED COFFEE and crunched on a slice of toast while she gazed from her bedroom window over grass and gravestones wet with winter rain. She was relieved she hadn't had to commute to Manchester on a day like this. Spending the week here, away from the office, had been very relaxing. She sighed. Better get on. She'd make the beds, take her breakfast tray down, then…

Men bearing a coffin had emerged from the church, followed by Andrew, imposing in his long black cape. An acolyte was sharing a huge black umbrella with him; undertakers were holding umbrellas over the heads of the gaunt Mrs Dalton and her plump daughter. The other mourners had to protect themselves against the pouring rain as they processed towards the grave.

Rites of passage: birth, marriage, death. Andrew presided over them all with a gentle dignity. And his height, his athletic build, his handsome features, made him attractive to the female members of his congregation and his prowess on the sports field brought admiration from the men. Zelda smiled. She was sure the first-year teacher at the village school was in love with him. She gave him such adoring looks. And no doubt there were others with a secret yearning for her husband. She watched the mourners gather around the newly-dug grave. Iron-grey sky, grime-blackened church, black figures: a real rain-swept Lowry landscape.

Andrew would be home in half-an-hour, wet through, freezing cold. She'd make him a mug of proper coffee and a bacon sandwich. She knew she neglected him, but an affection for men, an instinct to care for them, wasn't part of her nature. He'd known that from the beginning, accepted it without complaint, almost seemed to welcome it; God and the parishioners would have no rival for his affections.

Zelda trotted down the stairs, put coffee and water in the percolator and switched it on before returning along the hall to Andrew's study to gather up the cups that had accumulated there. She found one of her best china mugs on a filing cabinet, saw a cup and saucer hiding beneath the papers on his desk. A red-leather bound copy of *Hymns Ancient and Modern* lay open on the blotter, the verses of *Abide With Me* half-covered by an old envelope. Numbers had been scribbled on it: 4, 329, 116, 534. Hymn numbers. Andrew had been choosing hymns, probably for the funeral service he'd just conducted. Something began to fret away at the edges of her memory, something that had been vaguely troubling her for days. The black-haired woman with the compelling eyes who'd burst into her office; she'd shown her one of her own business cards, *Zelda Unwin Head of Criminal Law*, and said it had been found in the flat of a missing girl. A similar list of seemingly unrelated numbers had been scribbled on the back. Zelda gathered up the mug and the cup and saucer and headed for the kitchen.

The woman had said she'd been a pupil at the Martha Hemmingway School for Girls; had mockingly recited the school motto as she was leaving. It had been a good school, a very expensive school, but it wasn't all that well known. Either the woman really had been a scholar there, or she'd been checking on her. Zelda tried to remember what was printed on the woman's ID card. She'd been so busy, so harassed, all she'd wanted to do was get her out of the office and she'd hardly paid any attention, but she remembered the words *Serious Crime* had headed one of the documents in the wallet. And yesterday Julia had told her the woman had been to the village, talked about her to the man who helped the sexton dig the graves. Why would one of her business cards be in the flat of a missing prostitute? A client must have left it there, a client who made lists of numbers....

'How did the funeral go?' Zelda and Andrew were sitting at the circular table in the bay window off the kitchen.

'Better than I expected, thanks to you. I told Mrs Dalton I'd visit her. I'll walk over later if the rain eases.'

Keeping her voice casual, Zelda said, 'I forgot to tell you, a woman came to see me at the office, she was from some special police unit. She said they'd found one of my business cards in the flat of a missing prostitute.' She watched Andrew's expression freeze. Nervous blue eyes began to flicker over her face, as if trying to read her thoughts. The news had meant something to him. She twisted the knife: 'The same woman came to the village a few days ago, talked to the young man who digs the graves, asked him about the woods and the marshes. She talked to him about you.'

Andrew's breathing became rapid and shallow. He closed his eyes and whispered, 'You say this woman was from the police?'

'Some sort of special police.' Zelda continued to watch him over the rim of her cup. His broad shoulders had sagged, his back had hunched, as if he were cringing from her. 'You know something about it, don't you, Andrew?' she asked softly.

'Know something?' He stared down at the table. Zelda heard him whimper, 'Jesus help me. Dear Jesus help me.'

A hardness, a coldness, crept over her. She slipped into professional mode, the table became her desk, the trembling man on the other side of it someone who had to be made to tell her everything. 'You went to her flat, didn't you, Andrew? You must have dropped one of my cards there. Numbers were scribbled on the back. You'd used it to note down hymn numbers.'

He began to sob.

'I think you'd better tell me all about it, Andrew. Then we'll decide what we're going to do.'

He was silent for moment, then he dragged in a breath and said, 'I used to go and see her. She was called Brenda Baxter. She had a flat, just outside Manchester; she shared it with another girl. It was miles away from Enderley, no one would know—'

'Did she pick you up?'

'Pick me up?'

'Was she soliciting when you met her?'

'She advertised. I telephoned, made an appointment.'

'This girl she shared with, did she ever see you?'

'I don't think so. She was never there when I visited.'

They fell into another silence. Then, suddenly filled with an angry loathing, Zelda demanded, 'What was she like?'

'Does it matter?'

'I'm your wife, Andrew. I've a right to be curious.'

'Small, thin, waif-like.'

'Was she very young? Was she pretty?'

'Late twenties, possibly thirty. Not particularly attractive.'

'Why, Andrew?'

'I don't know why. If I knew why, I'd—'

'Of course you know why.'

'It's something I can't put into words.'

Zelda rested her arms on the table, leaned towards him and hissed, 'Try, Andrew. You're a highly educated man. I'm sure you can put it into words.'

He turned from her, watched the rain streaming down the bay window. 'It's a need,' he said presently. 'A nagging need that builds up inside me. It distracts me. I can't concentrate, can't pray, can't turn my heart and mind to God, and I have to find some release from it.'

'Then why on earth did you marry a woman like me, Andrew? What possessed you to agree to—'

He showed her his tear-streaked face. 'Because I loved you,' he sobbed. 'We were soul-mates.'

'Was she the first?'

He shook his head. 'There have been others, quite a few, but she's the only one I've seen since we came to Enderley.'

'Often?'

'Once or twice a month'

'And she was small and waif-like: are you telling me she looked like a child?'

His reply was inaudible.

'I can't hear you, Andrew.'

'Yes!' He was becoming angry at her probing. 'She looked like a child, she dressed like a child and she talked like a child.'

'The woman who came to see me said she remembered me, that she'd attended my school. I think she was lying, Andrew. I think she'd found out things. Did you talk to this prostitute about me?'

'She'd no idea who I was or where I came from. I told her to call me Edward. We never had what you'd call a proper conversation.'

Zelda didn't speak, just stared at him, listened to the patter of rain against the window, the hum of the big new refrigerator, the slow tick of the clock on the wall as its pendulum sliced away the hours.

Unable to meet her gaze, Andrew stared down at the table and continued to weep. When he spoke again, his voice was little more than a whisper. 'I took her some of your school dresses to wear. I found them in a trunk in the attic, the one you used when you were at boarding school.'

'They had name tapes in.'

'I cut them out.'

'But not the crest on the pocket?'

He shook his head.

'Why, Andrew, why?' she insisted.

'I thought I'd just told you why.'

'You haven't told me why you're attracted to pre-pubescent girls, why this prostitute had to dress like a child.' She stared at him, disgust shaping her features. He was still looking down at the table, sobbing quietly. Feeling a renewed surge of contempt, she raised her voice and made it harsh as she demanded, 'Tell me why, Andrew.'

He glanced up, his entire being crying out for compassion, then flinched when he saw the loathing in her eyes. 'Could you get me a drink?' he whispered. 'A whisky? I need one if I'm to explain things I can hardly understand.'

Zelda went through to the sitting-room and poured what was left of the whisky into a tumbler. When she returned to the kitchen he was wiping his eyes on the backs of his hands. He took the glass, drank from it, then waited until she'd resumed her seat.

'Things can happen to you when you're a child,' he faltered. 'Good things, bad things, things that influence you and help to shape the kind of a person you're going to become. Something like that happened to me in the summer of my seventh year. Edward, my twin brother, had become gravely ill. The doctor had diagnosed an infectious kind of meningitis, and I had to be sent away. My father took me to a maiden aunt's. She lived in Derbyshire, in a dark old house that was full of strange noises.

'A little girl called Nancy lived across the street. I wasn't used to girls. There were girls at school, but I'd always had Edward, and being twins we were so close we didn't really get involved with other children. But I was lonely and frightened, and my aunt was rather forbidding, so Nancy's company was a great comfort. We were playing together in the back garden. The lawn was lush and green and bordered by all kinds of flowers. Some men had just creosoted a wooden fence. The sun was baking it and it was giving off a smoky, nose-tickling smell. I'd brought a toy I'd been given for my birthday; two cars, one red one blue, that raced around a figure-of-eight track. The cars kept jamming under the bridge where the tracks crossed, and I was searching for a pebble to lift it when I heard Nancy giggling. I can hear it now, such a happy sound, rippling out over that sunlit summer afternoon.'

Andrew closed his eyes and sipped the whisky. The tick of the clock seemed ominously loud in the silence. It was distracting him. He took a deep breath and began to speak more quickly, as if desperate to get the ordeal over. 'She was wearing a blue gingham dress, and blue ribbons in her hair, and white ankle socks and those shiny black shoes with rounded toes like the ones Minnie Mouse used to wear in the cartoons. She said, "Come over here, Andrew. Come over here and look." I didn't take any notice, I was trying to make the cars run on the track, so she said, "I've got something to show you. I've got a secret. Hurry, hurry, hurry." When I looked round, she was lying on her back, her legs in the air, her knickers around her ankles. She was giggling. She said, "Don't just sit there, silly, come over here and look," so I did. I was shocked. There was nothing there, no penis, just this tiny cleft in a swelling of pink flesh. It disturbed and fascinated me. I reached out, laid my hand over it, began to stroke and squeeze…' Andrew swallowed. His breathing had slowed and deepened.

'Then I heard this woman screaming, "You filthy little boy. You dirty disgusting little boy." She was glaring down at us, over the fence the men had creosoted. She yelled other things, but I was too shocked to take them in. Nancy started crying. She tried to pull her knickers up, but they were tangled in her shoes so she kicked them off and ran down the path, screaming for her mother. I ran into the house and hid under the kitchen table. Then there was this banging on the front door. I heard my aunt opening it and the woman saying, "You've taken something evil into your home, Sarah. He undressed that little girl. He'd got her down on the grass and he was molesting her. God knows what he'd have done if I'd not seen him." Then the woman burst into tears and went away.

'My aunt ran through the kitchen and out into the garden, calling me. Eventually she found me under the table, dragged me out and asked me what I'd been doing. I said, "Nothing". I was crying. She waved the knickers at me and said, "If you've been doing nothing, why were these on the lawn?"

'She made me sit on a chair while she went into the hall and phoned my father. She told him she couldn't cope with me; she insisted he come and collect me right away. Then there was this hammering on the door. It was the little girl's father. He started yelling at my aunt, said I'd interfered with his daughter, called me a disgusting little bugger, said for two pins he'd call the police and have me locked up.

'I was beside myself, hysterical, but my aunt wouldn't speak to me. She just left me in the kitchen until my father arrived. When we got home a neighbour came round, said something to Father, and he started to cry. He turned to me and said, "Your brother died ten minutes ago, and I had to leave his bedside because of the disgusting thing you did. I hope you're ashamed."

'When my mother came home she'd changed. She looked older and behaved like a stranger towards me. She didn't want to hold me; she couldn't bear to even look at me. At the end of the summer they packed me off to this dreadful boarding school. All I remember of it are loneliness and unkindness and cold rooms and rowdy boys and the smell of disgusting food.'

Andrew closed his eyes again. His face was ashen. He'd dribbled whisky down his grey silk stock. 'That summer,' he went on, 'the summer of my seventh year, I lost my twin brother, my father's respect, and my mother's love. In the autumn, I was cast out of the family home,' he opened his eyes and challenged Zelda's unblinking stare, 'and I'd felt the first stirrings of sexual desire. As it grew, I tried to suppress it, to mortify the flesh—God knows how I've tried—but whenever the urges come, unbidden, to torment me, I'm back on that green lawn with the giggling girl, her knickers down, her gingham dress pulled up around her waist, my hand stroking her soft warm flesh.'

Zelda gazed across the table at Andrew, trying to make some sense of what he'd said. She felt no pity for him, just a confusion of loathing and disgust and anger. After a long silence, she asked, 'And this prostitute, this woman who looked like a child, what happened to her? Did you kill her?'

He nodded.

'Why, Andrew, why?

'A rush of blood to the head, a loss of control. I told her she had to lie there, say nothing, be passive, but that last time she started to say things, lewd things, and touch me and do things to me. It wasn't the way little girls behave. I told her to stop, but she just laughed. It wasn't Nancy's happy giggle, it was a coarse nasty laugh, and she went on and on and I had to stop her and I...'

'And you what?'

'Put my hands around her throat and squeezed and squeezed to stop the silly laughter, the awful lewdness, and when the rage had passed, she was dead.' Face ugly with anguish, he began to sob again. Then, his voice suddenly raucous, he cried, 'I didn't mean to do it. I was in a frenzy, a blind frenzy. I'd no idea what I was doing.'

Loathing and contempt finally overwhelmed Zelda. She felt physically sick. How often had she sat in police interview rooms listening to men say, 'I didn't know what I was doing; I don't know what came over me?' But these men were from the legions of the deprived: men who could scarcely read or write, men who led lives of angry desperation. Andrew was educated, cultured, privileged. He had no excuses.

He pressed his face into his hands and his voice was muffled as he asked, 'What are you going to do?'

'Nothing.'

He looked up at her.

'I don't see why my life should be ruined because of your craving for skinny little tarts. But if you're found out, I'll insist I knew nothing. How long ago was this?'

'A month, perhaps a little less.'

'And there's been no mention of it in the newspapers or on television?'

He shook his head. 'I haven't seen anything.'

'What did you do with the body?'

'I found a big suitcase in the flat. I managed to squeeze her inside and zip it up, then wheeled her to the car; I'd parked a couple of streets away. It was dark, curtains were drawn, I'm sure no one saw me.'

'And how did you get rid of the suitcase?'

'It's in the church crypt. I pushed it under an old Victorian coffin that stands on marble blocks.'

Zelda let out a disparaging snort. 'The crypt's the first place they'll look if you're suspected of the girl's murder.'

He flinched when she said murder. 'But where would—'

'Don't ask me. I don't even want to know. It's your mess, you sort it out.'

'FANCY ANOTHER BREW?'

Gavin watched the water swirling into the grate at the bottom of the steps. 'No thanks, Daniel. I just want this rain to stop so we can get on.'

Daniel Shoesmith pursed his lips and blew out a plume of smoke. 'If it don't stop soon we'll have to get the waterproofs on and make a start. Can't leave Matthew lyin' there, all uncovered.' He pointed the stem of his pipe at Gavin and his wrinkled old face parted in a grin. 'Hear you've been takin' women into the woods. Fancy women, good lookin' women, by all accounts.' He laughed. 'Hur, hur, hur.' It was like the contented purring of a cat.

'Can't fart in Enderley without everybody getting a whiff,' Gavin muttered. 'She was from the police. I was helping her.'

'Helpin' her? That's what they're callin' it now, is it? You'll have to come to the House of Correction, present yourself to His Reverence, ask him for a penance.'

'Be a long time before I ask him for anything. And I was only helping her with her enquiries.'

'Hur, hur, hur,' Daniel purred. Suddenly remembering something, he became serious. 'You got the grave dug for Jack Turgoose's widow?'

'Bottomed it out late yesterday. Looked a bit shallow, but I had to leave a few inches on top of her old man's coffin. It's all sheeted over and ready.'

'Good lad.' Daniel settled his battered trilby further back on his head and scowled down at the bowl of his pipe. 'Somethin' I need to tell yer,' he prodded the smouldering tobacco with the end of a pencil, 'just in case I'm not here. Vicar mentioned it yesterday. Going to be a military funeral next week. Boy killed in Afghanistan. Members of his regiment comin', buglers and such like. Thing is, grave's going to be three deep: boy in first with room for the mother and father on top. And it's going to be one of those big fancy caskets, so we've got to give it a bit more room all round. Can't put him side-by-side with old Matthew Dalton; earth will still be loose after only a week and the whole lot could fall in on us. We've got to start another row, put the boy in the middle, head to toe with Jack Turgoose and his widow. That way there'll be plenty of space and the crowd won't be trampling over the old graves.'

SAMANTHA WAS HEADING out of Manchester having done what she'd intended to do the previous evening, before Marcus diverted her with his request for a talk: she'd visited the girl who shared the flat with Brenda Baxter and shown her the photograph she'd torn from the church magazine. The girl had said she'd seen the man only once, and then fleetingly, but she'd been pretty sure the man in the photograph was the client who'd visited Brenda regularly.

Lorries were rumbling along the inside lane, throwing up clouds of spray, and the wipers were having difficulty clearing the wind-screen. She'd find some-where to eat, have a late and leisurely lunch. Then, by the time she reached the church, dusk would be deep-ening into darkness.

THIRTEEN

WIND, MOANING ACROSS winter fields, had swept the sky
clear of clouds and exposed the first faint stars of the
evening. Brighter lights gleamed behind the windows
of distant houses, and on the crest of the hill the tower
of St Michael and the Angels could be seen fading into
the darkness. Another ten minutes and it would be safe
to leave the field gateway and drive into Enderley.

A ringing sound, muffled but insistent, disturbed the
silence. Samantha patted her coat pockets, then clicked
open her bag. The ringing became louder. Snatching up
her mobile from amongst the clutter, she clicked it on
and pressed it to her ear.

'Miss Grey... Is that you, Miss Grey?'

'It is, Father.'

'Hope you don't mind my giving you a call, but it's
been a while now and I was wondering if you'd any
news of Brenda.'

'I'm almost certain she's dead, Father, murdered by
a client.'

'But why would anyone want to do a thing like that?'

'Don't know why, but I think I know who. I'm pretty
sure it was a clergyman, a vicar.'

'A man of the cloth? That's monstrous. Surely you're
wrong?'

'I'll know within the hour. How's Paula Hamilton?'

'She's in hospital. She's very poorly.'

'Very poorly?'

'I don't think she'll see the week out.'

Samantha gazed across darkening fields and hedge-rows. The moon was rising, its narrow crescent just visible against a ribbon of still luminous sky. 'How's Benjamin?' she asked.

'A neighbour's caring for him. The boy's coping, but he's missing his mother. I told the neighbour not to take him to the hospital; Paula looks so desperately ill.'

'And what's going to become of him?'

There was a heavy sigh, then a tired voice said, 'I've been making some enquiries. Paula's husband's people in Ireland don't want to know, and the neighbour's made it plain she's only caring for him on a short-term basis.'

'If Paula dies he'll be traumatized, Father. The loss will affect him more than it would an ordinary child. He won't understand. He'll think she's abandoned him.'

'I've been worrying and praying about that, trying to think of some way of explaining it, but he has such strange notions about the living and the dead.' There was a silence, then a faltering voice asked, 'Will you call me when you know for sure about Brenda? I baptised the child, gave her her first Holy Communion. I can't believe she's—'

'I'll phone you, Father. Probably tomorrow.'

Troubled by what she'd just heard, impatient to get the evening's business over with, she keyed the ignition, pulled out of the gateway and drove up the rise to Enderley. After parking beneath the huge trees that bordered the village green, she walked over to the church.

The iron gate at the top of the steps was hooked back against the stonework. Gavin had told her the gate and the door below were never locked; the last vicar had allowed the occasional passing tramp to use the crypt as a refuge, and Andrew Leyton had issued no instructions for the arrangement to be changed. When Samantha descended the steps and tried the door, it opened. She ran her hand along the wall, flicked a switch and light from a scattering of unshaded bulbs sent shadows darting into the gloom around the outer walls. She closed the door. There were no rough sleepers, no gentlemen of the road, just the gravediggers' picks and spades, their ladders and wheelbarrow, the planks and props they used to hold back the loose sandy earth, all neatly stored. Two unwashed mugs, a spoon and a bag of sugar rested on a table made from trestles and boards. She found her torch, clicked it on, then switched off the lights and headed towards the door that separated the living from the dead.

The size and position of the keyhole told her the lock was big and old and probably bolted on to the inner face of the door. Samantha shone the torch into her bag. The picks in the wallet were too short, too flexible; they were designed for more modern, more sophisticated things. She rummaged deeper, found a leather pouch, slid from it a long steel pick with two shafts, one revolving inside the other, both fitted with wards to simulate a key and knurled grips to enable the contraption to be turned. She laid her bag on the floor, propped the torch against it, then examined the scrolled escutcheon that decorated the keyhole. The lock had been oiled recently; traces still darkened the rust on the iron. She slid the pick into the lock and began to probe its ancient mechanism. After struggling in the semi-darkness for what seemed like an age she felt the wards move into alignment, but when she tried to turn the simulated key it wouldn't budge. She grabbed the huge ring handle and pulled the door tightly into its frame. When she tried again, the pick turned and the bolt slid back. Bag under her arm, torch in hand, she pushed open the massive door and stepped inside the necropolis.

The torch was made up of a great many tiny bulbs that emitted an intense bluish-white light. She swept its beam down a wide central aisle that probably extended beneath the altar. Dark passageways, just wide enough to permit a coffin to be manoeuvred with some dignity, ran off to the left and right. Bracing herself, she closed the door behind her and stood for a moment in the darkness and the silence. The dead were all around her; their bones, teeth, hair, the dessicated remains of flesh and skin, all wrapped in rotting shrouds and sealed in musty caskets.

She headed down the aisle and turned into the first passageway. Coffins, some plain, some varnished, all displaying signs of age, filled small chambers off either side. Most were arranged in tiers on stone shelves. A few, usually the grandest and most ornate, rested on stone plinths in individual niches.

The cold light of the torch probed every recess. Gritty debris from ancient brick and stone filled corners and formed a film of dust over coffins and floors. Like the breath of the dead, the air was still and strangely dry; the only odours were those of dust and age, of old wood and crumbling stone.

After searching the niches and chambers off the first passageway, Samantha progressed to the next. The coffins there seemed older; some were quite crude affairs, no more than rough-hewn boards secured by iron nails. In a niche beside an outer wall, one had succumbed to decay. Its side and end had tumbled into the gritty debris and the lid had collapsed on to what remained of its owner. The dust lay undisturbed. There was no green canvas suitcase, no still-moist corpse hidden here.

The entrance to the third passageway had been bricked up. Perhaps the coffins had become so decayed decency demanded that what remained of the dead be hidden from the eyes of the living. The bricks and mortar were old.

Samantha walked on until she reached the end of the central aisle. What had once been an archway had been closed off and crudely plastered over. A stone tablet was inscribed: *The Winstans of Enderley, 1407–1573, and Four Priests of the Roman Rite. This tomb sealed by order of Nathaniel Brightman, Bishop of the Diocese, December 1603.*

As she made her way back to the entrance, she searched the warren of niches and chambers on the other side of aisle and found what she was looking for in the gallery nearest the door. A tiny wheel glinted in the torchlight, and she glimpsed the curve of a handle and part of a metal frame. She crawled into the niche. The suitcase had been laid flat behind a marble block that supported the end of a large and ornately panelled Victorian coffin. Moisture was oozing from dark patches on the green canvas, and there was a faint and sickly-sweet odour of putrefaction. Brenda Baxter was decomposing.

Samantha wriggled out of the narrow space, brushed dust and grit from her coat and returned to the outer passageway. She closed the door, adjusted the pick in the lock and turned it. The old mechanism grated as the bolt slid home. She'd been right to trust her instincts; where else would the Vicar of Enderley have hidden the body of his victim?

She stood for a moment in the shadows at the top of the steps, gazing out over the graveyard, breathing in cold clean air. From across frozen fields came the bark of a starving fox. It was answered by dogs, yelping on a distant farm. The graveyard and the lane beyond were deserted. She walked off, down the side of the nave. When she rounded the end of the church she could see lights glimmering in the windows of houses and cottages on the far side of the village green, the occasional street lamp illuminating frosty pavements. She was back amongst the living.

There was a public phone booth on the post office forecourt. Samantha left the church yard and half-walked, half-ran, silent over the grass, towards it. Her breath was making clouds when she snatched up the handset and punched in 999. After she'd dealt with the operator, the line clicked and a bored male voice said, 'Police.'

'Put me through to the person who deals with homicide. I want to report a murder.'

'Can I have your name address and telephone number, please madam?'

'No. Just put me through to homicide.'

'I must have your—'

'I'm trying to make an anonymous call. Do you want the details or don't you?'

'One moment.' A click, a faint hum, then another male voice asked, 'How can I help you?'

'I'm going to give you details of a murder.'

'Who's calling?'

'Judy Garland's mother. It's an anonymous call. Do you want the information, or shall I ring off?'

'OK, OK. Go ahead.'

'The dead woman's called Brenda Baxter.' Samantha gave the address of the flat in Manchester. 'She was reported missing a few weeks ago. Her body's in a green canvas suitcase in the crypt of Saint Michael and the Angels, Enderley. She was probably murdered by a client, the Reverend Andrew Leyton, Vicar of St Michael's. There's a rug and clothing stored in a wardrobe in the girl's flat. You might want to check the items.'

'And how do you know all—'

'Just go to the crypt. The body's in a green canvas suitcase that's been hidden under a coffin. The coffin's in a niche down the first passageway on the right hand side as you enter the crypt; a big black ornate thing standing on marble blocks.' She cradled the phone.

MISS SPRY'S FINGERS settled on keys; her feet, lumpy with bunions, pressed pedals, and the organ sounded the final chord of the last hymn. Andrew recited the concluding prayers, then began to read the announcements. The Sunday morning service had ended. Zelda sighed with relief. Sitting through it, keeping up appearances, was always a chore. Today, with Andrew's revelations hanging over her like a poisonous cloud, it had been well nigh unbearable. His sermon had been lack-lustre, his usually fine singing voice sadly off-key, and the congregation must have noticed how preoccupied and exhausted he looked.

She'd heard him leave the house a little after ten the previous night. She hadn't heard him return. He'd probably telephoned a prostitute and slunk off to relieve his puerile urges. She didn't want to know. It was his problem, his secret. If he was found out, she'd leave him. Her husband was pathetic, a man who searched out waif-like little tarts to assuage his lust for pre-pubescent girls, a man who'd married her because she reminded him of the mother who'd rejected him when he was a child.

Julia Farrell was still in her pew. She was alone. Jeremy wasn't with her today. Beneath carefully applied make-up she looked agitated and distressed, and quite a few of the congregation were giving her pitying looks as they drifted towards the door. Zelda waited until she could hear them chattering in the porch, receiving Andrew's handshake, exchanging parting words, then crossed the aisle and whispered, 'What's wrong, Julia? You look absolutely desolate.'

'I thought you'd know. Everyone else seems to. It's on the front page of that dreadful Sunday paper.'

'I don't read the Sunday papers.'

'*Minister for Culture and the Arts, Jeremy Farrell, in All-night Sex Romp:* I think that's what the headline said.'

Zelda slid into the pew beside her and reached for her hand. 'I'm so sorry, Julia. I'd no idea. Where's your car?'

'Parked across the road, under the trees.'

'I'll take you out through the vestry door, keep you away from all the Nosy Parkers jostling around Andrew.'

Julia rose to her feet. 'Will you stay with me? I don't want to be on my own, and I desperately need someone to talk to.' Still holding Zelda's hand, she followed her into the choir.

Miss Spry was lowering the cover over the organ console. She stared at Julia, hand-in-hand with the vicr's wife; watched as they disappeared into the shadows behind the choir stalls, then heard the vestry door open and close.

The two women emerged into the cold greyness of the winter morning. Julia dipped her hand into her bag and took out a bunch of keys. 'Would you drive?' She held them out to Zelda. 'I'm just a bundle nerves. I can't stop shaking. I'm not really fit…'

Zelda took the keys to the silver Audi, unlocked the doors and helped Julia into the passenger seat. After she'd settled herself behind the wheel, she glanced in the mirrors. Churchgoers were spilling out into the lane and quite a few were watching. This could be me if Andrew's crime were discovered, she reflected: people staring, pointing, making cruel remarks. She started the car and they swept off around the village green, past the shop and post office, then turned into Old Forge Lane. Seconds later the roof and upper storey of the Grange loomed over tall hedges. Zelda turned into the drive and parked in front of the rather impressive rustic brick and grey stone house. Its many windows were divided into small panes, and fluted columns supported a pedimented canopy that sheltered the front door.

It was opulent, Zelda discovered, as Julia led her into the sitting room, and cosy and comfortable. 'Where's the kitchen?' she asked. 'You sit down while I make you a cup of tea.'

Julia waved a slender hand towards what looked like a Chippendale sideboard. 'Let's have a gin and tonic. Tea won't hit the spot for me at the moment. Glasses are in the middle compartment.'

'You found out about it from the newspapers?' Zelda poured a large measure of gin into a glass and added tonic, then poured tonic into another. She handed Julia the glass with the gin, then lowered herself on to the sofa beside her.

Julia closed her eyes and sipped her drink. 'Someone sent me a video, about a week ago. I sat here for almost an hour watching my lardy-arsed husband having sex with a beautiful young girl. I could see everything, hear every rustle, every grunt, every faint little cry. After a couple of minutes I was feeling sorry for the girl. You could tell she was hating it. I hope they paid her well. Half-way through he stopped for a rest, she fetched him a drink and they lay on the bed, talking. That was the worst part. Jeremy said some vile things about me. God, it was so humiliating; I'll never forgive the treacherous little shit.' Julia gulped desperately at the gin and tonic, then glanced at Zelda and said apologetically, 'I'm sorry, love. I'm really quite common. When I'm upset, I return to my roots.'

Zelda smiled. 'Don't apologize. Just let the anger come out.' She experienced a sudden rush of tenderness towards Julia, and with it an intense desire to make love to her. Stress usually made her crave the distraction of sexual release, and right now she was finding her fears about her own husband deeply worrying. She slid her glass on to a low table, put her arm around Julia and drew her close. Julia's grey eyes, brimming with tears, were heartbreaking; her tiny mouth was crying out to be kissed. Be careful, Zelda warned herself, don't rush things, don't frighten her. She pressed her cheek against Julia's and began to stroke the hollow of her arm where a tracery of fine blue veins lay just beneath the skin. The urge to lean forward and kiss it was unbearable.

Julia drained her glass. 'And you wouldn't believe the utter insensitivity of those bastards at Westminster. Chief Whip phoned me yesterday, asked me if I'd stand by Jeremy, said the Party was reeling after the PM's death and Edward Ashton's suicide, and would I stay with him, at least until the furore was over. I slammed the phone down.'

Zelda stroked Julia's hand. 'What are you going to do?'

'Do?'

'Stay with him or separate?'

'I'm going to divorce him. I'd like you to act for me, be my lawyer.'

'I'm a criminal lawyer, Julia. Divorce isn't my speciality, but one of the partners is very good: Samuel Weinman, I could arrange a meeting.'

'Would you? I've got to have someone decent. I hate Jeremy. He's absolutely vile. I don't want to leave him a pot to piss in.' The triple gin on an empty stomach was beginning to hit the spot.

'I presume your daughter knows?'

'I told Jeremy he had to tell her. He must have, because she phoned me, very angry and bitter. She's at university, in the middle of exams, so she's not coming home. God knows what she's made of the newspapers today.'

'You're still living here on your own, even after what's happened?'

'I've always lived here on my own. Jeremy's spent his entire bloody life at Westminster. I used to feel grateful when I saw him at weekends.'

'Why don't I arrange an afternoon meeting with Samuel Weinman. We could stay on in Manchester, have dinner together in the evening, book into a hotel so we could have a drink without worrying about driving home.'

'I'd like that.'

'It would probably have to be later in the week. Samuel's diary is always full.'

'The sooner the better.'

'Shall I book two singles or a double room?'

'A double would be fine. I'd rather not be on my own at the moment.'

There was a pounding on the front door, the bell began to ring in long persistent bursts, and they could hear a babble of voices.

'Sit there.' Zelda struggled up from the overstuffed sofa and strode over to the window. She glanced back at Julia. 'Looks like the press; about half-a-dozen of them under the porch, and there are quite a few cars parked in the lane. Do you want me to get rid of them?'

'The press!' Julia's eyes widened with alarm. 'I can't face anyone at the moment. Could you?'

Zelda marched into the hall. Distorted faces were peering through the small leaded windows set on either side of the front door. Resting her hand on the latch, she glanced into a gilt-framed mirror hanging behind a vase of flowers. Mouth set in a firm line, eyes hard, her expression conveyed an authority that verged on the ruthless. She tucked a stray lock of brown hair behind her ear and opened the door.

Loud male voices assailed her. 'Mrs Farrell, is she at home? How is she taking the news? Does she have any message for—'

'Gentlemen, gentlemen.' Zelda's tone was commanding. They fell silent. 'I'm Zelda Unwin of Weinman, Wallace and Webster. We've been instructed to act for Mrs Farrell, and I have to tell you she's too distraught to speak to anyone at the moment.'

'You're representing her; she's divorcing her husband?'

'Please, gentlemen, try to put yourselves in her position. She first knew of this when she saw the papers this morning. She's in a state of shock. She hasn't even begun to think about the consequences of it all.'

'Jeremy Farrell; is Jeremy Farrell here? Can we talk—'

'I understand Mr Farrell is in London.'

'You say Mrs Farrell was completely unaware of her husband's—'

'You heard me say the first she knew of this was when she read the report in the newspapers. She's very distraught. I must ask you to respect her feelings and give her time to collect herself. She may then instruct me to make a statement on her behalf, but I don't expect that to be for some days.'

ANDREW LEYTON CRADLED the phone. Zelda had just told him Julia Farrell was having marital problems and she was at the Grange, comforting her. He felt uneasy, hoped his wife wouldn't be too comforting, that she'd restrain herself and be discreet. And despite her accusing looks, her cold anger, he needed her with him; needed the comfort of another human presence in the big old house. He glanced at his watch. Lunch: he'd better put something together. He headed down the hall and along the kitchen passageway. There'd probably be something he could heat up in the microwave.

The door bell rang, then rang again. Andrew turned, retraced his steps down the hall and opened the door.

'Reverend Andrew Leyton?' The man had dark hair and narrow eyes. His skin was sallow and there was a faint scar high on his left cheek.

Andrew nodded.

'I'm DCI Tinsley,' he flicked open a wallet to reveal a badge and photograph, 'and this is DI Bardeen.' He inclined his head towards a man with close cropped blond hair. They were both wearing grey overcoats over dark suits. 'Could we come inside and have a word with you, sir?'

Andrew's heart was thudding, his stomach lurched, he felt faint. 'Of course.' He managed a smile, then stood aside while they entered the hall. He took them into his study, cleared books from a couple of chairs, invited them to sit down, then settled himself in his swivel chair, glad his shaking legs were hidden behind the desk.

The man with the sallow face flashed him a genial

smile. 'Are you acquainted with a woman called Brenda Baxter?' His fairhaired colleague was gazing around the cluttered room.

Andrew frowned, pretended to think, then shrugged and said, 'I don't recall the name. I'm pretty sure she's not a parishioner of mine.'

'She's not from Enderley, sir; she's from Manchester. Reported missing about three weeks ago.'

'In that case, I'm certain I don't know her.'

'We've received a report that her body's been hidden in the crypt of your church.'

'In the crypt of Saint Michael's?'

Tinsley nodded. Bardeen fixed Andrew in an un-blinking stare.

'It's locked and I have the only key. It's not possi-ble—'

'Do you mind if we take a look, sir?' Tinsley's voice became apologetic. 'We've had a report, so we're obliged to investigate the matter.'

Andrew swallowed against the dryness in his throat and pressed his legs together to control the trembling. Reaching down, he slid open a drawer and took out a heavy iron key. 'Would you like me to come over with you?'

'That would be very kind of you, sir.'

'You have torches? There are no lights in there.'

'We've an inspection lamp in the car.' DCI Tinsley looked at DI Bardeen. 'Could you bring it, Dave?'

The inspector nodded, they rose to their feet and filed out into the hall. Hands trembling, Andrew took his coat from the hall stand and drew it on as they stepped out into the chilly winter dampness.

'We can go this way,' Andrew said, trying to keep the tremor out of his voice. 'There's an opening in the garden wall that leads through to the churchyard. No need to go back down the lane.'

They waited until DI Bardeen returned from the car, a leather battery box hanging by a strap from his shoulder and a lamp like a small searchlight in his hand. Then they walked around the front of the vicarage and began to trudge along a gravel path that led up the rise to the church.

'Does it bother you, sir; living on top of a graveyard?' The man with the sallow face was making conversation.

'Not in the least. It's very peaceful, and dealing with death is part of a clergyman's job.'

They reached the steps by the side of the church and Andrew swung the heavy iron gate open. His legs were shaking uncontrollably now. He stumbled and had to grab the handrail to stop himself falling.

'You OK, sir?'

'Not too good, Inspector. I think I'm getting flu. Felt groggy when I woke and it got worse while I was conducting morning service. Heaven knows what the congregation made of the sermon.' He opened the door at the foot of the steps and clicked on the light. 'This way. The necropolis starts under the nave and extends beneath the sanctuary.' He led them between columns supporting ancient vaulting, then down a short passageway that ended in a massive door. A light, intensely bright, suddenly flared behind him. He slid the key into the lock, turned it, then heaved the door open. The police officers followed him inside.

'There hasn't been an interment down here for more than a hundred years,' Andrew said. 'The most recent are nearest the door; the oldest are under the sanctuary.'

The beam of light traversed the central aisle and picked out a plastered-over archway at the end. DI Bardeen worked it slowly back, held it for a moment on each of the openings to the side passages, then brought it to rest on the nearest opening on their right.

Without uttering a word, the men left Andrew in the doorway and entered the passage. Andrew followed, saw them standing by the niche that held the ornate black coffin. His heart was pounding. They knew something. Someone must have been in here, searched the chambers and found the suitcase. Who? He was sure that his was the only key. Perhaps there was another at the diocesan offices in Manchester, perhaps the sexton....

Tinsley was on his hands and knees, inside the low vault, peering behind the marble block that supported the coffin. He glanced over his shoulder. 'Pass me the light, Dave.' He reached out, took the lamp and swept the beam beneath and beyond the coffin, probing every recess in the narrow space.

Andrew closed his eyes. Sweet Jesus, help me. Jesus—

'Anything there, Chief?' They were the first words the fair-haired inspector had spoken.

'Just dust.' DCI Tinsley scrambled out and handed the lamp back to Bardeen. 'We'd better take a look at the rest.'

They walked the central aisle, entered all the passageways, shone the powerful torch into every niche and over every shelf. Andrew followed, trembling, glad to be in the darkness behind the savage glare of that dreadful light.

'These spaces been bricked up long?' Tinsley turned and looked at Andrew.

'About a hundred years I'd say. The vaults closer to the sanctuary were sealed a long time ago; there's a date on one. When the coffins disintegrate and there's a danger of the contents being exposed, the remains are gathered together in a niche and it's bricked up.'

'Nothing recent then?'

Andrew managed a shaky laugh. 'Nothing one would call recent, no.'

They returned to the outer passage. While Andrew was locking the door, Tinsley asked, 'There's no other way into this part of the crypt?'

'No other way.'

'And there's no other key?'

'As far as I'm aware, this is the only key and it's kept in my desk drawer.'

'And no one knows it's there?'

'No one, not even my wife. I took charge of it along with the other keys when I accepted the living.' Andrew led them up the steps, into an afternoon that was suddenly even more grey and overcast. Darkness would come early.

'Thank you very much indeed for you time, sir.' DCI Tinsley smiled apologetically. 'We get reports; we have to investigate.'

'Don't apologize, Inspector. I completely understand. May I ask who telephoned you?'

'We've no idea, sir. We recorded the call. Woman's voice, refined, rather assertive. She refused to give her name. It was from a public phone, in the village, the one outside the post office. Perhaps someone has a grudge, sir?'

'It's possible.' Andrew managed another laugh. 'You wouldn't believe how easy it is to upset some parishioners.'

FOURTEEN

SAMANTHA SWUNG THE Ferrari into the cul-de-sac, cruised on for a hundred yards, then keyed the remote. The door to the garage beneath her small three-storey house rose and she swept inside. The garage, a utility room, a tiny entrance hall and stairs, took up the ground floor of what the developers had proudly called their Regency Villa: a fine-sounding name for an unremarkable little house on a cramped estate. Hidden in the quiet suburbs of a dreary little town, it was a place where she could come and go unnoticed.

Tiredness was tempting her to ignore the security check. She reproached herself. If she became careless, if she abandoned the rituals, she might soon be dead. Tapping keys on her i-phone, she interrogated the system. Utility, stairs, landing, sitting-room, bedrooms, bathroom, were all deserted. When she flicked to the kitchen, Crispin appeared on the screen. He was standing at a worktop, wearing his blue-striped apron, stirring something in a mug. She felt a surge of affection, immensely glad to find him still here. Gathering up her bag, she headed for the stairs.

'Thought you might need this.' Crispin handed her the drink as she walked into the kitchen. 'Brandy and hot chocolate.'

She sipped at it, then closed her eyes. 'It's heavenly. How did you know I was here?'

'Heard you when the doors rattled up and you rumbled into the garage. It's like a pit stop at Le Mans when you arrive in the Ferrari.'

'Stay and have supper with me.'

'Can't, love. Going round to Julian's place with Timothy for drinks and nibbles.' He frowned. 'You're making a mess of that Ralph Lauren coat; put it in the spare room and I'll brush it and give it a good sponging tomorrow.' He untied his apron and hung it behind the door.

Samantha slid her mug on to a worktop, then reached up and straightened his dusky-pink silk tie. 'I don't think I've ever seen you looking quite so handsome, Crispin.' She took hold of the lapels of his deep-blue velvet jacket and settled it on his shoulders. His dark hair had been carefully barbered, and he'd shaved away the stubble that usually covered his cheeks and chin.

He beamed; compliments delighted him. His smile suddenly faded. 'And you look exhausted.' He was gazing down at her in a concerned way now. 'You're seeing too many clients. Has someone been unpleasant?'

'They've all been perfect gentlemen.' She retrieved her hot chocolate. Crispin was convinced she was a high-class whore: the car, the clothes, the frequent absences from the flat. It was fortunate that he did. A woman who sold herself for sex didn't trouble him at all, but if he knew she dealt in death he'd be appalled.

'There's a casserole in the oven, wine in the rack, and your dry cleaning's laid out on the spare bed.' Tuttutting, he reached forward and began to unbutton her coat. 'You really have made a mess of this, love.' He helped her out of it. 'The fabric's full of dust.'

'Don't shake it in here,' she said, remembering the crypt and the coffins. She took it from him and laid it over a stool.

He made a surprised face. 'Now who's getting all

house-proud? As if you ever cared. The place was a tip
when I came over yesterday. Took me all morning to
get it straight.'

Samantha stood on tip-toe and kissed him on the
cheek. 'You're very sweet, Crispin, and I love you dearly.
How would I manage without you?'

'Want me to run your bath?' He turned and headed
across the landing. 'I'll do that, then I'm off.'

She sipped the hot chocolate. Crispin had been generous with the brandy. She heard a door open, a light
switch click, shoes tapping on tiles, then water rushing
from taps. When she followed him into the bathroom
he was pouring scented oil from a flask.

'Sit down,' he dragged a stool over, 'and I'll take your
boots off.' She obeyed and stretched out a leg. The bathroom was filling with steam.

Crispin knelt on a towel, slid off the long boots, stood
them against the wall, then began to massage her feet.
'You look exhausted, Sam. You really are seeing too
many men.'

'I don't know how you dare say that, Crispin. You've
had more than your share of boyfriends.'

'But I do it for love, dear.' He sighed, then added
softly, 'Or the expectation of it.'

'Until the real thing comes along?'

He let out a bitter little laugh. 'Until the real thing
comes along.' He glanced at his watch. 'Got to go, Sam.'
He released her foot. 'Put the coat in the spare room. I'll
sponge it for you tomorrow.'

When the outer door had slammed, Samantha rose
from the stool, turned off the taps and began to undress.
The priest: she'd promised to call him. She padded into
the kitchen and picked up her bag. On her way back to

the bathroom she found her mobile phone and keyed in the number.'

'Father Ryan?'

'Georgina.'

'Sorry I didn't call you yesterday, Father. Brenda Baxter: I'm afraid she's dead.'

An Irish voice, tired and sad, mumbled, 'She was such a tiny little thing, more like a child than a woman. Where did you find her?'

'It's best you don't know that, Father.'

'Did you discover who did it?'

'I'm certain it was the clergyman. I notified the police last night. I did it anonymously. You've got to forget our conversations. I don't want it known that I've been involved.' She listened to a silence, then asked, 'How's Paula Hamilton?'

'Went to see her after evening mass. They're trying some new treatment and she's rallying. She was able to talk to me. She's desperately worried about Benjamin.'

'Keep me informed, Father.'

'I will, I will. And thanks for Brenda. I'll offer my mass for her tomorrow. And for her mother. She's going to be mortified. She won't be able to lie about her daughter any more.'

Samantha kicked her tights and underwear into a corner, slid into the hot bath, relaxed back and closed her eyes. Too many men, too much sex. She smiled. Crispin had no idea. Too much travelling, too much watching and stalking, too much killing. Now crypts and coffins. She must have been brain-dead, agreeing to find the girl for Father Ryan. Crispin was right: she had to distance herself. More than anything, she had to stop listening to smarmy old Marcus when he tried to bribe her with generous short-term contracts.

A bleeping dragged her back from the edge of sleep. Bleeping, not ringing. Reaching over the rim of the bath, she groped in her bag and picked out the encrypted mobile.

'That you, Sam?'

She put a note of resignation in her voice. 'I'm here, Marcus.'

'Where's here?'

'At home, soaking in a hot bath.'

'Is your manservant with you?'

'He's not my manservant, Marcus.'

'Your valet, then?'

'I thought only men had valets. He's my friend, Marcus. My dearest friend. And I'm alone; he's not with me.' Irritated by his patronising references to Crispin, she brought the conversation round to business. 'The coach they used for the pilgrimages, did you have it checked?'

'Customs diverted it in Plymouth when it came off the ferry from Santander. We had a forensics team waiting. They locked it in a shed and searched it. There'd been a partition in the luggage bay. You could see where it had been fixed: depressions in the carpet, holes where the screws had been. They vacuumed the space, took fibre samples, checked for body fluids. I got the report an hour ago.'

'And?'

'Nothing. Just human and animal hairs, assorted fibres, the sort of things you'd expect to find in a luggage hold. No traces of blood or body fluids. Nothing to link the bus with the Cosgrave boys. We did uncover something interesting, though. Two of the men working as labourers on the Pimlico art gallery refurbishment sometimes clean coaches when they dock in the Bassingers' depot in Stepney. That could explain why the bodies ended up where they did.'

'Do you think the Bassingers realize we're watching?'

'They're bound to be wary, but I'd hope not. Customs people searched the passengers' luggage, stopped another two coaches and some cars. Their bus wasn't singled out.'

'What does Fallon make of it?'

'She's come round to your way of thinking. The Prime Minister, his sons, Edward Ashton, now Jeremy Farrell: the Bassingers are avenging the dead. Government's trying to limit the damage from the Farrell exposé, but the media's obsessed with it. They're like a dog with a bone.'

Samantha reached forward, turned on the hot tap, restored the temperature, then relaxed back again. 'And how is our Minister for Culture and the Arts?'

'Unrepentant. He's declined invitations to resign. He was taken into hospital yesterday evening. Seems he returned home to Enderley to collect clothes and papers. He'd paid off the taxi and was walking down the drive when somebody grabbed him and beat the living daylights out of him. House is isolated, surrounded by tall hedges, it was dark and no one was at home, so no witnesses. Farrell told the police it was a tall well-built youth, possibly the boyfriend of the young woman he'd spent the night with. She told him they'd parted years ago, but Farrell thought she might have been lying.'

'Is he very bad?'

'Broken ribs, jaw, teeth; face is quite a mess. They're hoping a few days in hospital will make him think again about resigning. He's become a bit of an embarrassment.'

Samantha slid lower in the bath. 'What's the next move?'

'Not sure. We need a lead from the politicians. I've had an informal meeting with the DPP. There's no way he'd agree to arrest and trial. What evidence we have is circumstantial at best.'

'The surveillance, the phone taps?'

'Nothing. Just domestic stuff, not even business. They're being very careful. Lot of chat about the wedding. Your research team's gathering the details.'

'The flat in Knightsbridge: were you able to establish a link with the Bassingers?'

Marcus shook his head. 'It's owned by a French woman living in New York. Her London agents let it three months ago to a party claiming to be Charles Swinburne who gave them a Glasgow address. He paid a big deposit, supplied references, paid six months rent in advance. Charles Swinburne died six years ago in a car crash. Whoever rented the London flat stole his ID. The Glasgow address was for a small terrace house located in the north of the city. Neighbours said they'd never seen anyone there; landlord was owed rent; they'd probably used the place as a mail box, then abandoned it. Like I said, they've been careful.'

'Do you think Loretta might hand it over to the Met?'

'Doubtful. They don't know a thing about this; they're still interrogating terrorist suspects. Loretta's been called to a meeting at Number Ten, first thing tomorrow; Deputy PM, Home Secretary, and they've invited the DPP along. I hope to know a little more after that.'

'How's Mrs Cosgrave?'

'Back home. They've improved security in and around the house and stationed people on the street outside. The Met don't like it, but she refused to stay at Chequers any longer. I might give her a call; make sure she's OK.'

'Collect another Boy Scout badge?'

Marcus chuckled. 'You're a cynical little witch, Sam. I'll keep you informed.'

'I'VE GOT A raging thirst. Fancy a drink?'

'Wouldn't mind.' Lewis Bassinger checked the carriage clock on the mantelpiece. 'I'll see you in the local: ten minutes. Get a round in.' He flicked his mobile off then glanced at Sharon. She was still reading her fashion magazines: she'd done nothing else for the past two weeks. Weddings! Still, the prospect of a new outfit, a bit of a knees-up, had mollified her, made her more amenable. She'd even accepted Dad's assurances that the marriage wouldn't change things, that Velma coming into the family wouldn't affect them. It would. Dad and his new bride were going to fade from the scene. He and brother Mark were taking over the firm. He'd have even less time for domestic affairs. Sharon wouldn't like that.

'Got to go out, love.'

'Again? You're never in.' She let out an annoyed little sigh, then turned the page. The cream silk suit was rather nice. It might be cold, travelling from Alma's place to the hotel, and her mink stole would go well with it.

'Business, love. Got to call Brendan from a public phone.'

'Don't know why you can't use your mobiles, like the rest of the human race.' She flicked back a page. The pale-blue dress would be very slimming, though, and with that coat she'd seen in Harvey Nichols....

'They can trace mobile calls, and they can tap house phones. Public phones are safe, 'specially if you keep changing.'

Sharon didn't answer. She was trying to decide: suit or dress and coat, or maybe she should look for something completely different. Trouble was, the wedding was only a week away now. She had to make her mind up and choose something.

Five minutes later Lewis Bassinger was in the foyer of the hospital dropping coins into a slot. He keyed in the number of the pub in Stepney. The line clicked open. He could hear voices, laughter; the pub was crowded. 'That you, Brendan?'

'Yeah. Just let me shut this door.' The talk and laughter faded, then an East-end voice said, 'Customs stopped Trevor's tour coach when it came off the ferry. Emptied it, took it into a shed and kept it there for a couple of hours. Pilgrims got very pissed off.'

'Just Trevor's bus?'

'They stopped two other coaches and about half-a-dozen cars.'

'Did they say anything?'

'Apologized. Told the driver they'd had a non-specific drugs tipoff.'

'And they let the coach go?'

'Yeah. Helped the driver re-load the luggage.'

'Sounds like a coincidence. I presume the partition had been taken out?'

'Yeah. And the carpet cleaned and hoovered.'

'Nothing for them to find then,' Lewis said.

'Just thought you ought to know.'

'Thanks, Brendan. You did right to phone. Keep me posted.'

THE REVEREND ANDREW Leyton sat back in his swivel chair. He had to pen a panegyric for the soldier they were going to bury this coming week, but he couldn't concentrate. He'd had no difficulty putting something together for the Turgoose funeral; the daughter had told him her mother's life history, almost written it for him, but the soldier…

He ran his eye down the sheet of notes from the boy's commanding officer: a soldier's soldier, whatever that might mean. He was brave, loyal, good humoured in adversity; a warrior who'd be greatly missed by his comrades, killed by a roadside explosion, a great loss to the Regiment. Andrew turned the sheet. Date enlisted, tours of Iraq and Afghanistan, promotions, decorations; the officer had listed everything about the soldier, nothing about the man. He'd go and see the boy's parents, first thing tomorrow. Not easy eliciting information from people who are grieving deeply, but if he commiserated and let them talk, they'd probably tell him something about their only son.

Where had Zelda got to? He glanced at the desk clock; it was after eleven. She'd spent most of Sunday with Julia Farrell, she'd had her here at the vicarage until late last night, and when she'd arrived home this evening she'd snatched a meal and dashed straight over to see her at the Grange. Legal business, she'd said. Didn't she realize that *he* needed her, needed the comforting presence of another human being in the house. That visit from the police had greatly unnerved him. He'd not mentioned it to Zelda. He still trembled at the thought of it. It was guilt, of course, guilt and fear. He heard the gate clang shut, then footsteps approaching along the path. He rose from his desk, went through to the hall and opened the front door. Zelda stepped up into the porch and strode into the house. She kept her back towards him, avoided his gaze while she unbuttoned her coat.

He helped her out of it and hung it on the hall stand. 'Can I make you a drink? Some supper?'

'I had something at Julia's. I'm going up to my room.'

Zelda's voice was cold and matter of fact. Her tone, her demeanour, were just like his mother's had been after his brother had died, after she'd been told about...

Still avoiding his gaze, Zelda crossed the hall and began to climb the stairs.

He called after her, 'I haven't had a chance to tell you. The police came on Sunday afternoon.' His need to unburden himself, to confide in someone, had become unbearable.

She turned and looked down at him.

'Two of them, plain clothes. They searched the crypt.'

'And?'

'They didn't find anything, because—'

'Don't tell me. I don't want to know. This is your nasty little mess, Andrew, and if you're found out I want to be able to say I knew nothing at all about it.'

He gave up. 'How's Julia?'

'Still devastated. The police contacted her this morning to tell her Jeremy's in hospital: Stepping Hill, Stockport. Seems he came home yesterday evening to collect some things and a man attacked him on the drive and beat him half to death. Julia was here, so she'd no idea it had happened. She refused to go and see him. She's very bitter.'

'Wouldn't visit him in hospital?' Andrew was shocked.

'Jeremy said some awful things about her on the video—truly unspeakable things. She'll never forgive him.' Zelda resumed her climb up the stairs.

Andrew followed her with his gaze. He needed her, needed her compassion, needed her to be with him, but she'd spent the entire evening, yet another evening, with Julia Farrell. Now she was going up to her room, deserting him again. 'What's going to happen?' he called after her.

'Happen?'

'About Julia and Jeremy.'

'She's suing for divorce. We're representing her. I've fixed up a meeting with Weinman tomorrow afternoon.' Zelda began to climb again, then paused. 'Oh, by the way, I'll be staying over in Manchester. I'm having dinner with Julia, then we're going to a hotel. I won't be back until Thursday evening.'

'Is that wise?'

'What do you mean, *is that wise*?'

'You know what I mean: spending the night with Julia.'

'What's wrong with spending the night with someone who's a friend and a client?'

'Are you sharing a room?'

'What if we are?'

'You might surprise her, shock her. She might gossip.'

'I'm not insensitive, Andrew, and I'm quite experienced. I can always tell if the other party's not interested before they even realize they're being propositioned. And how dare you warn me to be careful after the shockingly sick and wicked things you've done: things we might not have heard the last of.' She turned and stamped on up the stairs.

'Zelda, don't go. Stay with me for a while. It's been awful these past few days. I need…' He heard her bedroom door slam. He hadn't wanted to be alone tonight. He'd wanted her to stay with him for a while, he'd wanted to hold her hand. He turned and headed back to his study. Going up to her would be a waste of time. Her contempt, her disgust, were palpable. She wouldn't even look him in the face. He was alone, like Jesus had been alone in the Garden of Gethsemane, tormented by fear and dread while the people who claimed to love Him were lying asleep all around. Andrew shivered, suddenly gripped by his own fears, and he prayed to God that this night in the garden wasn't to be followed by a walk to Calvary.

VELMA REMOVED PINS and her long blond hair tumbled around her shoulders. She picked up an ivory and silver brush and began to tease out the ends while she studied Henry's reflection in the dressing-table mirror. He was sitting on the bed, wearing his black dressing-gown, still engrossed in his newspaper. 'You're gloating, Henry,' she murmured. 'You've been staring at that paper since seven this morning. I think you've fallen in love with the girl.'

'She's OK. Did you give her the bonus?'

'When I put her on the plane.' She smiled. 'It really is the girl, isn't it? You can't take your eyes off those pictures.'

'She's not in your league, love. Wouldn't give her a second glance. It's the article. Journalist's a bit of a word artist, been spinning it out for days. Farrell must be spitting feathers.'

'Don't think he's spitting anything at the moment.' Velma watched Henry look up from the paper and smile at her reflection. 'On the television news tonight,' she went on. 'You missed it. You were talking to Lewis. Farrell's in hospital. Someone's given him a beating.' She held his gaze. 'Did you have anything to do with it?'

He shook his head. 'Wish I knew who had. I'd send him ten grand.' She resumed her brushing. He continued to gaze at her through the mirror. 'Sexy pyjamas, Velma.'

'You've seen them before, lots of times.'

'Still as sexy and gorgeous as the first time,' he

said huskily. 'Anyway, it's not the silk pyjamas, it's the woman in the pyjamas.'

Velma smiled at him with her eyes and began to sweep the brush through her hair with long, slow strokes. He'd relaxed over the past few days. That tense remoteness that had distressed her, that had made her think everything was over, had gone. He'd become very loving and tender, more affectionate than he'd ever been. And he wasn't just trying to please her; she could sense his deep yearning for her, a longing for happiness after all the heartbreak and pain. She shivered. He was so strong, such huge shoulders, such big powerful hands. No one could ever harm him, no one would dare, yet he was so gentle with her. She said, 'Wait until you see the things I've bought to take to Spain; wait until you see my wedding outfit.' She made her voice contrite. 'I've spent quite a lot of money. I hope you don't—'

'That's fine, love. Get whatever you want. Whatever makes you happy.' He tossed the paper on the floor, kicked off his slippers and swung his legs up on the bed.

'Abraham's making you a suit. He's used your last measurements, but he wants you to go in tomorrow for a final fitting.'

'I've got a wardrobe full of suits.'

'This one's for you to get married in. And I've bought you a special shirt and tie and some shoes, but I only booked the hotel suite for five days. I thought we'd travel. Trevor's laid a car on for us.'

Henry's face clouded. Mention of his nephew's name had reminded him of his conversation with Lewis about the bus being searched. Still, it was probably nothing; just a coincidence, like Lewis said.

Velma laid down her brush, rose and crossed over

to the bed. She gazed down at Henry. 'I think I should move out.'

Craggy eyebrows rose. 'Move out?'

'These last few days before the wedding. Stay at Alma's.'

'Stay at Alma's?'

'It would feel nicer, somehow. It doesn't seem quite right, climbing out of bed together on our wedding day, then driving off to get married.'

He began to laugh, slid an arm around her waist and drew her down beside him. Then he lifted her hand to his lips, kissed it, and his deep voice whispered, 'You're crazy, Velma. Wedding's not for another week. There's no way I'm going to lose you for a week.'

'A couple of nights, then. I think we should part for a couple of nights.'

'You can stay at Alma's the night before. Mark can collect you in the Rolls and take you to the Cranbourne from there.'

FIFTEEN

An hour after dawn. In the east, a faint glow of light was challenging the darkness, but the neon signs advertising food franchises were still a bright blood-red in the freezing gloom. Samantha gazed across the car park towards the motorway service station. Marcus was late. It wasn't like him to be late. While she'd been waiting, her thoughts had dwelt on little Benjamin and his grandmother, Paula, the woman who'd pretended to be his mother, and Helen Cosgrave, the widow of the man who'd fathered the child. The sexual urge, the urge to procreate, could bring misery as well as joy.

Beyond the expanse of parked cars, a huge container lorry was rumbling towards the motorway. Closer, a family; father, mother, son and daughter were making their way towards the service station, hungry for breakfast. She suddenly caught sight of a tall figure in a trilby hat and belted overcoat. Marcus was striding across the tarmac towards her, carrying a briefcase. As he drew near he peered through the windscreen and recognized her, then the door swung open and he slid his long legs beneath the dash and settled himself in the passenger seat.

'You've changed the car. I was looking for the silver Modena.' He slammed the door. Broad shoulders, the smell of cold morning air, old-fashioned shaving soap and peppermints filled the cab. He dropped his hat in the foot well and rested the ancient briefcase on his knees.

'Getting weary, Marcus. I traded it in.' She turned and studied his shadowy features. 'You said there'd been developments...'

'Politicians have been in a quandary, been wrangling about the Bassinger business for days, couldn't seem to reach a decision. They're relieved it's not terrorism, Islamic or Dissident Republicans, but concerned that it's going to take time, and perhaps prove impossible, to gather evidence that would support a trial and convictions. I suspect that some of them are afraid that if it's not stopped soon, they could be next on the hit list; quite a few of the politicians who openly supported the Bassinger sequestration have something to hide. They called Loretta to Number Ten yesterday evening. She could tell they'd made a decision as soon as she walked into the room. They'd sent the Cabinet Secretary out— didn't want any minutes taking—and they'd invited the leader of the opposition and the shadow Home Secretary along. Matter of national security, so they thought the opposition should be kept informed.'

'Wanted them to be implicated.'

'Probably. Anyway, Deputy PM didn't beat about the bush. She reminded Loretta that the security of the state and its institutions was ultimately her responsibility. Prime Minister had been assassinated, his sons murdered, the personal lives of cabinet ministers exposed and their careers ruined: in short, there'd been an unprecedented attack on the elected government.' He held Samantha's gaze. 'And, having been advised that it would be futile to bring the culprits to trial, the committee had no alternative but to instruct her to take whatever measures she considered necessary to remove the threat to national security.'

'You're going to put people in to—'

'Loretta wants you to go in.'

'I'm tired of killing, Marcus.'

'Cosgrave's widow's in danger; you're in danger. Surely this is something you'd want to resolve yourself, not trust to others?'

'When we were racing to find Benjamin, any Bassinger who saw me, any of their minders who saw me, died. They can't identify me. If they could, I'd have been the first to be killed.'

'They retrieved an image of you from Vincent Bassinger's security system.'

'I've got a copy. It was indistinct.'

'It was recognizable.' Marcus made his voice urgent. 'Do this one, Sam. Do it for your own peace of mind.'

'If they'd been going to kill me, they'd have killed me by now. Put someone else in.'

'Loretta wants to be as certain as she can be of a successful outcome. You know these people, you've confronted them before. She wants you to deal with it.' He tried to read Samantha's expression, but the green eyes gazing back at him revealed nothing. Her body in the elegant coat with the huge lapels, her black-gloved hands, were perfectly still. She seemed calm, almost detached. 'You'd be protecting Cosgrave's widow,' he went on. 'Henry Bassinger's wife died a couple of months after you'd killed their son. Could well have been the grief and trauma. An eye for an eye: they might try to kill Helen Cosgrave when the security's lifted. And, whatever you say, it's likely they're still searching for you. They'll never forget, Sam.'

Samantha knew he was right, at least about Cosgrave's widow. An inexplicable feeling that Helen Cosgrave's life was profoundly important, that it had to be protected, began to override her reluctance. 'They'll gather for the wedding,' she said. 'The wedding's on Saturday. Today is Thursday. That doesn't give me much time to prepare.'

'We've been monitoring phones and emails around the clock.' He unbuckled his briefcase and took out a file. 'Everything's in here: transcript of all calls, wedding invitation list, venues, timetable. Velma and Stanley Bassinger's widow, Alma, have been making the arrangements.'

Samantha took the file. 'Just give me the essentials.'

'Civil ceremony, eleven o'clock, at the Cranbourne hotel—an exclusive place on the rise to the moors east of Stockport. Velma's staying with Alma the night before the wedding and the other women and children are gathering there on the day. The men are meeting at Henry Bassinger's place, about twenty miles away. Henry's son, Mark, is collecting Velma on the morning of the wedding and taking her to the Cranbourne; he's giving her away. The other son, Lewis, is Henry's best man. It's a very small affair, just close family, and there's not much close family left.'

'What about Barry Clovis, the cousin who killed Cosgrave?'

'He's not on the guest list. They're probably being careful and staying well clear of one another.'

'And Morris Bassinger's widow, Elaine, the one who runs the bus tour company, is she attending?'

'With her son, Trevor. And Trevor's as close as we'll get to the men who murdered Cosgrave's sons. He'll have hired the killers and arranged for the bodies to be shipped back to the UK.'

Samantha gazed out over the service station car park. 'There are going to be women and children there, Marcus. It's all very risky and unpredictable.'

'Read the transcripts, Sam, study the arrangements. It's a perfect opportunity. Mark's daughters are bridesmaids, Lewis's son's a pageboy; they'll be with the women at Alma's. As far as we can see, there are no other children. The men are having some sort of meeting at Henry Bassinger's place before the proceedings get under way. We won't get a better opportunity.'

'Anyone been in Henry Bassinger's house?'

'Too risky. Always someone there.'

'What's it like?'

'Big, detached, not overlooked; it's set well back with extensive grounds at the back. It's a few miles from Sheffield, on the Manchester road.'

'I'll need some incendiary devices; intense heat but not as bright as those white phosphorous things, if that's possible.'

'I'll have whatever we've got delivered to you. Where do you want to collect it?'

Samantha pondered. She had to locate Barry Clovis. 'Tell the courier to call me on the encrypted phone. I'll agree a drop-off place. I'd like six; one fitted with a timer.'

Marcus retrieved his hat, pushed open the door and climbed out. 'We'll keep on monitoring right up to the wedding. If there's a change in the arrangements, I'll let you know.'

DANIEL SHOESMITH PUFFED contentedly on his pipe; the tobacco was fragrant and burning evenly in the bowl. 'Be over soon. We'll wait a few minutes after the bugler's played the last post, then go up and see if the crowd's cleared.' He stretched his short plump legs and made himself more comfortable in his chair. 'Grave's three coffins deep, that's a bit more than eight feet, take us a couple of hours to get it back filled.' He blew out a plume of smoke. 'Ground was a bit loose, there's more gravel in the sand as you get further down the bank, and we didn't have enough long planks for the shuttering. There's only struts wedged across the top end next to the Turgoose grave; I didn't like that.'

'No one's going to stand there,' Gavin said. 'They wouldn't trample on a fresh grave.'

'Buggers would trample anywhere,' Daniel muttered. 'Anyway, probably wouldn't matter if they did. Widow went on top, not very far down, and we left a good space between her and the soldier.' He pointed with the stem of his pipe. 'What you done to your hand?'

'Scraped it on the planking when I was bottoming out the grave.' Gavin's voice had become tense; its Welsh lilt more noticeable.

'Didn't see yer.'

'It's nothing.'

'Needs a clean bandage, it's swollen. Hope you washed it. Funny diseases lurkin' around graves.'

Keen to change the subject, Gavin nodded towards the open door. 'At least the rain's held off.' A band of brightness suddenly appeared on the wall at the foot of the steps. 'And the sun's come out for him now. Always better when there's a bit of sunshine.'

'What do you make of old Farrell, having a bit of how's-yer-father with that woman in the flat?'

'Can't think why he'd want to, bloke with a lovely wife like that.'

Daniel took his pipe from his mouth. 'Little Julia? Putting on the posh voice and fancy clothes, strutting around the village as if she owned it; I wouldn't call her lovely.'

'She's not like that,' Gavin protested. 'She's really

nice. You can talk to her. She listens to what you've got to say.'

'Bit on the skinny side.' Daniel was puffing at his pipe again.

'She's not skinny. She's slender; slender and curvy.'

'Hur, hur, hur.' Daniel's purry laugh rustled around the crypt. 'You fancy her, don't yer, young Gavin.'

Gavin blushed. 'Course I don't fancy her.'

'Yes you do. Hur, hur. You fancies her. And I can tell yer, she's not all she seems. Julia Briggs they called her, born in a back-to-back down Sidings Lane in Stockport. Health Department condemned it. Her dad used to work for the Council, when he worked at all. Rat catcher. Not many people know that.'

'Don't care what her dad did,' Gavin said. 'All I do is dig graves and a bit of building work.'

'Do work at her house, don't yer? Hur, hur, hur.'

'Now and then.'

'Hope you've not been giving her one, young Gavin.'

Gavin blushed. When he'd called a couple of days earlier to collect his sealant gun and bucket, he'd found her crying in the kitchen. She'd allowed him to put his arms around her and hold her close. Her body had been hot and trembling, and her breasts had seemed surprisingly round and firm through his sweater. She'd pushed him away, but he'd never forget those few blissful seconds. 'She's nice. She's not like that. She's not like her husband. Don't know what he was thinking about, treating her that way.' He rubbed his swollen hand and with the pain came a glow of satisfaction.

Daniel firmed the tobacco in his pipe with his thumb. 'Skinny piece, I reckon. Hur, hur. What yer need, young Gavin, is a real woman. Woman like the vicar's wife,

Zelda. Now there's a lovely woman. I tell yer, if I had her spread out on this bench I'd make them trestles shake.'

'You're a dirty old man, Daniel.' Gavin didn't try to hide the disgust in his voice.

'Dirty? Dirty? Don't mind old, because I am old, but there's nothin' dirty about fancyin' a woman, and the vicar's wife's a fine, handsome...' He fell silent. Up the steps and across the graveyard, the bugler had begun to sound the last post.

PRAYERBOOK CLUTCHED TO his breast, the Reverend Andrew Leyton watched the casket being lowered into the grave. The funeral service had gone well; the military and religious rituals had merged seamlessly to make the event one of great dignity. He was wearing a new white surplice trimmed with Belgian lace, and the gold tassels on his purple stole were hanging just below its hem. The soldiers were in uniform, khaki and crimson, buttons and badges and medals gleaming.

The polished casket came to rest on the levelled earth, black nylon straps were tugged free, bearers came to attention, and the bugler began to sound the last post, the long clear notes rising sorrowfully on the still morning air.

There was a rumble like distant thunder, a drumming of earth and stones on the casket lid. Andrew felt a stab of alarm. The earth face at the head of the grave was collapsing. His alarm turned to horror; the green canvas suitcase was sliding out on the torrent. Suddenly its metal frame caught on a wooden strut, it tilted, burst open and disgorged its contents.

Mind numb, Andrew watched what was left of Brenda Baxter's body tumble down on to the mound of displaced sand and gravel. Her shrivelled flesh was dark with putrefaction, clumps of hair had become detached from her scalp. Sockets that had once held bright brown eyes were filled with a white mould. Stained but still recognizable, the hem of the pink satin dressing-gown he'd wrapped her in had ridden above her hips.

This was unbelievable. He'd been so careful, so thorough. He'd concealed the case in the grave they'd prepared for Molly Turgoose. He hadn't been able to dig straight down because her husband's coffin was there, so he'd tunnelled outwards and downwards, made a space big enough for the case, then slid it in and packed earth around it. He thought she'd lie there until the Resurrection, but here she was, staring up at him with those sightless eyes; the woman whose warm body he'd fondled and caressed while her soft sweet mouth had talked the talk of little girls. There was no soft mouth now, just teeth, leering up at him out of the putrefaction; no smooth warm skin, just rotting flesh, puckered with decay.

As the bugler sounded the final note, Andrew dragged in a shuddering breath and raised his head. Every eye was staring at the intruder in the grave. Then, one by one, the mourners turned and gazed at him. It was as if they were commanding him to speak; to give them an explanation. His throat was dry. He couldn't think. All he could do was feel, and he was feeling a shame and terror more intense than any he could have imagined. Surrendering to instinct, he turned, hitched up his cassock, and began to run over the wet grass. He plunged through the bushes, vaulted over the graveyard wall, then scampered on, heading down the lane that led to the vicarage.

SOFT FOOTSTEPS SOUNDED on the stairs. Lewis Bassinger stopped watching the match and peered through the half-open door into the hall. Sharon shuffled past, her feet in furry-cat slippers, her hair in huge rollers. Lewis muted the sound on the television and called out, 'How is he?'

She padded into the sitting-room. 'Headache, feels sick, bit feverish. Could be something coming on or it could be the excitement.'

'Didn't think he was all that excited about being a page boy. He's probably trying to get out of it. Am I taking you round to Almas?'

'He's not well, Lewis. He's not trying to get out of it. Let's wait another half-hour, then we'll decide.'

'It's well after ten now.'

'All right then, run us over early in the morning. I'll give Alma a ring.'

'What if he really is ill?'

'Then I'll ask Lilly to come over and keep her eye on him.'

'Lilly?'

'Lilly Jackson, the woman who cleans for us. She's OK. She's had plenty of kids herself.'

He grinned at her grotesque slippers, her denim skirt and faded jumper. 'That your wedding outfit?'

'Cheeky sod.' She turned towards the door.

'What's it like?'

'What's what like?'

'Your wedding outfit.'

'You'll see it tomorrow,' she called from the hallway. 'Alma likes it. She helped me choose it.'

Lewis turned back to the television and restored the sound. The crowd was ecstatic. Someone must have scored. The phone began to ring. Every time there was a decent game on…He snatched it up.

'Fancy a drink? I'm dying of thirst.'

'It's a bit late. And I'm watching the match. Do you need one very bad?'

'Parched. I'm at the club, not the pub.'

'I'll be there in fifteen minutes.'

Lewis switched off the set and ambled through to the kitchen. 'Just had a call. Got to go to a public phone. Be about half-an-hour.'

'Don't know why you bother coming home. You're always going out.'

Lewis parked outside the railway station, walked through the entrance and over to the phone booths beside the ticket office. He lifted a handset, fed coins into the slot, and keyed in the number.

The line clicked. An East-end voice asked, 'That you, Lewis?'

'It's me. What's happened?'

'Barry Clovis is dead.'

'Jesus. How?'

'Crushed under a truck he was fixing. Jack collapsed. Ella called me because she thought there might be something strange about it. Seems that when she came home from work she saw a woman sitting in a parked car close to the house. Barry came in soon after, they had a quick meal, then he went back to the workshop to finish a job. She watched him leave from the bedroom window; saw the woman's car pull out and follow him. When he'd not come back an hour later, she got suspicious. Cousin Carl used to fix him up with all the skirt he could handle. Ella knows that. She thought the woman in the car might be an old flame who'd gone to meet him at the garage. When she went to check, she found him and called the ambulance; the ambulance men called the police as soon as they arrived.'

'He was using a trolley jack?'

'Yeah. Police checked it, said it was still raised, it hadn't collapsed or been let down. Truck had shifted and slipped off the support. Truck wasn't in gear, brakes were off, wheels weren't chocked.'

'Barry would never be that careless.'

'Could have been tired. We all get careless when we're tired.'

'Not Barry. The woman in the car; did Ella see what she looked like?'

'It was dark and the street lighting's not wonderful, but she noticed black hair, a pale complexion and bright red lipstick. Ella admits she's always been crazily jealous, so it could mean nothing. Woman had probably visited someone and was just driving off.'

'Thanks,' Lewis said. 'Tell Ella she'll be well looked after. Tell her someone will be in touch.'

'Give your old man my very best for tomorrow.'

'Will do. Keep me posted, Brendan.'

The line clicked, then went dead.

SIXTEEN

Showered, shaved, carefully barbered, dressed in a bespoke dove-grey three-piece suit, Henry Bassinger relaxed on a sofa in the sitting-room and gazed across at Mark and Lewis.

They were reclining on the sofa facing his. They were all identically dressed, right down to their pale-blue silk ties and pocket handkerchiefs. They'd been co-ordinated. Velma had sweet-talked the tailors into doing a rush job. His nephew, Trevor, smart in a dark-blue pinstripe, not long arrived from Spain, was sitting in an armchair, smiling expectantly at the assembled company, his gaze flitting from face to face.

Henry was feeling a stirring of excitement: a happiness shadowed by poignant memories. He gazed lovingly at his sons for a long moment, then his deep voice began to rumble up from his vast chest and rustle out through the gravel in his throat. 'Wanted a quiet moment with you before we set off, to say things that couldn't be said at the wedding.' He sniffed, and his voice began to shake with emotion. 'You're my flesh and blood, my very own flesh and blood. I want you to know that my marrying Velma doesn't diminish your mother. She was the light of my life, the melody that lingered on after the song had ended. She gave you to me, made this fine home for us. Velma's had the good sense to keep it just the way she left it.'

A little embarrassed by his father's sentimentality, Lewis kept his eyes fixed on a bottle and glasses arranged on a low table between the sofas. His brother, Mark, stared down the garden through big glass patio doors. Trevor had stopped smiling.

'But it's not good for a man to be alone,' his father went on. 'A man needs a woman. It's nature. And I didn't like living over the brush with Velma. It disrespected her, it wasn't right; not for my generation, anyway. I'd have asked her to marry me sooner, but there was outstanding business, family business, that had to be sorted before any of us could get on with our lives. It's mostly dealt with now. Cosgrave's dead, that deviant little bastard Edward Ashton's dead, Farrell's ruined.' He turned his gaze towards Trevor and lowered his voice, 'And Cosgrave's sons are dead. Your father would have been proud of you, Trev. He can rest now. He can hold your brother Carl in his arms and they can sleep the everlasting sleep in peace.

'I'd have liked Barry to be here. He and Carl were close, like brothers. Barry didn't need any persuading to do the Cosgrave kill; he begged me to let him do it. But it would have been too dangerous for him to come to the wedding. He's got to keep his distance; and we've all got to keep our heads down for a while. That's why I told Velma not to invite Stanley's boys, Ian and Hugh, and Ronald's son, Luke. Australia's half-a-world away, and we'd be building up a crowd, starting to make a bit of a commotion. We don't want that right now.'

Lawrence glanced up. His father's eyes were bright with unshed tears; his heavy features flushed. Can't tell him about Barry now, he decided. Can't interrupt his speech. Can't spoil his day. I'll tell him when he's ready to leave for the airport.

'But it's not over yet,' the deep voice rumbled on.

'When the bastards killed Clifford and left him to rot on the moors, they killed your mother, too. Broke her heart, drove her insane; been kinder if they'd killed her with a bullet. When they've relaxed the security, when they've begun to forget, we'll deal with Cosgrave's widow. Then there's that black-haired bitch who murdered Vincent, the woman on the video. God knows how many more of the family she killed. We've got to find her. No matter how long it takes, no matter how much it costs, we've got to find her. We've got to make her pay; make her beg to die.'

Black hair, pale face, lipstick. Lawrence felt a growing unease. Should he say something? His father was reaching for the bottle on the table. No, not now, later, after the celebration.

SAMANTHA HAD WATCHED the house for almost an hour, hidden amongst the bushes and brambles and trees that formed a wilderness at the end of a vast back garden. A few moments ago the men, all tall and broad and powerfully built, had gathered in what looked like a sitting room. The family resemblance was so strong she'd hardly needed the binoculars to confirm that they were Bassinger males. They were waiting for the cars that would take them to the wedding. She could see them now, through big glass sliding doors that opened on to a patio. She glanced at her watch. The first of the cars, the one that would take Mark to collect the bride, was due in twenty minutes. It might be early. She picked up her canvas holdall. Time to move in.

She retreated through the bushes, left the garden by a door she'd levered open earlier, then stepped down on to a narrow track that ran beside a high boundary wall. Clutching the heavy canvas bag, she hurried back towards the main road and the front of the house.

Weathered oak gates had been pegged back in readiness for the arrival of the wedding cars. Dark windows glowered at her out of walls of grimy brown stone. There was no cover to hide her approach, just a brick paved drive curving across an acre of lawn to a three-bay garage. Two black cars, an Audi and a BMW, had arrived since she'd first looked the place over. They were parked on a hard standing.

She studied the house and grounds again, searching for security cameras. There were none to be seen. Perhaps they'd been carefully concealed, or perhaps Henry Bassinger had no fear of intruders. He was with his sons and nephew in the room at the back, and her long watch hadn't revealed any other occupants. She'd have to take a chance. Moving across the lawn to deaden her footsteps, she ran towards the house, climbed steps guarded by stone lions and stood in an open porch. The wide front door was locked. She listened to the silence for a few seconds, then crept around the side and entered a passageway between the garage block and the house. Light gleamed beyond the rippled glass panel of a door. She peered through. There were no signs of movement. She turned the handle. The door wouldn't open, but when she pressed her knee against it, it parted from the frame. It was secured by the eye-level cylinder latch, not the dead lock.

She slid the canvas holdall beneath a meter cabinet, then searched her coat pockets, found her locksmith's friend, and forced the postcard-sized piece of springy plastic into the gap between door and frame. She rocked it to and fro, working it around the latch until it slid from its keep. When she turned the handle and pushed, the door opened. Gun gripped in gloved hands, she entered the house.

A door on her left opened into a laundry and utility room, a door on her right into a spectacular kitchen. Both were deserted. Up ahead, at the end of a tiled corridor, an archway gave her a view across a blue-carpeted hallway. When she moved from tiles to carpet she heard a voice that was unusually deep, a voice heavy with emotion. It seemed to be coming from beyond an impressive flight of stairs. She crossed the hall, passed beneath another archway, then paused beside a half-open door. She heard a cork being drawn from a bottle, the sound of wine being poured, the deep voice saying: 'Del Orte Amontillado; the finest Spanish port. It was your mother's favourite tipple. I got Trevor to bring a case over so we could toast her memory.' Glasses clinked, then, 'To Carla, wonderful wife and mother, and to all the Bassinger dead: fathers, sons, uncles, brothers. May they rest in—'

Samantha heaved the door open, heard it crash against the wall as she took in the scene, aimed the gun and fired two shots. Henry Bassinger fell back on the sofa, legs sprawling. Trevor's body convulsed then collapsed in a heap beside his chair. Lewis and Mark spun round, eyes wide, features slack with shock. She squeezed the trigger again. A bullet tore a dark hole above Mark's right eye. Blood and brains spurted across the rug and he crashed down on the low table. Lewis dropped to his knees screaming, 'Bitch, bitch, you crazy murdering bitch.' Gun held in both hands, arms extended, she approached the sofa and stared over the back at the powerfully built man in a dove-grey suit, cowering on the rug. His whimpering mouth was twisted with hate, his eyes were huge with fear. She squeezed the trigger, felt the recoil, watched his face relax, the terror and rage fade from his eyes as he slumped beside his brother.

The wedding cars would be here soon. Samantha used her mobile to capture images of the dead, then ran back to the outer door and returned with the canvas holdall. She dragged the zip across: incendiaries, half-a-dozen, as she'd requested; just one would melt the inside of an armoured tank. She distributed the grey metal canisters amongst the bodies, then examined the package equipped with a timer. Beneath an army part number and the MOD crest, the instructions were brief and clear:

To set timer, rotate cap until desired delay is indicated against the arrow. To start timer and activate device, grip red ring and withdraw rod.

The cars would be arriving soon. The blaze had to be well under way. She set the delay at one minute, pulled out the rod, then pushed the canister beneath the body of Henry Bassinger.

PARKED IN A lay-by on the crest of a hill, Samantha looked back towards the Bassinger residence. Urlrick the armourer had sent white phosphorous incendiaries. Presumably she had no others. Even at this distance, the glare was alarmingly bright; a chemical flame that couldn't be extinguished. The bodies would be totally consumed, the house reduced to a blackened shell.

She was shaking. These things affected her deeply now. They filled her with self-loathing, reminded her that she was no more than a hired killer, a dealer in death, employed to act when the institutions of state failed. Suddenly feeling cold, she decided to change into her furs, find a pub up on the moors, have a whisky, a meal, try to recover her composure. She was reaching behind the seat for her coat when she heard a faint ringing. Ringing, not bleeping. Marcus wouldn't contact her again for a while. He'd leave her alone now she'd given him what he wanted. She found the phone in her bag and keyed it on.

'Miss Grey? Georgina? I've been trying to reach you for days, but you never answer.'

'Been busy, Father. Must have missed your calls. What's happened?'

'Sad news, I'm afraid. Paula Hamilton's died.'

The iron-grey sky began to shed its burden. Large flakes of snow were swirling out of the gloom. Samantha took a breath. 'I thought she was recovering.'

'It seems the treatment was a last resort. It didn't work. She died the night you phoned to tell me about Brenda.'

'And Benjamin?'

'Disturbed.' There was a silence, then, 'Very disturbed.'

'Who's caring for him?'

'Mrs Shepherd, the neighbour. I went to see her the morning after Paula died, did my best to explain to Benjamin, but he couldn't grasp what had happened. Just kept on asking me when his mummy was coming home. Mrs Shepherd made it clear she wasn't going to mind him much longer. Said she'd have him until after the funeral, then he'd have to be taken into care.'

'He's being difficult?'

'Not at all. He reads his books, watches a little television, doesn't give her any trouble, apart from endlessly asking when his mother's coming home. Mrs Shepherd's no longer young, that's the problem.'

'When is the funeral?'

'This afternoon. Requiem mass at twelve, then over to Stockport Cemetery. We should be at the graveside around half-past one.'

'I hope Benjamin's not going?'

There was a sigh. 'Sister Winifred thought it best that he did.'

'He's only seven, Father. He's intelligent, highly sensitive, has a vivid imagination; he'll be traumatized.'

'But it might help him to accept that his mother's died,' the old priest protested. 'I've talked to him, the nuns have talked to him, but he still persists in this bizarre notion that she's coming home. Sister thought attending the funeral would make him grasp the finality of it all. Then he'd be able to start grieving and move on.'

'It'll traumatize him. He'll never get over it.'

'He can't go on expecting his mother to come home. He's got to come to terms with it, accept that she's gone to Jesus.'

'You've told him she's gone to Jesus?'

'How else should one explain death to a young child?'

Samantha closed her eyes, tried to control her anger, then dragged in a breath and said, 'There's something about Benjamin you don't know, Father. The man who married Paula's daughter, Janos Tyminsky, the man you thought had died in a car crash, the man you thought you'd buried: well, you didn't. God knows who or what the police put in the coffin for you to bury. After Janos had given evidence at the Bassinger trial they had to protect him, they staged his death, gave him a new name, a new identity. He went to live in Carlisle, but on one occasion he came back to Stockport and took Benjamin to relatives in Cheltenham. Benjamin saw him, touched him, spoke to him. The child's being completely rational when he thinks people come back from the dead.'

'I didn't bury Janos? Where is he now?'

'In a home for the mentally ill, near Carlisle. You must forget what I've just told you, Father. And you can't let Benjamin go to the funeral. He won't understand why you're burying his mother in a box.'

'Janos Tyminsky or no Janos Tyminsky, sooner or later he has to accept the reality of his mother's death. And it's all arranged. Sister Winifred's taking him.'

'No, Father,' Samantha insisted. 'He mustn't go.'

'I'm not changing things now, Miss Grey, I'm—'

Samantha switched off the phone, too angry to argue. She glanced at her watch; it was after eleven. She was already on the Manchester Road, west of Sheffield. It wasn't far to Stockport, bit more than twenty miles, but it was snowing hard now and the old road across the moors would become treacherous. She searched in her handbag, took out a leather-bound notebook and flicked through the pages until she found the number she wanted. She keyed it into her mobile.

'Hullo?' The woman's voice sounded surprised, a little apprehensive, as if she'd not been expecting, or not wanted, anyone to call.

'Mrs Cosgrave?'

'Miss Grey!' How did you know I was back at home?'

'Marcus Soames told me.'

'I'm still pestered by security people, but I'm so glad to be away from that dismal Chequers place. How are—'

'Paula Hamilton's died.'

There was the faint drone of a hoover being pushed to and fro. Helen Cosgrave asked, 'When?'

'A few days ago. The funeral's today. She's being buried this afternoon.'

'And Benjamin?'

'Very distressed. They're taking him to the funeral. I'm going to drive over and try to persuade them not to.'

'And after the funeral?'

'He's going to be taken into care.'

'By the local authority?'

'Presumably.'

'God help him.'

The droning of the hoover became louder, the phone rattled down, a door slammed, then out of the silence Helen Cosgrave said, 'Bring him to me.'

'You mean that?'

'I've lost my husband. I've lost my sons. Benjamin is my husband's child. I'll make some use of my life caring for him. I'll watch him become a man. Hopefully, I'll grow to love him.'

'He'll remember me,' Samantha said. 'He'll come to me. Whatever they say, I'll just take him and bring him to you. You can sort out the formalities later.'

Samantha swung the car on to the road and accelerated hard up the rise, hoping to cross the moors and negotiate the Snake Pass before it became blocked by snow.

IN THE SUBURBS of Stockport salt and traffic had reduced the snow to slush, but up on the moors the winding road had become almost impassable and the journey had taken too long. The requiem mass would be over now, the mourners assembled by the graveside. Samantha's hopes of rescuing Benjamin were fading as she made her way to the cemetery. She turned on to Buxton Road. The traffic was heavier here. After moving with it for a couple of miles, she saw the sign, signalled, waited for a gap in the oncoming cars, then turned through the gates. She cruised past offices and a chapel, then drove on down a hearse-wide strip of tarmac that ran between endless rows of graves. In the distance, ghostly behind a veil of falling snow, the domed tower of the crematorium rose out of the whiteness.

Monuments and gravestones were obscuring her

view from the low car. Up ahead, an angel on a pedestal marked a turning circle at a crossing in the narrow roadways. She parked, climbed out, grabbed a foot and hoisted herself above the forest of grime-blackened stones. She peered into the swirling snow. A sudden wind flurried the heavy flakes and she glimpsed the hearse and the car that had brought the mourners, two specks of black at the edge of the advancing line of burials. She returned to the Ferrari and drove on.

The graves became more modest. Soon she was speeding past squat marble headstones and there was nothing to obstruct her view across the burial ground. The hearse and the black limousine were no more than a hundred yards away now. She braked, turned on to a narrower strip of tarmac and closed on the funeral party.

Samantha gathered her furs around her, emerged from the car and strode off between the headstones, heading towards the group around the grave. She could see Father Ryan, sharing an umbrella with a nun. Another nun was holding an umbrella over a child. Two elderly women with scarves over their heads were hunched against the cold.

'No… No… I want my mummy.' The gently falling snow deadened Benjamin's cries, but didn't hide the terror in his high thin voice. 'You mustn't do this to my mummy. Let her out.' His voice rose to a scream. 'Let her out. Let her out. I want my—'

'Benjamin.' Samantha called his name and began to run towards the grave.

Benjamin paused, mid-scream. He knew that low husky voice. It still filled his dreams. He peered through the swirling snow. It was the lady with the green eyes; the one who'd killed the minotaur. Jesus had sent her again. She'd stop them. She wouldn't let them do this terrible thing. He tugged his hand free from Sister Winifred's, scrambled over plastic grass and stood at the foot of the grave. 'They've locked my mummy in a box.' His voice became a wail. 'They're going to bury her in a hole.'

'Your mummy's not in the box, Benjamin.'

'She is. She is. Sister Winifred said she is.'

'She's wrong, Benjamin. Her old clothes and shoes are in the box, that's all. They're going to bury her old things because she doesn't need them any more.'

She was close to him now. He was gazing up at her, fear and bewilderment chasing one another across a face made raw by the freezing cold. A renewed frenzy of terror suddenly gripped him. 'I want my mummy,' he screamed. 'I want my—'

'I've come to take you to her.' Samantha held out her hand. Benjamin fell silent, the tension ebbed from his body. He reached up and slid ice-cold fingers into hers.

'Really, Miss Grey, this is absolutely monstrous.' Father Ryan's protest was chorused by angry gasps and muttering from the nuns and the elderly women. 'How dare you interrupt the burial service? How dare you tell the child such a dreadful lie?'

Ignoring them, wanting to hurry Benjamin away, she led him between the graves and settled him inside the car. She slid behind the wheel, reversed at speed down the narrow track, then turned on to the wider access road and rolled to a stop.

She looked down at him. What had she said? What had she done? But she'd had to do something; the child was going out of his mind. Snow was beginning to melt on his hair and on the shoulders of his dark-blue raincoat. He gazed up at her without speaking while the Ferrari's engine murmured and its exhaust growled, then bewildered eyes slid down to her coat. Reaching out, he ran his fingers into the thick, silvery-grey fur.

'Why is your coat like this?'

'Because it's made from the pelts of wolves.'

'Pelts of wolves?'

'The skins of animals that roam the Arctic wastes of ice and snow.'

He parted the folds and stared at the silk lining. 'Where are the wolves now?'

'Their spirits are in me. They give me courage.'

'Courage?'

Drawing him close, she wrapped him in a great swathe of fur, held him tight, and whispered, 'Now their spirits are flowing into you, making you brave. Can you feel them?'

He gazed up at her, eyes wide with wonder behind his wire-rimmed spectacles, and nodded.

Still holding him tight, Samantha murmured, 'Your mother's been to Jesus.'

'Like Uncle Janos?'

'Like Uncle Janos. Jesus has made her well. She looks younger now; younger than she did when you were born. Her hair's brown, not white, and she's strong and healthy and pretty again.'

'She's been...' he groped for a word, '...transfigured, like Jesus on the mountain?'

'She's been made new. But it's exhausting going to Jesus, and you lose your memories. She'll need you to help her to recover; remind her about past things if she sometimes forgets. Can you do that?'

He nodded. He was still peering up at her through the fur.

Samantha held him very tight. 'The wolves will help you. They'll make you strong, fill you with courage. Shall we go to her? She's found you a new home. It's bigger than the old one. She's fit and well. She can care for a bigger home now.'

'My books and things, will they be—'

'Do you have a key to your old house?'

He nodded.

'We'll stop off on the way. You can gather up what you want for tonight. Your mummy will take you back again tomorrow.'

She released him from her arms, fastened his seat-belt, then drew her furs around her. How was she going to tell Helen Cosgrave? And when Benjamin saw her, would he continue to believe? She slid the gear stick over, let out the clutch, and roared off between the grave-stones.

HELEN COSGRAVE'S HOME on Ludlow Hill was surprisingly modest. A detached house of red brick and pebble-dashed stucco, it was located along a tree-lined road amongst the urban sprawl that links Stockport to Manchester.

While Benjamin had been gathering things into carrier bags, Samantha had called her, made her aware that he thought he was coming home to a mother Jesus had made young again. Too amazed to comment, a shocked Helen Cosgrave had whispered, 'I'll be waiting for you. I'll cook him some tea.'

Samantha drove down the quiet avenue, past security guards hunched in a four-by-four, and turned into a gateway. A man in a visibility jacket climbed out of a car and ambled over. She lowered the window and showed him her ID wallet. 'Georgina Grey and Benjamin Hamilton. We're expected.'

He studied the photograph on the card, handed it back, then went over to the gates and swung them open. Samantha eased the Ferrari through and parked beside a double garage.

The front door opened and Helen Cosgrave was silhouetted against the brightness of the hall. Samantha reached over and released Benjamin's seat belt. He tumbled out of the car, ran past the bonnet and began to climb the steps leading up to the house. Samantha watched and listened.

Benjamin faltered, then paused and looked up at Helen Cosgrave's brown curls, at her lipstick and powder and eye-shadow, at the elegant red dress, the glittering ear studs. 'You're crying,' he said. 'Why are you crying?'

Helen Cosgrave dropped to her knees. 'Because I'm so happy to see you.' She opened her arms.

He climbed another step. 'Mummy?' He sounded bewildered, uncertain.

'Benjamin.' Helen Cosgrave reached out to him. When he moved closer, she folded him in her arms and clutched him to her breast.

Presently he freed himself and gazed up into her face. 'You're different.'

'Jesus has made me young again.'

He touched her hair. 'Your hair's brown now; brown and curly, and you smell nice.'

Helen laughed. 'Do I, dear? How about some tea?'

'I've got to fetch my things from the car.'

'Your tea's going to get cold. Let me put you in the

dining-room, then I'll come back for your things while you're eating your tea.'

'You won't go away again?'

'I'll never go away.'

Helen Cosgrave took the last of the carrier bags into the hall then joined Samantha in the car. 'Won't you come in and have a meal with us?'

Samantha reached past her and closed the door. 'Don't forget what I told you while you were at Chequers. They'll have bugged every room in the house. If there are things you want to keep secret, go somewhere else to talk. It's best that we stay out here.'

'I must go back to Benjamin, I can't leave him—'

'We won't be a moment. I just want to tell you that the man who killed your husband died yesterday. The man who arranged the murder of your sons and the men who organized the whole thing, died this morning. You're not in danger any more. In a while they'll lift the security. Then you can get someone in to check the house and remove the listening devices.'

'Was Benjamin very upset?'

'Beside himself. Utterly terrified. He thought they'd nailed his mother in a box and they were going to bury her alive. I had to say something, so I told him his mother was waiting for him in his new home.'

'Does he believe it? Will he go on believing it?'

'He'll believe for as long as he wants to.'

'If I need you, how can I contact you?'

'I don't think you're going to need me any more, but if you do, speak to Marcus Soames. He'll get a message to me.'

Helen Cosgrave pushed open the door and swung her legs from the car. She looked back at Samantha. 'I'm a party to a truly breathtaking lie, Miss Grey. And I'm going to have to live the lie, and probably make up more lies as I go along.'

'It's an act of great kindness, Helen. And there are times when a few kind lies can be worth more than a thousand truths.'

* * * * *

ReaderService.com

Manage your account online!

- Review your order history
- Manage your payments
- Update your address

> *We've designed
> the Harlequin® Reader Service
> website just for you.*

Enjoy all the features!

- Reader excerpts from any series
- Respond to mailings and
  special monthly offers
- Discover new series available to you
- Browse the Bonus Bucks catalog
- Share your feedback

Visit us at:
ReaderService.com

RS13

REQUEST YOUR FREE BOOKS!

2 FREE NOVELS
PLUS 2 FREE GIFTS!

WORLDWIDE LIBRARY®
Your Partner in Crime

YES! Please send me 2 FREE novels from the Worldwide Library® series and my 2 FREE gifts (gifts are worth about $10). After receiving them, if I don't wish to receive any more books, I can return the shipping statement marked "cancel." If I don't cancel, I will receive 4 brand-new novels every month and be billed just $5.49 per book in the U.S. or $6.24 per book in Canada. That's a savings of at least 31% off the cover price. It's quite a bargain! Shipping and handling is just 50¢ per book in the U.S. and 75¢ per book in Canada.* I understand that accepting the 2 free books and gifts places me under no obligation to buy anything. I can always return a shipment and cancel at any time. Even if I never buy another book, the two free books and gifts are mine to keep forever.

414/424 WDN F4WY

Name _____ (PLEASE PRINT) _____

Address _____ Apt. # _____

City _____ State/Prov. _____ Zip/Postal Code _____

Signature (if under 18, a parent or guardian must sign)

Mail to the **Harlequin® Reader Service:**
IN U.S.A.: P.O. Box 1867, Buffalo, NY 14240-1867
IN CANADA: P.O. Box 609, Fort Erie, Ontario L2A 5X3

Want to try two free books from another line?
Call 1-800-873-8635 or visit www.ReaderService.com.

* Terms and prices subject to change without notice. Prices do not include applicable taxes. Sales tax applicable in N.Y. Canadian residents will be charged applicable taxes. Offer not valid in Quebec. This offer is limited to one order per household. Not valid for current subscribers to the Worldwide Library series. All orders subject to credit approval. Credit or debit balances in a customer's account(s) may be offset by any other outstanding balance owed by or to the customer. Please allow 4 to 6 weeks for delivery. Offer available while quantities last.

Your Privacy—The Harlequin® Reader Service is committed to protecting your privacy. Our Privacy Policy is available online at www.ReaderService.com or upon request from the Harlequin Reader Service.

We make a portion of our mailing list available to reputable third parties that offer products we believe may interest you. If you prefer that we not exchange your name with third parties, or if you wish to clarify or modify your communication preferences, please visit us at www.ReaderService.com/consumerschoice or write to us at Harlequin Reader Service Preference Service, P.O. Box 9062, Buffalo, NY 14269. Include your complete name and address.

WWL13R